HOLLYWOOD
STRIP

HOLLYWOOD STRIP

Shamron Moore

A Tom Doherty Associates Book · New York

This is a work of fiction. All of the characters, organizations, and events portrayed in this novel are either products of the author's imagination or are used fictitiously.

HOLLYWOOD STRIP

Copyright © 2013 by Shamron Moore

A Forge Book
Published by Tom Doherty Associates, LLC
175 Fifth Avenue
New York, NY 10010

www.tor-forge.com

Forge® is a registered trademark of Tom Doherty Associates, LLC.

Library of Congress Cataloging-in-Publication Data

Moore, Shamron.
   Hollywood strip / Shamron Moore.—1st ed.
      p. cm.
   "A Tom Doherty Associates book."
   ISBN 978-0-7653-3230-1 (hardcover)
   ISBN 978-1-4299-6021-2 (e-book)
   1. Young women—California—Los Angeles—Fiction.   2. Self-realization in women—Fiction.   3. Hollywood (Los Angeles, Calif.)—Fiction.   I. Title.
   PS3613.O56688H65 2013
   813'.6—dc23

                                                                              2012049515

Forge books may be purchased for educational, business, or promotional use. For information on bulk purchases, please contact Macmillan Corporate and Premium Sales Department at 1-800-221-7945 extension 5442 or write specialmarkets@macmillan.com.

First Edition: June 2013

Printed in the United States of America

0 9 8 7 6 5 4 3 2 1

For my grandmother,
Frances Schifano Rozyla
(1921–2010)

and

My friend,
Adam Bascomb Ross
(1972–2010)

Acknowledgments

Hollywood Strip is a product of various themes that dominated my life in 2009 and 2010—loss, turmoil, and awakening. Writing a novel was a daunting experience, and I sometimes thought I would never overcome the self-doubt and block that came along with it. All in all, though, this proved to be a most cathartic experience. Many creatures inspired and supported me in my journey. A shout-out to the following is in order:

Walter Mosely—*This Year You Write Your Novel* was incredibly helpful. Thank you for penning a gem of a tutorial.

Mona Gable—Several years ago I took one of your courses and learned valuable advice, such as to "make every word count." I often thought of your plethora of tips while writing and appreciate the knowledge you shared.

George—I'm grateful you introduced me to the proper people and helped push this project forward.

Dr. Freedman—It was in your office that the idea for *Hollywood Strip* was born, at a time when I was going through a metamorphosis. Thank you for keeping me focused and believing in my creativity.

The crew at Vigliano Associates and Tor/Forge, particularly David Peak, David Vigliano, and Bob Gleason—I'm thankful you saw the potential in both me and my "baby."

Last, but certainly not least, a special thanks goes to Z., my Hemingway cats, Grandpa, Aunt Paula, Toby, and the neurotic, always amusing devotees of the Four Seasons.

HOLLYWOOD STRIP

Callie stared at her semi-nude reflection in the makeup room and exhaled. *Lord, these lights are harsh. Calm yourself; Coquette magazine is known for its stellar lighting.* She shifted her weight to her left hip and scrutinized her backside. Was that a dimple of cellulite? Impossible! Cellulite at just twenty-three wasn't logical. She adjusted the band of her lace thong and squinted. Well, even if there were trace amounts of cottage cheese, the editors would make her skin cherub-smooth. Digital retouching was as common as bark on a tree trunk. It was just last week that she met December's cover model and was stunned to see the girl's face was as dewy as a slice of freeze-dried pineapple. In her photos, though, she appeared supple and luminous. Yessiree, it was all just a matter of retouching and lighting, a goof-proof formula.

"You look fabulous," she told her reflection. Her concentration was interrupted by a knock on the door.

"Callie? You ready, babe?" Hannah, one of *Coquette*'s long-term makeup artists, poked her head in the dressing room.

"Ready as I'll ever be," she said, and tied a silken robe around her waist. Her heart rate soared but she managed a smile. "Let's do it."

Hannah clapped her hands. "Now, that's what I like to hear, my kind of girl. Everyone's ready for you. I'll do touch-ups on set."

"Sounds good," Callie muttered. *Maybe they keep a supply of Patrón nearby. . . .*

Hannah strode through the winding hallway with Callie trailing. Framed life-size photos of girls who had been in the magazine over the past four decades adorned the walls—maddeningly lush creatures who beckoned with parted, lacquered lips and eyes steeped in lust. Callie's skin tingled. *I can do that. That's going to be me. I'm going to be up there with all of you bitches.*

"We're doing the classic fairy-tale bedroom setup. It's the easiest way to get in the mood. Trust me, after twenty-two years, I know. Can't go wrong with it," said Hannah. She tapped the shoulder of a man peering through a tripod-propped camera. "Phil, our girl has arrived."

Phil, an affable sixty-something man with a cropped white beard, looked up from his lens. "Wonderful. How are you today?"

Callie dug at her cuticles. "Good, thank you."

"Go ahead and step into frame."

She tiptoed to the middle of the room next to the four-poster bed. The satin sheets were perfectly rumpled. Perfume bottles and pearly trinkets covered the vintage-looking vanity. Airy curtains masked a mock bay window.

"Watch out, coming through!" A scruffy assistant narrowly missed bumping into her with an armful of cable cord.

"Yep, let's start by the bed," said Phil in response to Callie's questioning look. "We'll take it easy, let you get comfortable. I work slower than most photographers. I like to make sure I've got the shot; that could mean twenty frames or five hundred frames. We'll shoot till I'm certain we've got the right look."

"Gotcha," she chirped while Hannah teased her roots.

"And don't be nervous—I know you'll be great." Easy for him to say; he wasn't about to balance in five-inch stilettos stark naked. "Don't be afraid to move and mix it up, I'll follow you. We'll start off with some lingerie shots and gradually move into nudes. I want you to feel comfortable. Hannah, can you smooth that little piece behind her ear? That's it . . . perfect."

"I'll take your robe," Hannah said. Callie slid out of the garment and draped it over the older woman's arm.

"And just remember, most importantly, Callie—don't forget to have fun." Phil's smile crinkled the skin around his bright eyes. He couldn't be any more different from what she had envisioned. Surely a man who photographed naked women for a living must be a lecherous pig, yes? But no. The complete opposite, in fact. She breathed a sigh of relief and her shoulders loosened. Perhaps she wasn't going to need a shot of tequila after all!

She positioned her rear toward Phil, feet apart, breasts lightly pressed against the bedpost.

"Nice, dear, very nice. Tush out more, twist your upper half towards me . . . show me more of your breasts. Perfect. Hold that." *Click, click.* "Flip your hair back for me."

The tendrils cascaded down her back like curled ribbons and she gazed at him over her shoulder. This wasn't so difficult. . . .

"Let's lose the thong," he said.

Already? She swallowed and timidly removed the garment. *Screw it. What have I got to lose? All or nothing, baby.* She faced Phil head-on and her eyes bored into the lens with laser-beam intensity. Hands cocked on hips, stark naked. The unanticipated adrenaline rush made her nipples erect. *Coquette* had found its next great sex symbol, she was certain.

Hours flew by at jet speed and by the end of the shoot she felt like a seasoned pro. Not that she was a novice to modeling; before moving to Los Angeles, she had posed for clothing catalogs and bridal ads in her hometown of Troy, Michigan, and filmed a commercial for a hair care company. But those jobs were for local and regional companies. And the biggest difference—she had been fully clothed.

Coquette was a global phenomenon. Founded in 1964 by French-born entrepreneur Yves Rousseau, the magazine was a clever mix of celebrity interviews, self-help, and fashion tips for the modern man. Each month a young woman was featured in a multipage layout in various states of undress. Though not considered smut by the majority of the public, the periodical grew racier with each passing year—legs became farther spread and pubic hair reached extinction—and the more Rousseau pushed the taste level, the farther *Coquette* slipped on the relevancy meter. Its heyday of the 1970s was long gone, but still, public interest remained and there was never a shortage of women hoping to be the next discovery.

The day she discovered *Coquette* was seared in Callie's brain. "Come look at this," Susannah, her next-door neighbor, had whispered, and pulled a stack of magazines out of a cardboard box. Two twelve-year-old girls on a Saturday afternoon in February. Snooping in Susannah's basement. Virginia, Callie's mother, allowed her to play at someone else's house, for once. (Usually her chums had to come over to Callie's. "It's safer that way," Virginia reasoned.) The models' hips, breasts, and windblown tresses mesmerized the sixth-graders. "I hope I'm this beautiful when I grow up," Callie sighed, and Susannah nodded her pigtailed head in agreement. Neither of their prepubescent bodies were developing fast enough for their liking. Callie especially desired a figure like her mother's, a Jayne Mansfield build to replace her coltish shape. But the hips and breasts never fully sprouted. Her body remained several inches shy of the va-va-voom frame she craved.

Five cups of coffee and a can of hairspray later, Callie exited the set and gathered her belongings in the dressing room. Caffeine combined with adrenaline made her euphoric—high. She had given Phil her best and her poise hadn't faltered during the entire shoot. Spot on. The come-hither smile (despite the agony of the back-snapping poses), the pout, the attitude . . . it all felt so right, so *on*. She eased her sore feet into a pair of Havaianas and rummaged through her purse. Where had she placed her car keys? Girlish chatter echoed from the hallway and a young woman entered the room. Her wheat-blond hair was pulled high in a ponytail and her nose was sprinkled with freckles. Without a speck of makeup, the girl was radiant. Callie's confidence plunged several rungs.

"Hi, I'm Callie." Better to break the ice.

"Rachel." The girl snapped her chewing gum and threw her oversized tote on the makeup chair.

"Are you doing a test shoot, too?"

"Yeah, but I feel like hell. I do *not* want to be here. My head is killing me and I'm sore." Rachel stretched her neck from side to side.

Wait until you're under a slew of hot lights in skyscraper heels for hours, your body contorted in positions you never knew were possible, thought Callie. *You want to talk about sore!* "I hate photo shoots when I'm sick, too. The makeup artist has some Advil—I saw her taking some earlier."

"What, are you, like, in kindergarten?" Rachel said. "Why don't I just munch on Flintstones chewables and call it a day? Only a bottle of Vicodin could cure the way I feel. I'm so fucking hungover, I can't even see straight, but what else is new. Welcome to the raw and randy world of Rachel O'Connor." She looked Callie over with a curled lip and plopped on the floor. She drew her thighs up tight against her chest to shield any light from her face.

Must find keys ASAP. . . . She spotted them next to Rachel's small but shapely derriere.

"Good luck," Callie said, and darted out the door.

Rachel's raspy reply came when Callie was halfway down the hall: "Yeah, whatever . . ."

The sun singed Callie's forehead as she whipped her Mustang convertible into Casa Vega's parking lot. Four o'clock happy hour with Candice. She scanned the dining room for her friend but the muted lighting made it difficult to adjust her eyes.

"Hey, girlie!" called a girl from the bar. She bear-hugged Callie and slid a drink in front of her.

"Thanks, but I don't like salt on mine," said Callie.

"Perfect. More for me." Candice called to the bartender and ordered a salt-less margarita. "What's the latest? Have you heard back from *Coquette*?"

Callie shook her head. "They said I'd hear a yea or nay within a month but it's been six weeks. I thought the shoot went so well, but now I don't even know."

"Of course you'll get it. You're hot and *I* recommended you." Candice swirled her tongue along the salty rim.

Callie shrugged, unconvinced.

Candice had been featured in the May issue that year. As stunning as her pictorial was, she was more striking in person. On the short end of the stick at five foot four, she boasted 36-24-35 measurements, the kind of curves Monsieur Rousseau was partial to. She had hair so black, it was almost blue, and her personality was equally intense. Candice Boyd was a dynamo with energy to burn and keeping pace with her was often draining. She walked and talked with dizzying speed and gobbled life in giant mouthfuls, be it men, drugs, alcohol, or bucketloads of Jimmy Choos. Her adventurous spirit ("After all, I am a Sagittarius") attracted admirers at the dry cleaner's as easily as at any nightclub. It was during high school French class of freshman year when Callie first fell under her sassy older classmate's spell. ("Excuse me, do you have a pencil I can borrow?" she had asked Candice. "Tell me you love me and I just may let you keep it," Candice snickered.) Her brashness was—most of the time—infectious.

"I almost forgot. Look, can you tell?" Candice tipped her head in the light and pursed her lips.

"I spotted that pucker before I even saw you. I kid. They look great, plump but natural," said Callie.

"Thanks. He used two cc's. They're still swollen."

"I was wondering why you wanted to meet in the Valley," laughed Callie. "And in a dark place, too. Now it all makes sense."

"Of course. You know me, gotta keep up appearances." Her light eyes turned cloudy. "Actually, I need to ask you something. If you say no, I completely understand. But I could really use your help."

"Candy, you and I both hate beating around the bush. Spill it."

Candice polished off her margarita and slammed the glass down. "As you know, Lars and I have been fighting like cats and dogs. I've had a burning suspicion he's been whoring around so I played detective and guess what? I was right. He's been cheating on me. And with a crusty, pathetic fossil, no less."

Callie's kohl-rimmed eyes widened. "Who is she?"

"Some thirty-eight-year-old who calls herself a model," Candice snorted. "I found all sorts of disgusting texts and e-mails. He's a total douche bag, a dog. It's not like it hasn't been a long time coming. Our relationship has had more ups and downs than a goddamned yo-yo. But this time it's different. I'm done with him, finished, kaput. Sayonara, pal. So, my question is this: What do you think about me staying with you for a month or two while I look for my own place? We could split the rent. No pressure."

Callie suppressed a groan. As much as she adored Candice, she didn't want to live with her. She didn't want to live with anyone in her cramped studio apartment on Orchid Avenue, be it boyfriend, girlfriend, or four-legged friend; she treasured her privacy. But she couldn't turn down her friend in her moment of need. And besides—five hundred dollars a month in rent was leagues better than a thousand.

"How can I resist? Absolutely."

"Awesome!" yelped Candice. "Thank you, mama. I really, *really* appreciate it. You know I wouldn't ask this unless I was serious."

"I know. Lars has never been a favorite of mine and now I like him even less, if that's possible."

"That's the thing. For all of his acquaintances, I don't know too many people who genuinely like Lars. What was I thinking? For six months, *oy vey*. I guess I'm just a sucker for a hot body," Candice sighed.

"That you are. There are far worse crimes, though, that's for sure." Callie dipped a tortilla chip in guacamole and crunched. "Needless to say, you're not going to his birthday party tomorrow night at Skybar."

"Are you kidding me? But of course I'm going. And you better bust out a sick-looking dress because you're coming with me."

3

Callie lay curled on her couch and shuffled through Friday's mail: an electric bill, a flyer advertising a local house on the market, a preapproved credit card from Caring-Thru-Credit—and a letter from *Coquette*. Her pulse quickened and she tore open the envelope.

> *Dear Ms. Lambert,*
>
> *Thank you for your interest in becoming a model for Co-quette magazine. Regretfully, you are not what we are looking for at this time. We encourage you to try again in six months.*

She crumpled the letter and threw it across the room. Her eyes stung with shame and she couldn't control the large teardrops that ran down her cheeks. "Try again in six months"? The nerve! Was she supposed to get prettier by then? What was currently wrong with her? Were her breasts too small? Was her bone structure not adequately chiseled? Was she too thin or not thin enough? This didn't make any sense!

She swiped a compact from her purse and examined her heart-shaped face: the high cheekbones and round eyes suggested Eastern European blood. She was fortunate to have naturally full lips and straight teeth. Her nose was small but imperfect; she rubbed the tiny bump on her bridge and wondered what she'd look like with it streamlined. This imperfection had always bothered her; was *Coquette* bothered by it, too? She needed someone else's opinion and immediately thought of her friend Tyler. He possessed the subtlety of a nuclear bomb and always gave it to her straight. He answered her call on the first ring.

"What up, skank?" His favorite moniker—"skank"—was reserved only for those he held dearest. She informed him of the rejection letter. "That sucks. But you know that rag goes for bigger girls. You're small-boned, and that's not a bad thing."

"I know, but Candice was sure I'd get it and I figured she'd know since she was their girl in May—"

"Candice has a rump to rival Mama Cass, which is exactly what that Rousseau creep likes. I don't get it, but, then, I have a better shot at figuring out the thought process of an alien versus a straight male. You remember Tracy, the model I introduced you to at my birthday? Sweet as pie and a fabulous body, but in person, her face looks like what I dropped off in my toilet this morning. Their logic is lost on me." In the four years they had known one another—it felt closer to a lifetime due to their similar naughty senses of humor, plucky drive, and single-mother, Midwestern upbringing—he never held his feelings back, regardless of whom he spoke to.

"I don't understand it. I really thought I nailed it, but I guess not."

"You can't predict what the decision-makers are looking for. Half the time, *they* don't even know. I found that out when I first moved here to be an actor. Thank God I fell into makeup instead." Having been an Angeleno for two years, Tyler was quickly becoming a much-sought-after makeup artist after abandoning his short-lived acting aspirations. He figured if he couldn't rise to be the next Brad Pitt in record time, there was zero point in playing the game. "Just remember, Cal, it doesn't mean there's something wrong with you or you're not gorgeous."

"What does it mean, then?"

"It means if you want to be in their magazine, you need to gorge on Popeye's and Big Macs. Other than that, there's nothing you can do about it. Most girls would die to be pin-thin, so try to look on the bright side."

Tyler's point was valid. "So, what's new with you?" she asked.

"A soap actress has been keeping me super busy—Barbara Hickey, ever heard of her?"

"No, I don't watch soaps."

"She's been booking me for lots of events and I'm thinking of charging her extra. That old bag's all shades of crazy. I'm ready to say, 'Look, honey, I'm here to put your face on, I'm not your shrink.' Just wait till you book a role—you'll see what I mean. And you better not turn into a neurotic mess, either, or I'll ship you off to the loony bin. Actresses, they're all nuts. Barbara told me she spends four hundred dollars an hour on her doctor. Heavens to Betsy, for that price, a blow job better be included."

"And how. I'll call you later, Ty; I have to comb through the casting breakdowns. Hopefully I'll find a movie I can submit myself on."

"Sounds good. And cheer up, girl; it's not the end of the world. You've only been in L.A. a few months. Your time will come."

Tyler was probably right. Something was bound to come along.

The balmy temperature at eleven o'clock at night melted the cubes in Callie's Cape Cod. She watched the assortment of women and men with displeasure. Candice had pleaded with her to come, but Callie's mood was foul—thank you, *Coquette*. The last thing she felt like doing was mingling and pretending to care about arbitrary conversation. Despite her lack of enthusiasm, however, it was impossible not to appreciate the stunning view the establishment offered. Los Angeles stretched for miles below her, twinkling as if it were made up of the gems in Louis XIV's crown. Michigan never provided a view so grand.

Candice tapped her arm. "Look at Lars over there. How disgusting!" Lars Lindquist was surrounded by a group of women at the edge of the pool, his muscular body sprawled on a patio bed. A red-haired woman with a compact frame straddled him. Lars caught their glare and squeezed her buttocks. "That cocksucker. How dare he! That's the whore he's been cheating with. All two feet of her."

"She's not a complete troll but she's in dire need of a deep conditioning treatment," Callie noted.

"You should see the nude pictures she sent him. Ha! She's got more roast beef than Arby's. Rule number one, sweetheart: if you're going to show off your snatch, make sure it doesn't look like a goddamned grenade went off in your Frankie B's."

Callie scowled. "And why does he like her again?"

"Who knows. Unless her pussy drips Colombian emeralds, I don't see what's so special. Ewww, and look at that tramp stamp! That flower is bigger than my entire head," Candice sputtered.

"He's just trying to make you jealous. You should play ball with him, Candy, and give him a dose of his own medicine."

A tall man with well-defined features sauntered past. Candice eyed him and licked her lips. "Great minds think alike. Excuse me, Cal; I think I just found a late-night snack." She followed her prey across the deck and down the stairs.

The girls had officially been roommates for five hours. Following a bitter argument that began the previous night, Candice moved her possessions—which amounted to little more than clothes, shoes, and a collection of Chanel sunglasses—out of Lars's Beverly Hills condo and into Callie's Hollywood apartment. Lars begged her to stay with him—it was all a big misunderstanding, he said the dirty pictures meant nothing—but she refused to reconsider. When Candice's mind was made up, nothing or no one could waver her opinion. "Congrats, Lars, you are now free to fuck every Tom, Dick, and Jane you see with a clear conscience. Hell, fuck all of 'em at the same time. It's L.A., after all, so that's not too difficult, you asshole!" she had screeched amid a sea of flying shoes (Lars's shoes, certainly not her own).

"Hey, hot stuff. Can I buy you a drink?" A fortyish man with a mop of curly hair hovered next to her. A skull-embellished T-shirt stretched across his expansive chest and silver rings adorned each of his overly bronzed fingers.

"Sure, vodka cranberry." She wondered how he could get through airport security with all the hardware he sported. *Tool*.

"You got it." He turned to a nearby cocktail waitress. "Sweetheart, can I get a vodka cran and a vodka Red Bull? Thanks. So, let me guess what you do and don't tell me I'm wrong. You must be a model. What have you been in?"

"A few gigs in the Midwest where I'm from. I haven't been in L.A. that long."

"I can tell. You got an agent yet? If not, I can recommend a shitload. My list of contacts is longer than your legs." His smile revealed Chiclet-style teeth.

"I'm with Starr Talent but they mostly only handle print and commercials. I haven't found a theatrical agent yet so I submit myself on film and TV projects."

"Is that right?"

"Yeah. A friend e-mails me the casting breakdowns every day."

"I like your style; you're a hustler. You got a name?"

"Callie."

"Cool, an Italian girl. I'm a dago, too. Amir, nice to meet you."

"Actually, Callie is Greek for 'most beautiful,' but I'm also Czech." Why did Middle Eastern men in L.A. refer to themselves as Italian? Her landlord had an Israeli accent thicker than a sumo wrestler yet he insisted he hailed from Palermo. More important, how much longer until her cocktail arrived? She hated shallow banter but on a waitress's salary with drinks priced at fifteen bucks a pop, it was wise to stay put.

"Want a bump?" he said.

She had tried cocaine twice in her life—both times with Candice—and enjoyed the euphoric sensation, the inflated self-confidence. That Friday night, exhausted and depressed, she sampled it for a third.

Amir reached in his pocket and took out a set of car keys and a plastic bag. He dredged his key through the powder and held it in front of her nose.

"Thanks. Honestly, it's been one of those days," she said, and wiped her nostril.

"Why? Tell me about it." He took a sniff and hid the stash in his jeans as the waitress returned.

Callie recounted the *Coquette* debacle but glossed over how rejected she felt by concluding, "It's just the nature of the business. Besides, I'm an actress first and foremost. I got my SAG card a few months ago." A clump of coke passed through her sinuses and settled in the back of her throat. She had forgotten how much she enjoyed the drip, when her tongue and gums—every nerve in her body from the neck up—shimmied with numbness. Elation surged through her loins like a lightning bolt.

"If *Coquette* isn't interested, there's something wrong with them, not you," Amir said. He gave her another generous snort and took one himself. "An ex-girlfriend of mine tried out for them, too. Gorgeous girl, sexy as hell, but she was too thin for their taste. Man, they're behind the times. Give me an anorexic over a beached whale any day. Besides, you say you're an actress. My buddy directs music videos, union. I'm pretty sure he's got one cooking this week, matter of fact. Why don't you give me your digits and I'll hook you up with all the details?"

"Sure, why not." She scribbled her number on a cocktail napkin.

"Cool beans. Here, take my business card. Call me and I'll show you around town." He flashed a blindingly white smile before abruptly darting off.

AMIR YAVARI
Actor/Producer
Hollywood Extraordinaire

Callie rolled her eyes; he probably only wanted up her skirt and didn't have a music video connection, but what the hey—it was La La Land. Stranger things happened every day. She tucked the card in her purse and set off to locate Candice. Maybe her friend was having a better time of it.

The sun poured through the windows onto the sleeper-sofa where Callie and Candice slept. Callie groaned and pulled the covers over her face. Her head felt as if it would split in half like the *Titanic*. How much did she drink last night, anyway? She remembered downing four vodka cranberries—or was it five? There was the nose candy Mr. Tan Man had given her, too. Damn him. What was his name? Armand? Her brain was foggy. . . . She looked at the stove's digital clock. Ten past two. She flipped on the TV and a Britney Spears video blared, jarring her memory. That's right—the "Hollywood Extraordinaire" supposedly had a link to a director. *Please.* She regretted giving him her number. Oh, well. Candice stirred next to her but remained in a deep slumber. Canoodling with the genetically blessed specimen she found had failed to spark Lars's jealousy, to her immense disappointment. After downing a bottle of champagne and engaging in an hour-long make-out session, she tired of the charade and, to the relief of Callie, called it a night. "The one time I want his panties in a bunch and it doesn't happen. Humph. Go figure," she fumed during the cab ride home.

The high-pitched ring of her cell phone made her jump and, wearily, she answered it. It was her grandmother, Esme.

"Hi, honey, what's going on?" asked the elderly woman.

"I'm great, Grandma, how are you?" She wanted to gripe about how lousy she felt from the booze and blow. Grandma Esme was cool, but that would be pushing it.

Thirty minutes ticked by as she listened to details of her grandmother's week—gardening, the Michigan weather report, and how wonderful the employees were at her local post office. "There aren't enough hours in the day, I'm telling you. It's just a rat race," said Esme with a dramatic sigh.

Esme, her paternal grandmother, enjoyed a warm rapport with her granddaughter and was the only relative Callie spoke to on a weekly basis. Not that she had many family members to talk to, anyway. Her father had died of a brain aneurysm when she was just five and she didn't get on well with her mother. Mother and daughter were opposite in every way; Callie was off-the-cuff and affectionate, Virginia rigid and reserved. If Virginia wanted pancakes for breakfast, Callie wanted scrambled eggs; if Callie viewed a shade of gray as charcoal, Virginia argued that it was, in fact, pewter. With the exception of their dark eyes and high foreheads, the two had little in common. Their squabbling increased during her teenage years when Virginia married Tony, a supervisor at the General Motors plant. His reasoning ("Why go to a restaurant and pay twenty bucks for a piece of fish when I can go Up North and catch my own?") and crude babble ("That Candice sure does have a sweet set of knockers!") exasperated her. How could her mother go from choosing a sensitive, refined man such as her father to a loud-mouthed, vulgar hillbilly?

"Have you met any nice men yet?" asked Esme. Ever since Callie moved to L.A. three months ago, her grandma asked if she had snagged a man whenever they spoke. "You need a stable partner, someone to settle down with who worships the ground you walk on. Like how Grandpa was with me."

"Grandma, I don't want to be tied down. I moved for the weather and my career, not to find a man," Callie insisted.

"But you're all alone out there, honey, and I worry about you. Are you eating properly? Do you need any money?"

Callie assured her she had her own cash. Waiting tables produced meager but steady income and she had two thousand dollars in savings. The last thing she wanted was to be financially dependent on someone, especially a person as generous as her grandmother. Callie was determined to pay her own way.

The beep on her phone indicated call waiting. "I'll call you back, Grandma," she said, and switched to the second line.

"Is this Callie?" a man asked. His voice was baritone and unfamiliar.

"Speaking. Who is this?"

"I'm Jeremy Granger. I just got a call from my friend Amir. Says he met you last night and you're very cool, but more importantly, you're brunette and hot. I'm directing a music video tomorrow in Burbank and my lead girl got into a nasty car wreck last night. She can't make it to the set and I need a replacement. I saw your pictures on IMDb and you two could be twins. Are you interested?"

"Absolutely!" She couldn't believe it was even a question.

"Excellent. You've made my job a lot easier. Harold, the production assistant, will call you tonight with location details. See you tomorrow morning."

Harold rapped on the trailer door, startling Callie. She spilled the Styrofoam cup of coffee on her lap and cursed.

"They're ready for you, Miss Lambert!" he shouted.

"Got it!" she hollered back, dabbing herself with a paper towel. Finally! After four false alarms, she was antsy. She had checked in with Harold at 6 A.M., chipper and eager to work. They needed her as soon as possible, she was informed, and she was whisked into the hair and makeup trailer. An hour later she emerged, coiffed, glossed, and ready for her close-up. Jeremy was amazed how closely she resembled the girl originally cast in the video, the unlucky car crash victim. "I just can't believe it," he marveled, his bloated but friendly face cocked to one side. "You and Stephanie could be twins. What luck! Pure, unadulterated luck. By the way, minor change in plans—it's going be an hour, at most, before we need you." An hour passed, then came an update—at least another hour, technical difficulties. Another delay, the lead singer hadn't arrived yet. And then another . . .

Callie reclined in her trailer, napped, read a few magazines, and dozed off again. Hardly strenuous activity and not too shabby for a first-time *real* acting gig. CALLIE LAMBERT was displayed in bold print on the door and she felt proud. Her trailer, with its chipped paint and discolored flooring, contained little more than an oversized chair, a sink, and a toilet, but that was fine. It was air-conditioned and quiet and sitting here certainly beat waitressing. What was more, she didn't have to audition for the part. How fabulous was that? And the crew was welcoming, too.

Callie exited the trailer and walked alongside Harold as he chatted away. "The set isn't far off, just over this little hill here," he said. "Boy, one delay after another on this one. Hope you weren't too bored. You never can predict how long some of these shots will take. Thirty-three years in this business and I still get surprised. We just finished up Evan's first scene."

"Who's Evan?" she asked. With all of the hustle and bustle, she hadn't heard—or inquired—who the artist was.

Harold chuckled. "Evan Marquardt, the singer. You never heard of him?"

"Never."

"He's made a pretty big name for himself overseas. Good-lookin' fella. All the girls go ga-ga for him."

"Is he nice?"

"Very. Real easygoing and smooth. Talented, too, he sure can hit some notes, let me tell ya."

They walked up to the director's chair where Jeremy sat, his hands resting on top of his belly. "Thanks for hanging in there, Callie. Your scene isn't very long, but it's an important part. This is the dream sequence Evan sings about halfway through the song. What I'm going to have you do—" Jeremy threw his bulky body on the ground to demonstrate. "—is lay like this while I shoot you from a few different angles. Just look off in the distance, like you're daydreaming. No eye contact with the camera. Think you can handle that?"

"I definitely can," she said.

"Excellent." Jeremy turned to his crew. "Can I get a rehearsal up, please?"

Callie, barefoot, trotted to the designated filming spot and lay in the grass, her hair splayed around her head in a halo. Her chiffon gown billowed across her legs in wispy layers.

"And . . . action!" yelled the director. One of the crew members cranked Evan's "Keep It Sexy," an acoustic guitar–laden tune with a thumping backbeat. Callie performed as instructed, looking like an ethereal sphinx. The cameraman glided back and forth on the dolly, panning over her body and zooming in on her face.

"Cut! That's it, Callie, you got it. Can I get last looks, please?"

She felt someone staring at her, and it wasn't the people fluffing her curls and powdering her face. A man with rich dark hair stood several yards away, arms folded across his broad chest. He wore a mischievous smirk and his eyes were carnal. She turned her head several times to sneak a look at him, much to the frustration of the makeup artist touching up her lipstick. It was impossible to ignore this creature; he was the most gorgeous man she had ever laid eyes on.

Jeremy called out from his chair. "Okay, guys and gals, this time we're rolling film. And . . . action!"

Callie tried to focus but was distracted by Bedroom Eyes. She fantasized about dragging him back to her trailer and writhing around with him on the floor, naked and sweat-drenched. She hadn't had sex in six months and was tired of celibacy. Her most recent relationship had been with a maturity-challenged twenty-one-year-old psychology major and had lasted all of two weeks. She was beyond ready to wade into the waters again. *Bring on unbridled passion and toe-curling orgasms!* her brain chanted.

"Cut! You're dynamite. Give me one more for backup. Ready . . . and—"

"Jeremy, hold it. Let me see the playback." Bedroom Eyes walked past Callie, his brow furrowed. He examined the footage on the monitor and shook his head. "It's not sexy enough. She should change into something else, don't you think?"

"Sure, Evan, we can do that. Wardrobe, can you take Callie back to the trailer and see what else you can come up with?"

Callie caught the wicked glint in Evan's eye and flushed. *Dirty boy.*

Scott, the stylist, led her to the wardrobe trailer and combed the racks of clothing. He grabbed a micromini and held it up to her body, biting his lower lip in concentration.

"What do you know about Evan?" she asked. "Is he single?"

"Ooh, we have the hots for him, do we?" Scott bounced from one clothing rack to another in search of the perfect outfit. "I have no idea what his status is, but I'd jump all over that, too. Yum. What are we going to put you in? Hmm . . . I hate it when they scrap my entire outfit, those bitches. Here, try this on. If Evan wants sexy, we'll give him sexy." He handed her a purple gown with a plunging neckline. The dress fit her like a sausage casing and she felt self-conscious. Scott slid an armful of bangles on her wrist. "If this doesn't make Evan want to jump your bones, then I give up. Even *I'm* getting moist and I like clam as much as a vomit sandwich. March out of here, sister, and work it like a champ."

Bedroom Eyes was in deep conversation with Jeremy. His concentration shifted when Callie strolled back to the set. "Now, that's more like it. By the way, I don't believe we've had the pleasure of being introduced. I'm Evan."

Callie mumbled her name, spellbound by the intensity of his eyes. Her brain, spitting out one filthy thought after another, was in overdrive and ready to explode. Jeremy interrupted her reverie, anxious to resume work. "Is that sexy enough for you, Evan?"

"It'll work," Evan said with a wink.

"Great. Let's knock this out, everyone."

The set quieted and filming recommenced. An hour later, the scene wrapped amongst a smattering of applause from the crew. Piece of cake. Child's play. She could definitely get used to this.

Evan called her name as she was about to go back to her trailer and sign the necessary paperwork.

"So, tell me—what's your story? Boyfriend? Don't tell me a girl-friend?" he said. His voice was deep and sensual, a British accent audible.

"No and no. Free as a bird, the way I like it. And you?" she asked.

"Same. I've got a lot of filming left but I should be off by eleven. Join me for a bite to eat."

"I'd love to, but I have other plans." Callie ardently wished she didn't have to waitress that evening.

He didn't miss a beat. "How about Wednesday, then?"

"That sounds nice. Do you like sushi?"

"Doesn't everyone in L.A.? It's a prerequisite. Katana is my favorite. Does nine work for you?"

"Nine is fine. Until then . . ." She grinned and turned on her heel. He admired her ass as she wiggled down the hill.

"José, can I get an extra side of gravy?" asked Callie. She looked at the clock for the tenth time that hour—4 P.M. Two hours until her shift ended and five more until her date with Evan.

"Did you ring it up?" José, the short-order cook, flipped a hamburger on his griddle. His forehead was dotted with sweat.

"Not yet, I will in a minute. Everyone wants everything all at once and I can't get caught up."

"I gotta see a ticket. Adam said don't give out no nothing until you guys ring it up."

Callie filled a ramekin with Ranch dressing. "I'm the only one on the floor right now, José, and I'm in the weeds. This guy asked for a side of gravy ten minutes ago and I forgot it."

"Sorry, muchacha. No ticket, no gravy."

"Jesus Christ!" Callie dashed to the computer. Waitressing

challenged her patience. Knee-deep in customers and the only thing the cook could worry about was a seventy-five-cent bowl of slop. Couldn't she just be on a set again, participating in something artistic? There was nothing creative in slinging hash. Her job in Michigan—working as a dental assistant in small but affluent Farmington Hills—wasn't nearly as frustrating. In fact, she enjoyed working on people's teeth and the employee discount that came along with the job. (She prided herself on keeping her pearly whites in pristine condition.) But if she wanted to audition for gigs during the day, she was left little choice but to work nights. And the only people who worked nights, of course, were hookers and waitresses.

Callie had thought of nothing but Bedroom Eyes for the past three days. She hated to admit just how intrigued she was by him, but her interest was thoroughly piqued. She cleared grimy plates and refilled sodas with the vigor of a zombie, so sidetracked was she with intimate Evan details. How rare did he like his steak? Which side of the bed did he prefer? How did he want his women in bed? . . . When Wednesday rolled around, her hormones had reached lunatic level. She felt distracted, crazed with desire. When six o'clock finally struck, she was ready to tear out of Harry's like a bat out of hell, but she had at least an extra hour attending to menial side-work: wiping down ketchup bottles, stocking sugar bowls, and rolling sets of silverware. By the time she arrived home, she was left with little more than an hour to primp for her date.

Velcro rollers bobbed on her head as she raced around the three-hundred-square-foot apartment in search of the perfect outfit. Sexy but simple—she didn't want to come off as though she were trying too hard. Candice sat Indian-style on the living room floor with her laptop and a can of Diet Pepsi.

"This guy, Evan, is a pretty big deal in Europe," said Candice between gulps. "It says on Wikipedia he's had four Top Forty hits. He's an only child, like you, Cal."

"I'm impressed, tell me more. How old is he?"

"He just turned twenty-eight. Oh, no!" Horror was etched on her face.

"What's wrong with that?"

"He's a Leo. This could be a problem. Damn those Leos. Cocky pricks."

"That's silly. Astrology is a bunch of bunk. Just because Lars is a Leo . . ."

"And Trey and Kevin and Duke, too." Candice scowled. "Of all the men I've dated, every one of the main players has been a Leo. I am lion, hear me roar. And let's not forget the last guy in Michigan you dated for a minute. He was one, too. But Lars has them all beat."

Callie swiped her lashes with mascara. "Speaking of the devil, has he still been calling?"

"Yes, and I refuse to speak to him. He can go to hell in a hand-bag, especially after the way he behaved on Friday with Carrot Tramp. Whatever, it's old news. I'm moving on to greener pastures. Did I tell you I have a call-back for a film tomorrow morning?"

"The Jim Carrey flick? Yeah, you told me. I have an audition tomorrow, too, at one o'clock. One of the leads in a horror film."

"A *lead,* really? How did you manage that?"

"I submitted myself. Threw a headshot and résumé in an enve-lope and dropped it off at the casting office."

Candice rubbed the lip of her soda can against her chin. "I should ask Doug if he can get me in to read for that. Hmmm . . ." Doug Starr represented both girls.

Her face bathed in concern, Callie turned from the mirrored medicine cabinet and faced Candice. "Honesty time, so give it to me straight: What do you think of my nose?"

Candice studied her friend's features before answering. "There's a little bump on the bridge, like Jessica Simpson's, but it's not big. It's cute and suits your face."

"I've never been a fan of hers or my bump," sighed Callie. "I guess it doesn't really matter, though, since I don't have the money to fix it."

"If you're really serious about it, you should look into getting one of those cards aimed specifically for surgery. I know a girl who's paid for a boob job, veneers, you name it. You pay a little each month and it's totally manageable. As a matter of fact, something came in the mail the other day from one of those companies."

Callie searched the pile of envelopes on the kitchen counter and located the letter. "Caring-Thru-Credit has preapproved you for an account with a five-thousand-dollar limit," she read. "That's not enough for a nose job, though, is it?"

"I've never had one so I have no idea. I'll ask Jackie, she'll know. We're going to a club later. Hopefully there will be a fine assortment of meat in stock." She wiggled her eyebrows suggestively. "You look hot, mama."

Outfitted in skinny jeans and a slinky camisole, Callie climbed into a pair of pumps and tucked her crocodile-embossed clutch underneath her arm. "Thanks, and I'm late. The story of my life. Wish me luck."

Candice jumped to her feet and gave Callie a peck on the cheek. "Have a blast and remember: don't do anything I wouldn't."

Katana bustled with hipsters in head-to-toe black, ready to mack-down and mingle. Callie inquired with the hostess if Evan had arrived; he hadn't. Nerves raw, she ordered a mojito. Men had never made her nervous in the past, but there she stood, palms damp, with gelatin knees. She caught a whiff of tobacco from the nearby patio and walked outside in search of a smoke. A friendly bystander offered her a cigarette. Taking a thick drag, she observed the restaurant-goers and wondered if they, like her, were L.A. transplants.

And, suddenly, there stood Bedroom Eyes, looking succulent as ever. She inhaled his musky scent as he greeted her with a strong embrace.

"Are you hungry?" he asked her.

Callie's stomach growled as if on cue. "Famished. This place looks fantastic."

"It is. I'll go see if our table is ready."

They were seated at a cozy table on the patio. Evan stared at her from across the table, eyes flickering mischievously. "So, what's your story?"

"You beat me to the question. I was just about to ask you the same thing," she said.

He rested his elbows on the table. "All right, I'll go first. You want specifics? I've been a singer, professionally, for nine years and I'm slowly branching out in producing, working behind the scenes. I split my time between London and L.A. I like my coffee black, my beaches powder white, and find brunettes with long legs to be ridiculously sexy. How's that for an abbreviated bio?"

She blushed and reached for the bowl of edamame. "Why London?" she asked.

"My mother's originally from the UK. When I was a kid, she divorced my dad and we moved across the pond. London's my home. Plus, my son is there."

"I never would have guessed you're a father. How old is he?"

"Riley's five. London is great, but the weather here is pretty unbeatable."

"Tell me about it. Where I'm from, if we get two sunny days in a row, it's only through an act of God."

"Which leads me to my next question: Where are you from?"

"I moved here fourteen weeks ago from a Detroit suburb. I worked as a dental assistant for a few years and modeled on the side, but what I really wanted to do was act. Always have. Actually, let me take that back. I took gymnastics classes every week as a little girl, thinking I was going to be the next Nadia Comăneci, but

I broke my ankle during a tumbling exercise. While I was recuperating, I watched movies all day long and decided I wanted to be an actress."

"And what movie was the deciding factor?"

"*Gilda*. But, obviously, if I wanted to be in movies, I couldn't stay in Michigan. There was really nothing to keep me there, anyway. My grandmother, that's about it."

"What about your parents?" He swirled the Pinot Noir in his glass.

"My dad's dead and my mom is . . . how do I put it? We're two entirely different species. Like night and day."

"That's how my father and I are. Definitely not cut from the same cloth. I haven't spoken to him in years. The last I heard he was living with a woman in Buenos Aires. Let's get some chow before we keel over from hunger."

Evan instinctively knew what she would enjoy and ordered with abandon—yellowtail, eel, tuna, Kobe beef—and his take-charge attitude appealed to her femininity. Whenever one dish was a bite away from being consumed, another heaping serving arrived. She had never tasted sashimi and she enjoyed sampling the various types he chose.

Evan regaled her with tales of his travels. After originally starting off as the lead singer in a boy band, his career took him from Australia to Iceland and everywhere in between. He had visited every continent at least once and performed for millions of people over the years. Callie was struck how he didn't possess an overly inflated ego, unlike others she'd met who weren't half as accomplished. He could almost be described as a gentleman, but his devilish eyes betrayed him. The last of their plates were cleared and he said, "I live off of Sunset Plaza, right around the corner. Would you care to join me for a nightcap at my place?"

Were birds equipped with wings? She couldn't refuse.

Callie followed his icy Carrera up the sinewy canyon road. His residence was a vision of modern architecture—lofty ceilings and rooms displayed incredible views of the city. She marveled that his home was everything her apartment was not.

"How does Vueve sound?" Evan asked. He popped open a bottle and handed her a flute. Holding his gaze, she placed the champagne on the granite-slab countertop without taking a sip. They stood so close, she could feel his breath on her face.

"I want you inside of me," she breathed in his ear. She slipped her hands under his shirt and ran her nails along his back. Evan gave her the longest, hungriest kiss she had ever experienced before feverishly tearing her clothing off and pulling her into the bedroom. Callie's six-month dry spell had finally come to an end.

Nympho Cheerleaders Attack! Callie read the script's title and chuckled. The plot of the low-budget horror film was farcical. Mildly entertaining, at best. She sat in the lobby, waiting for her name to be called, going over her lines. The audition couldn't be that difficult; the role of Layla, a bisexual college girl, wasn't exactly Blanche DuBois. Hell, it wasn't even Nomi Malone. But it was one of the leads in a low-budget film backed by a powerhouse studio and that was enough to excite her.

Focusing on the role was difficult—she kept replaying her debauchery-filled night, the multiple rounds of passion. Evan had not disappointed. The sex was intense, unbridled. She left his place at ten in the morning, bleary-eyed yet exhilarated, and returned to her apartment. Duty called. She showered after downing three cups of coffee and felt tip-top, but her mind was in another place. She couldn't stop thinking about him—those rock-solid arms, the way his body quivered when he was about to orgasm, the ravenousness of his tongue . . . *Concentrate. Nothing like a man to complicate things.* She tried to dismiss him but his memory nagged her like a premenstrual woman.

"Callie Lambert, you're up," said a woman, holding the sign-in sheet. Callie followed her into a small, musty-smelling room. Daniel Joyce, a slight, fey man in his forties, was seated next to a video camera operated by his pink-haired assistant, Rocket.

"State your name, height, and weight for the camera," said Daniel.

"Callie Lambert, five foot seven, one hundred and twelve pounds."

"And if you could show us both profiles and do a three-sixty."

She pulled her hair back from her face, displaying first her left profile, then her right, and slowly turned around.

"Rocket's going to read with you. She'll be Kiki. Whenever you're ready."

Callie cleared her throat and said in her best snarl, "I'd rather be dead than a homicidal maniac like you, Kiki."

"You've been itching to be in my shoes for years, bitch." Rocket's voice was devoid of emotion.

"Oh, you think so? I'm too good for you and your cheerleading team. I ooze class and you drip trash. I'll tell you this: no longer will I sit on the sidelines while you steal my thunder. Your time here is finished. Hell hath no fury like a cheerleader scorned!" Callie spit the last line.

"Good job. Thanks, Callie," said Daniel.

She was thrown off by the abrupt dismissal; there were two more pages' worth of dialogue between Layla and Kiki—surely they couldn't be finished with her yet. "You don't want me to finish the scene?"

"No, we have a lot of girls to get through today. We just want something on tape to show Tom, the director, so he can get to callbacks as quickly as possible."

"Thanks, guys. Have a good day." She stepped out of the room just as Daniel called her back.

"By the way," he said, "are you comfortable with nudity?"

"Totally."

"Good. Tom wants me to make sure. Some girls say they're fine then change their mind at the last minute. If we bring you back, he'll want to do a body check on camera."

"No problem. I was born naked."

"We'll be in touch."

Confused, she walked to her car. Perhaps they liked her read after all. Guessing what casting directors were looking for was so difficult. Maybe they'd end up going with a blonde, someone shorter, taller, fatter, paler, darker, blander. For all she knew, maybe they wanted a limping, one-eyed freak with buckteeth and a third nipple who suffered from Tourette's. One thing was crystal clear to her about the casting process: it was impossible for her to tell what the powers-that-be had in mind, so she may as well be herself. She had done her best; onward to the next project.

Starr Modeling and Talent hadn't called her in weeks. Had they forgotten about her? Their roster of talent was large and it was easy to get lost in the shuffle. She dialed their number and the receptionist patched her through to Doug Starr.

"Hey, girlie, I was just about to call you," Doug said. Funny, she thought—he always said the same thing whenever she called. His agency had first opened during the late 1980s, inconveniently located in Long Beach, but convenient for Doug, only five minutes from his house. His clients weren't at the top of the totem pole but the gigs he booked for his talent were steady—commercials, liquor ads, lingerie catalogs, swimsuit calendars, and the occasional part in film and television. Typical of a C-list agency. If a company was in need of spiky-haired beefcake or Rapunzel-tressed, globular-breasted women, Doug was the man to see.

"I beat you to it," Callie said. "Any auditions for me, Doug?"

"Actually, something better. I just got off the phone with the owner of this skin-care line—you've probably heard of it, Skyn by Symone. It's kind of last-minute, but they're doing a trade show in Vegas this weekend and want to book two of my girls, one of them being you. A grand for two days. What do you say?"

"I say hell-to-the-yes, book me."

"You got it. They'll have a booth set up for you. Just look pretty, ask passersby if they'd like to try their creams. Einstein shit like that," he said.

"Hmm, that sounds pretty heavy, I don't know if I can handle that, Doug. Who else did they book?" Callie merged onto the 101, homeward bound.

"Gabrielle Manx. You two will be sharing a hotel room. I'll call you when I know specifics regarding your flight and whatnot. In the meantime, I'll call them back to confirm you. Thanks, sweetheart."

"Ditto, talk with you later." How about that: Las Vegas. She had never visited but had always wanted to. Not that she was a gambler. Blackjack, occasionally. Two fewer days she had to be at Harry's, too. Adam, her manager, had a crush on her and getting out of work at the last minute wouldn't be a problem. She searched the radio for a Sinatra or Elvis tune—something to put her in the Sin City spirit—before stumbling on "Keep It Sexy" on 102.7. She swooned when Evan sang the familiar lines: *Keep it steady / Keep it sexy / Girl, I got it bad for you / Can't you see I'm mad for you.* . . . Damn you, Bedroom Eyes. As if she needed to be reminded of that luscious beast; she'd thought of nothing *but* him since leaving his mansion a couple of hours ago. Her cell beeped—a new text. Perhaps it was from Evan—she'd left her number on a Post-it next to his bed.

*Hey mama—can you pick me up? Westmount by Santa Monica.
xoxo*

Callie was a mile from 1778 Orchid Avenue—hardly close to Candice. Other than a 6 P.M. shift at Harry's, though, she didn't have anything going on; there was plenty of time to drive to West Hollywood.

Santa Monica Boulevard was a disaster; construction made traffic drip like molasses. Candice sat curbside and her appearance was startling; bags hung from her crepey eyes, red blotches splattered her porcelain skin, and stringy hair fell on her shoulders like tumbleweeds. She was clothed in the previous evening's cocktail dress. A loaf of month-old pumpernickel would have looked fresher.

"I haven't been to bed yet," said Candice in response to Callie's quizzical look.

"I gathered. What happened?"

"Jackie and I met these two French guys and we ended up partying in their room at the Four Seasons. Oh my God, Cal, it was *so* much fun, we were all crazy-smashed. Jackie and I went back to her apartment a few hours ago and she passed out. So there I was, stuck without a car."

"What happened to your call-back? Didn't you tell me it was this morning? Buckle up." Candice strapped the seat belt over her chest. "The call-back, yeah . . . that shouldn't be a problem. I called Doug and told him I couldn't make it and to just reschedule me."

"Umm . . . how do you plan on rescheduling a *call-back*?"

"I asked him to call the casting office to see if I could come in tomorrow but we haven't heard back yet. Please. It can't be that hard. I'm way too strung out to go in today. Anyway, I've auditioned twice for that casting director. What's her name? Shit, I can't remember, but she *loves* me. Tomorrow will work out so much better."

"Let me tell you about the night I had, Candy. We had an amazing time. Evan and I—"

"Can you fill me in on everything later? I'm exhausted and could really use a nap. So tired . . ." Eyes closed, Candice tilted her seat back and stretched her legs.

This was the thanks she got for driving to the other side of town?! Candice couldn't even give the simple courtesy of listening to the fantastic time she had? Callie pressed her lips in silence and vowed never to let a friend—especially one of ten years—take advantage of her again.

Callie panted as she lugged her suitcase and oversized duffel bag up three flights of stairs. The Vegas Motor Inn's elevator was out of order and she was wearing high-heeled ankle boots. *Room 320, where are you?* Of course; the very last door at the end of the open hallway. *Figures.* She flung the door open and tripped over a stiletto.

"I'm so sorry!" said a young woman. She dashed across the room and snatched her shoe off the floor. "Here, let me help you with your things."

"Thanks," Callie said, and turned her duffel over to the tall blonde.

"I nearly died, too. I always over-pack, and hauled three suitcases up here. I'm Gabrielle, by the way. Gabby, for short."

"Very nice to meet you. I'm Callie. You'd think Skyn by Symone would put us up in a nicer place, wouldn't you?"

"You certainly would. I got here an hour ago and called Doug to see if there was anything that could be done, but no such luck. Supposedly everything is sold out because of all the conventions going on." She placed the worn nylon sack next to her Louis Vuitton suitcase.

Callie flopped on one of the stiff queen-size beds. "It's probably because they don't want to fork over extra money. It's Vegas; how can everything be sold out?"

Gabrielle gestured toward the room and laughed good-naturedly. "Well, obviously, not *everything* is."

The Vegas Motor Inn held the stench of mothballs and looked like it was straight out of an amateur porno from the 1970s. Dark, braided carpeting; dingy floral bedspreads at least thirty years old; a rotary-dial telephone situated on a sad, weary desk. Callie was thankful her roommate was a good sport. Most women as beautiful as Gabrielle were cantankerous snoots or prima donnas. And she was more mature than the girls she'd met on castings; she guessed Gabby to be in her upper twenties.

"Want to do a little gambling? It's my first time in Sin City and I definitely don't want to stay cooped up in this dump," Callie said.

"Ooh, a virgin, are we? When I was married I lived here for four years. I know it like the back of my hand. I'll be your tour guide, come with me." Gabrielle pulled Callie to her feet and looped their arms together.

The girls hailed a taxi and rode it to the Hard Rock—Gabrielle had a few friends who worked there. Callie was stunned by the crowd's appearance—everyone was dressed in double-extra-large T-shirts and flimsy cotton shorts. Fanny packs sprouted from their blubbery bellies. Where were the Cavalli gowns, the wrists and necks swathed in jewels, the elaborate updos? Not a single pair of

Choos or Blahniks could be spotted. Even pedicured feet were scarce. What a disappointment!

"You know, I expected people to be much more glamorous and about two hundred pounds thinner. Like Sharon Stone in *Casino*." Callie coughed as they passed a row of Winston-puffing senior citizens at the slot machines.

Gabrielle giggled. "That's cute, hon, but you've watched too many movies. In Vegas, they rope 'em in with four-pound hot dogs that cost a buck. Cheap food and a big jackpot, that's the allure. There are tons of upscale places, though, way more than when I lived here."

Mouths of women and men alike dropped as Gabrielle Manx sashayed through the casino. She was a stunning spectacle. The cleavage spilling from her tank top—DDDs—coupled with forty-inch legs made it impossible not to gawk at least once and often thrice. She feigned indifference but her smile made it clear she relished the commotion.

The girls played several rounds of blackjack, but after an hour, their wallets were substantially lighter. "They're really cleaning us out. Would you like to have a drink and just talk?" Gabby asked. They took a seat at the casino's main bar. "I haven't been back to Vegas in quite some time. Too many memories."

"What happened?" Callie ordered an ice-cold beer.

"My husband and I lived here when we were married. The best years of my life. We had it all—we were happy and trying to have a baby, had lots of money . . . and then everything was thrown upside down when he died. So unexpected, too, a total freak accident."

"I'm so sorry. . . ."

"I wasn't in very good shape for a while. I guess you can say I'm still a mess because I can't find relationships that ever last. Justin was an amazing man and I compare every guy I meet to him. No one seems good enough. That's not too fair, is it?" Gabby's tigress eyes were distant.

"When did you move to L.A.?" Callie asked.

"Six years ago. Justin begged me to get my boobs done as big as possible then what does he do? He high-tails it to heaven. Well, what was I supposed to do with these girls except come to L.A. and bust into the business, so to speak? But I've had enough of that town. I'm thirty-two. I want a family. I'd really like to move back to Connecticut, where I'm originally from, and open my own bed-and-breakfast. Just abandon the entertainment business altogether and try something new."

As keen as Callie's imagination was, she couldn't picture Gabrielle stoking the fire and serving coffee and muffins to visiting Iowans.

"Do you have a man in your life?" Gabby asked.

"No, not really. There's this one guy I kind of like. . . ." She filled Gabby in on her night with Bedroom Eyes and was animated, giddy.

"He sounds like a great catch."

"I'm not pursuing a relationship," Callie quickly added. "Too complicated. It's just a little crush, a little nookie. I don't want a boyfriend."

Gabby grinned. "You lie like a rug. It's written all over your face. You may call it just a 'crush,' but do yourself a favor and be careful. Men in L.A. are all players and they can sense you're fresh off the boat. Guard your heart at all costs. That's the problem with me—I'm all heart." She sighed and reached for her champagne.

"I probably won't ever see him again. Besides, it's not like I can call him since I didn't get his number."

"But did you leave him your number?"

"Yep, I made sure of that."

"He'll call, all right. Why wouldn't he? You're beautiful and seem really sweet. There's this girl-next-door quality about you and guys love that. Say, would you like to join me for dinner tonight at TAO? We don't have to stay up late or get crazy—our call time is pretty early tomorrow. My friend is the manager and he'll comp everything."

"Try not to twist my arm. At the rate I just played, I could use a free meal."

11

Callie and Gabrielle sat in folding chairs in front of a large display booth. Skyn by Symone was one of hundreds of companies gathered at the Las Vegas Convention Center. Merchants from around the globe hawked every conceivable beauty product—follicle-smoothing conditioners, body butters that smelled like French patisseries, face masks thick enough to suffocate a small child . . . Callie handed out packet after packet of samples until her arm went limp. The owner of the company—Symone, of course—stopped by the booth throughout the day to check on sales, but for the most part, the girls were on their own.

"Hi, ma'am, would you like to give your skin the gift of moisture with Skyn by Symone? For an even forty dollars, you can purchase our best-selling kit that includes cleanser, toner, and anti-aging serum," Gabrielle told a dour-looking woman. Despite the frigid air-conditioning, the woman panted and fanned herself with a brochure. She appraised Gabrielle warily.

"Is it gonna give me skin like yours?" she said gruffly.

"Probably even better than mine," Gabby said.

"I need all the help I can get. Okay, give me two. My sister's got skin like a leper."

Callie chuckled as the woman walked off with her purchase. "God, Gabby, you could sell the Brooklyn Bridge to a cockroach."

"It's easy. Just be nice to people and tell them what they want to hear. Simple formula. I'll be glad to get out of this place soon, though, I'll tell you that. I should have brought a sweater." Gabby rubbed her bare shoulders.

"It's freezing," Callie agreed. "Any plans for tonight?"

"An old friend is taking me out."

"Nice. Is he cute?"

"Umm . . . no, not really." Gabrielle examined her French-manicured nails. Given her distracted demeanor, Callie decided not to press for details.

Seven o'clock marked the end of the girls' ten-hour shift. Gabrielle rushed to the motel to primp for her date while Callie pondered which show to see that evening. Her phone rang before she could decide. It was Tyler.

"Didn't you tell me you're in Vegas this weekend?" he said.

"Yeah, I just finished working a long trade show. What about you?"

"I'm in Vegas, too, last-minute thing. Old Bag Barbara flew me out because she's attending a red-carpet charity event tonight at the Hilton. What are you up to?"

"Nothing, unfortunately."

"Good—you're coming with us," said Tyler. "Barbara's limo is picking us up at our hotel at eight thirty. Why don't you meet us there and we can all ride to the party together?"

"Sounds great. What should I wear?"

"You're the only person I know who looks amazing in anything. Wear whatever you like. I swear if you threw on a potato sack, you'd still be one hot bitch. Whatever you do, don't be late, because Barbara will have a conniption and she's already on my last nerve. We're at the Bellagio, by the way."

"Awww, you poor baby. Such a tough life you live, Ty."

"I know, right? A three-thousand-square-foot suite. Poor me. Better get yourself ready, you big skank. I'll see you soon."

With little time to spare, Callie flew to her motel and threw on the only dress she'd packed—a clingy black number. She pulled her hair in a twist and slicked red lipstick on. A cab dropped her off at the Bellagio an hour later and she was proud of how early she was, for once. Tyler greeted her in the lobby with a big hug.

"You're *early*? Christ, hell really has frozen over. Let's go up to the room and grab a drink. Just to warn you, Barbara's been eating Vicodin like chocolate-covered cherries, so disregard anything she says." They rode the elevator to the top of the building. Tyler's heavily tattooed arm flung the suite's door open. Barbara Hickey sat in the opulent living room playing the grand piano. In a cracked, shrill voice, she sang so loudly, she didn't hear anyone enter.

"Barbara!" Tyler screamed. "I want you to meet my friend."

Barbara looked up from the keys and smiled broadly. At age sixty-two with countless plastic surgeries, her face was pulled tighter than a drum. Clusters of diamonds covered her well-wrinkled neck and hands. "I'd be delighted to," she said, and rose from the bench with gallantry. "I'm Barbara Hickey. I'm sure you know me from *Son of the Hamptons*."

"Thank you for inviting me, Barbara," said Callie.

"Callie and I met in Michigan. We worked for the same dentist," Tyler explained.

"How *fabulous*. I *adore* Tyler, I refuse to let anyone else touch my face. He's magic. I look ten years younger when he's done with me. Come have a glass of Dom, our car will be here shortly." She waltzed to the minibar, her ball gown rustling. Barbara knew drama like soap knew suds. She handed Tyler and Callie their drinks. "The gala is at the Hilton. It's a charity benefiting muscular dystrophy, such a wonderful organization. Marjorie, a dear friend of mine, is chairwoman. Very glam, very froufrou, *very* exclusive." She raised her sharp, penciled eyebrows and swilled Dom. "I'll probably know every battleax in that place and I'm told my fourth and fifth ex-husbands are attending. You two will undoubtedly be the youngest scamps there. Assuming, of course, hubby *número cuatro* doesn't bring his wife. Last time I checked, minors weren't allowed. I own girdles older than that one." She adjusted the pearl brooch on her bosom.

"As long as there are plenty of young and available men, I'm sure this soiree will be fantastic," piped Tyler.

"Darling, I hate to break it to you, but you'll be lucky if any man is under sixty," Barbara said.

"Damn it. Old queens are never any fun, and what's more, they don't die, either—they just move to Silver Lake."

Barbara flung her russet head back and cackled. The phone buzzed. "Hello? Yes, this is Mrs. Hickey. Thank you, I'll be down in a moment. That's our car, kiddies. Right on time. Tyler, you can touch me up en route. And here, take Mr. Pérignon with us for the road. I never let a good bottle of booze go to waste." She swayed in her satin pumps.

The partygoers at the Hilton made a Fort Myers retirement

community look young. Everyone Callie encountered was a senior citizen, or on the brink of becoming one. She and Tyler scanned the table of dried-out hors d'oeuvres while Barbara fluttered about, air-kissing one crony after another.

"Everything here is old," Tyler said incredulously. "The money, the people, and, good Lord, the food. Guess I'm on a liquid diet tonight."

Callie wanted to enjoy herself but felt lonesome. That's silly, she thought. She was in Las Vegas with one of her best friends, how could she be sad? Being surrounded by so many elderly people made her think of Grandma Esme; she missed her. And then there was the matter of her career, or lack thereof. In four months, she had auditioned for twenty commercials, one TV show, and twelve print gigs. Not one did she book. The music video was sheer luck. True, the trade show money wasn't shabby—and it was flattering they chose her out of hundreds of models—but doling out face cream wasn't exactly going to propel her up the entertainment ladder.

"The end of summer is always slow, babe. Trust me, I've seen it happen for seventeen years," Doug had told her. But then, he repped numerous pretty girls, too many similar-looking types to keep track of. It was easy to get lost in the shuffle. And with her skimpy résumé, it was difficult obtaining a primo agent. Other than Tyler and Candice, Callie knew few people—before moving to L.A. she had never been to the West Coast. Had she made a colossal blunder by leaving behind her familiar surroundings to pursue a career she knew nothing about? Her mother and friends back home were quick to point out it was an insane move, a misjudgment she'd come to regret. But she'd rather follow her heart than wonder what could have been. Screw sitting on the sidelines—that was for suckers. She wanted in on the action.

A glowing head of hair caught Tyler's attention. "That girl over there is gorgeous. Just look at those highlights! Wonder why she's at this geriatric convention?" Callie almost dropped her glass when she saw the girl's face—it was Gabrielle, wrapped in a cream, strapless sheath, all glowing skin and gravity-defying breasts. She clung to the arm of a much-older Asian man. "Skank, is that the girl you're doing the convention with? She looks how you described her to a T. Jesus, Mary, and Joseph—she's so hot, she could even make me go straight."

Callie guffawed. "Ty, please, you need dick the way a diabetic needs insulin."

"That's so true but I haven't been laid since the *Lusitania* set sail; a woman is almost looking better than my right hand about now."

Why didn't Gabby mention she was attending the gala? Why so secretive? She did say an "old friend" was taking her out and that was true; her friend was certainly old. But it was odd. . . . Gabby seemed to be enjoying herself, laughing at the man's jokes, looking at him attentively when he spoke. He clearly got a thrill from being seen with a beautiful, much younger woman. But what did she see in him? Callie considered saying hello but was uncomfortable. If Gabby spotted her first, that was fine—if not, even better. Too late, anyhow; she and the man had left.

Callie decided to call it a night, too, and wanted to say good-bye to Barbara but couldn't locate her. "Thank her again for me," she told Tyler. A bed—even one as uncomfortable as that at the Vegas Motor Inn—sounded nice. She could have peace and quiet and be alone with her thoughts.

Hours later as Callie lay in bed, the door creaked open and Gabrielle slipped in the room. She held her heels in one hand and tiptoed to the dresser, careful not to wake Callie. There was no need for her to be so quiet—Callie had tossed and turned for the last three hours, unable to sleep.

"Hi, Gabby," Callie said, sheets pulled to her chin.

Gabrielle jumped. "Oh! You scared me. I'm sorry, I didn't mean to wake you. I thought I was being quiet."

"You're fine, I just can't fall asleep. How was your night?"

"Pretty boring, actually. Dinner and a club, nothing special. What did you end up doing?" She grabbed a nightie out of the drawer.

"My friend Tyler and I went to a charity event at the Hilton." She waited for a response. It was too dark to make out Gabrielle's expression.

"That sounds fun. Did you enjoy yourself?"

"Not especially. I left early. Tyler's a makeup artist who works with this old soap actress, Barbara Hickey. She invited us. And man, is she ever a character."

Gabrielle unzipped her dress and walked to the bathroom. "I love Barbara Hickey! She's been on *Son of the Hamptons* for decades. I hear she's a real trip. Boy, do I ever reek of cigarettes. I'm going to shower and hit the sack. Good night. I hope you get some sleep, hon."

"Thanks. Pleasant dreams." Callie lay restless in bed, pondering Gabrielle's secrets. Finally, at four o'clock, sleep . . .

The clouds wafted by like strings of spun cotton and after a forty-minute flight, the plane landed in Burbank. Callie tapped her foot, anxious for the conveyor belt to spit out her luggage. Vegas had been a letdown, hardly the land of glamour she'd pictured. She'd seen women with more class pumping gas at the local Shell back in Michigan. The point of her visit, though, was to work. Mission accomplished. And then there was Gabby—meeting her was an unexpected pleasure and they had exchanged numbers before departing. During breakfast, Callie almost slipped and asked her where she had purchased her beautiful, creamy gown, but thought it wise not to mention the gala—it was too awkward. And, any-way, it was probably a bunch of nothing, Callie thought dismissively. She made a mental note to call Gabby later in the week. Gabby was a rarity, a combo of beauty *and* brains, and Callie wanted to keep in touch.

She pulled out of the parking lot and flipped on her cell; there was a new text from a number she didn't recognize: *What are you up to? You left your bra at my place.* Ah, Evan . . . She responded saying she didn't have any plans. Not that he'd be available; she was sure he was too busy to see her. But throwing a line out never hurt.

Your legs should be pinned behind your ears right now, he texted.

She shivered at the memory of him lying between her legs, clutching her hips as he kissed her inner thighs, removing her panties in a single forceful tug . . .

I want to wrap my cunt around your neck, Callie fired back. She slapped her hand over her mouth—where was this smut coming from? Never before had she spoken so filthy! But then, none of her previous boyfriends had been as uninhibited as Bedroom Eyes and her potty side hadn't been fully unleashed. Brian Belsam, her longest relationship, was as sexually exciting as a ball of lint. She asked him once to spank her and he balked. Eight months together and he couldn't indulge in minor S and M? He looked good on paper—a handsome six-footer, late twenties, with a solid job at Daddy's law firm—but in reality, he was blander than instant pudding. She dumped him the next day. Bedroom Eyes, God bless him, brought out her inner slut. What was she to do but embrace her racy side? Her phone beeped again.

Get your fine ass over here, sexy. I want to drink you.

Her wheels squealed as she made a U-turn. The farther she raced down Sunset Strip, the harder her heart pounded. Fast, faster she sped. She couldn't get to him quickly enough. One order of whore, served piping hot and delicious, coming up.

She found him lounging in bed, half naked, and pounced on

him. "What have you been up to, stranger? I missed you." She nuzzled his neck.

"What exactly did you miss?" said Evan.

"This." She grabbed the bulge in his Hudson's.

"Mmm," he moaned. "And why haven't you called me, again?"

"You didn't give me your number. Besides, I just got back from a job in Vegas."

"Vegas? Slinging pussy for high rollers again, is that it?"

Callie hit his stomach. "Exactly. Everyone else pays for it but you get it for free. By the way, 'Keep It Sexy' is everywhere! I must have heard it a hundred times this weekend. It's going to be huge." Callie was excited for Evan; not only had it been several years since he'd had a hit, he'd never before experienced a smash in the United States.

"It's tearing up the charts. Completely unexpected. Certainly puts my record label back in my court. The album drops September twenty-first. You'll have to come to the release party."

"I'll see if I can ease it in my schedule." She straddled Evan and ran her hands over his sculpted limbs.

"What a little tease you are." He ripped her top off and gripped Callie's shoulders. Without much effort, he tossed her on her back. His lips tickled her breast and her nipple grew hard between his teeth.

"*Fuuuuuuuck,*" Callie panted as goose bumps spread across her body.

"Fair warning," he growled, "I have an ambulance on standby. And I'm not stopping until the neighbors hear you scream."

"Please. Pretty please, Evan, give it to me. I can't wait any more. . . ."

13

Dr. Harlan C. Coop had practiced the art of plastic surgery in Newport Beach for sixteen years. He specialized in facial reconstruction and often traveled to third-world countries to repair cleft lips and other deformities for little to no salary. Callie was impressed with his credentials and, almost as important, he accepted Caring-Thru-Credit. He came highly regarded from Candice's friend Jackie; she was thrilled with the nose he had carved for her the previous summer. A last-minute patient cancellation enabled Callie to schedule a consultation right away. She had never undergone surgery of any kind and the idea of an operation to appease her vanity left her slightly unsettled. *It's a free consultation,* she thought. *No harm in that.* She could always back out of anything more.

A stern-looking man with a narrow face and bulbous eyes, the doctor listened to Callie describe what she disliked about her appearance. "It could be streamlined, to be sure," he said, and lightly ran his fingers over her nose. "Are you looking to thin out the bridge as well or do you only want the bump shaved down?"

She hadn't thought about changing the width of her nose. Was it necessary? Was a rhinoplasty *ever* necessary? "I haven't decided. What do you think is best?"

"Well, this is the way I look at it: if you're going to go through the procedure to begin with, shouldn't you do everything you can to get the most aesthetically pleasing result? Why take your car in for just an oil change when it needs new brakes, too? In my opinion, it would look best if I reset the nose and took out the bump. It's not a problematic nose—there's no deviated septum or the like. The procedure isn't very difficult. It would take an hour, maybe an hour and a half, max."

"How do you 'reset' a nose?" asked Callie.

"By breaking it. That's the easy part; it only takes a few taps. The healing time is longer—there's more swelling whenever anything is broken—but that's the only way to narrow it. The good news is you don't need much done. With just a little tweak, you'll see a subtle but substantial improvement." The doctor spoke breezily, as though reciting what he ate for breakfast.

"How much is all this going to cost?"

"Bethanny handles all that. She'll go over the cost in her office and I'll tell her to give you a discount, too, since you came here by referral. Jackie had a nose similar to yours, actually, only more hooked."

"I get it from my mom's side," sighed Callie. Although Virginia inherited a ski-jump nose, she passed her family's prominent feature to her daughter.

Bethanny, a mousy-looking woman, handed her a sheet of paper. "Here's the price breakdown, including the fee for the anesthesiologist and the facility. This reflects the thirty percent discount Dr. Coop is giving you, also." The grand total was six thousand dollars.

The cost wasn't surprising—in fact, Callie had expected the figure to be higher. She could dip into her savings and use the new credit card for the rest. Plus, she had money coming in from the trade show—$850, after Doug's cut. Life was too short to spend it being unhappy, she rationalized, especially when options were available. Every movie star she could think of had gone under the knife at some point in their career. How could they not when the camera magnified every feature and flaw? It was routine, like visiting the dentist for a cleaning. She worried about getting the necessary time off work, but no matter—she'd figure that end out later. Mind settled, she grabbed the fountain pen Bethanny dangled in front of her.

Person to be contacted in case of emergency. That was something Callie hadn't considered. She filled in her grandmother's name and pictured the older woman saying in a voice tinged with worry, "Honey, did you do something to yourself? You look different. No, it's not your hair and it's not your makeup, it's something else. I can't quite put my finger on it. . . ." Her mother's reaction—if she noticed at all—would be less kind. Callie brushed that aside and focused on how photogenic her profile would be. The notion greatly pleased her.

"Hi, this is Rocket from Daniel Joyce Casting. We would like to see you for a call-back this Tuesday for the role of Layla in *Nympho Cheerleaders Attack!*"

Callie couldn't believe her ears—Daniel actually liked her read! He wanted to see her again! It was a cheesy sleaze fest, but it was a call-back. "What time?" she asked.

"Four o'clock. Daniel wanted me to mention the director and producers will be there this time, so come prepared."

Check. If auditioning for Layla meant swinging from a trapeze by her labia, so be it. She'd show up to the audition waxed and ready.

Callie expected five or nine or twelve girls waiting in the lobby, but there were none, and she was called in immediately. Three new faces greeted her when she walked into Daniel's office: director Tom

Johannesburg and the producers, look-alike silver-haired brothers, Will and Wendell Wilder.

Callie performed her scene—this time in its entirety—with the same gusto she'd packed in the previous one. Inhibitions were checked at the door and she let the diva in her loose, screaming, stomping, arms flailing. With a name like *Nympho Cheerleaders Attack!* what was the point in playing it timid?

"I want to give you one adjustment," said Daniel. "For that last line, when Layla says 'It's always been my world and you cats are lucky just to live in it,' try to make her more vulnerable and less bitchy."

"Kiki is the bitch. Yes, Layla is cunty in her own way, but she's kinder. We want the audience to be on her side, so there needs to be a certain softness that comes through," added Tom, a hefty bear of a man.

Callie repeated her dialogue and Daniel nodded his head in approval. Tom, Wendell, and Will sat next to one another in silence.

"Great. Gentlemen, other than a body check, do you have anything else you'd like from Layla, here?" said Daniel. The Wilders shook their heads but Tom spoke up.

"The film features a few lesbian sex scenes and I have to ask if you're comfortable with that," said the director.

Although nudity didn't intimidate her, she had never filmed a sex scene, lesbian or otherwise. The thought made her nervous, but she couldn't afford to say so; the talent pool was too large. If she didn't tell Tom what he wanted to hear, he'd move on to the next girl, and there were hundreds of actresses who'd gladly take her place. Can you make your nipples more erect? Yes. Is simulated cunnilingus okay? Sure. Do you mind providing a stool sample at the beginning of every scene until filming wraps? Why, of course!

"Absolutely, I'm comfortable," she said.

"Great. So far there are only two, but we may add to that," Tom said nonchalantly.

"The four of us will step out while you remove your top and bottoms for the camera—you can keep your underwear on, but take your bra off—since nudity is required," Daniel said. The men shuffled off, leaving only Rocket and Callie in the room. She stripped to her G-string while Rocket stood behind the video camera.

"Show me your backside . . . turn left . . . now right . . . and face me where you started. Got it, thanks." Rocket flipped the camera off and yawned.

Callie looked at the clock and dashed through the lobby—her shift at Harry's started in five minutes. "Shit!" she said. A female voice called out to her; it was Gabrielle, dazzling, per usual, in a sleeveless dress. She paced the hallway clutching a sheet of paper. "Hi, Gabby! Small world. Are you here for the film, too?"

"*Nympho Cheerleaders Attack!*? Yes, I'm reading for the role of Kiki. I don't know if I can handle it, though; this is a little too Shake-spearean for me."

"Haha. Not exactly Oscar-worthy, that's for sure. I read for Layla."

"Wouldn't that be something if we both get it? Not very likely, but you never know. How about we do lunch this week?"

"Sure, that would be fun. I'd love to chat but gotta run—I'm late for work. I'll call you later. Break a leg!" Callie drove like a wily de-mon and made it to Harry's in fifteen minutes—her personal best. Not bad considering it was rush hour and all the way in Sherman Oaks. Hopefully, Adam, the manager, wouldn't notice her tardiness. Alas, that wasn't the case. He was standing outside the employee bathroom when she scurried out in her uniform, street clothes in hand.

"Hello, there, Callie Lambert," he said. "Glad you could make it."

"Hi, Adam. I didn't think my audition would take as long as it did. I called earlier to say I was running a little late. Kim didn't tell you?" She clocked in and threw her clothes in an overhead cabinet.

"No. I never got the message. I covered your shift last weekend—which wasn't easy since it was so last-minute. And this is the second time this week you've been late."

"I apologize. If it makes you feel any better, Adam, know I'll also be late to my funeral." She flashed a sheepish grin.

Adam wasn't smiling. "You're on thin ice, Cal. I like you, but I like my job more. Table five just got sat. Don't forget to pull your hair back."

She pulled the elastic off her wrist and looped it around her tresses. Quitting Harry's was going to be cause for a massive celebration—if the day ever came. The greasy spoon had employed her for three months and she was fortunate to have a job—even obtaining a table-waiting job was competitive in L.A.—but she wasn't cut out for manual labor.

"Hi, there; what can I get for you today?" Callie gave her best gosh-I'm-so-happy-to-be-your-server expression. The two customers—a decrepit, sour-looking couple—were startled by her cheerfulness.

"We both drink decaf. I'll have the number one, no cheese, no pickles, and heavy on the mustard. My wife would like your blue plate special, hold the sauce. She doesn't want corn, either."

"Do you have coleslaw?" asked the old woman.

"Yes, we do."

"Which kind? Because if it's made with vinegar, I don't want it, I only like the creamy kind."

"I'll check on that for you, ma'am."

"And I don't want the salad that comes with it. What can I get instead? Do you have Brussels sprouts?"

"No, we don't."

The woman looked pained. "You don't have *any*? What kind of restaurant doesn't serve Brussels sprouts?"

"Guess we won't be coming back here again," her husband grumbled.

"How about asparagus?" the woman asked.

"The only steamed vegetable we have is corn, which your husband says you don't want." Callie considered ripping one of the spongy curlers out of the woman's hair and beating her with it.

"Just give me the corn. Hopefully I won't have indigestion but if I do, I'm holding Harry's personally responsible."

You old bag. "Sure, ma'am, I understand." The day she no longer had to serve grub couldn't come fast enough.

"If you haven't tried the artichoke here, you're in for a treat," said Gabby, an avid health nut. She and Callie lunched at the Newsroom.

Callie sucked on the leaf and enjoyed the smoky flavor. She was trying to curb her unhealthy Midwest eating habits—fried food and anything with dairy—in favor of healthier fare. Every actress and model she met in L.A. seemed to be a vegetarian but Callie had no plans of giving up meat; she enjoyed a juicy steak too much.

"How are things going with Evan?"

"We saw each other again the other day. I'm not kidding, Gabby, the guy lasts for hours. He's not one of those awful ten-minute men."

"Those kind are the worst. What's the point? I'd rather be alone and do the job myself," said Gabby, picking at her tuna salad.

"Tell me about it. He's handsome, wealthy, great in bed, and has a hot career. The full package. I don't meet guys like him every day."

"Whoa, hold on a minute; you sound like you're in love with him. And judging from the starry look in your eyes, I'd say you definitely are."

"No, I'm not in love with him. I *like* him."

"You like him a *lot*," Gabrielle said with a mischievous smile. "I thought you said you didn't want a boyfriend?"

"I don't. Besides, he's not my boyfriend. We're just seeing each other. No ball and chain, no strings, no drama. Our video is debuting tonight. He invited me to watch it at his house and said to bring a friend. I know it's last-minute, but would you like to come?" Candice was supposed to accompany her but canceled last-minute after receiving an invite to a party in Miami via private jet. Gabrielle would make a fun replacement.

"Sure, count me in. How do you think you did on that audition yesterday?"

"I don't have a clue. I thought my first audition absolutely sucked, but they called me back, so go figure. How was yours?"

"Awful. I tripped over a few words and didn't feel on my game. But I've learned over the years it's when you think you've done horribly that you often book the job. Honestly, I'm too old for this, Callie."

"Are you kidding? You're young, Gabby, and you could definitely pass for someone in their twenties."

"Thirty-two isn't *that* young."

"But you *look* young. I mean it, you look better than most girls my age!"

"Playing the hot babe isn't something I'll be able to do much longer. Everyone has a shelf life. And, anyway, what have I accomplished? A few bit parts in film and television, a couple of sexy pictures in magazines—big whoop. When my mother was my age, she had three kids and a PhD! My sister is the vice president of a stock-holding company with a penthouse in Manhattan! Now, those are accomplishments. My mother was right all along. I should have done more with my life, something with substance. I look at women older than me, still playing the acting game, and feel sorry for them. It's pathetic: forty-year-olds trying to compete with women half their age. That's not going to be me. Nope, I'm getting out and the sooner the better." Gabrielle's gold-flecked eyes were dewy but her voice stayed steady.

"It sounds like you've given this a lot of thought," Callie said. She couldn't imagine discarding her own acting ambitions; she'd just as soon nosedive off a cliff.

"I have, trust me. I've thought of nothing but turning over a new leaf for the past year. Connecticut is so pretty this time of year, it will be nice going home soon. I've certainly had some good times here but Los Angeles has shown me the true definition of 'ego.' There's never a shortage. I've had my fun but I'm over it."

Chatter from a nearby table caught their attention. Two women in hot pink tracksuits and rhinestone-studded ball caps sipped smoothies. Their bronzy-orange skin was tight and waxy-looking. One of the bottle-blondes gesticulated wildly as she spoke, bangles clanking on her arms. "The director was blown away by my read," she said. "He said the younger girls aren't as talented as me and the ones my age or older aren't up to my caliber of beauty."

"You've got it in the bag for sure, Jill," the look-alike friend said. "That part was written for you."

"Was it ever. I'm used to being fawned over, but this was

something else entirely. By the way, did I tell you the paparazzi chased me down at LAX yesterday? The one time I get recognized and I didn't have a speck of makeup on. Go figure!"

"Wow. Murphy's Law."

Hmmm . . . Callie turned back to Gabby. "I'm beginning to see where you're coming from."

Gabrielle's expression was one of both sympathy and contempt. "See what I mean? Denial isn't just a river in Egypt."

"Sad."

"Completely. Two walking heaps of utter *sadness*."

16

Callie hopped in the seat of Gabrielle's Mercedes SLK. "Thanks for picking me up," Callie said. She rubbed the camel leather seat. "This car is beautiful, Gabby. Mmmm, and it smells brand-new, too."

"It is; I bought it just last week. We'll easily be there by nine since there's practically no traffic. How many people are coming?"

"He didn't say, but I'm guessing it's going to be just us. It's been a week since we've seen each other and I miss him! I can't wait to give him a giant smooch."

It was clear from the noise coming out of Evan's house that there was quite a crowd inside. The girls stood in the foyer and exchanged surprised glances. Clusters of orchids and Stargazer lilies sprouted from vases in all corners of the candlelit house and a DJ spun tunes from one of the four balconies. The stylishly outfitted guests, about fifty in total, danced and mingled.

"So much for my theory," Callie said in Gabby's ear. "We're so underdressed, look at us! You're at least wearing heels. I look like I'm going to a ball game."

"No, you don't, hon, you look pretty. Everyone wears jeans. Anyway, nothing we can do about it now. I just feel out of place being the only sober ones." Gabrielle grabbed two flutes of champagne off a tray. "Here, drink up."

Callie spotted Evan on a balcony talking to several scantily clad women. He gave her a hug and squeezed her waist.

"Thanks for coming. You look great. Who's your friend?" he said. He was drop-dead handsome in a pair of black slacks and a simple button-down.

"Evan meet Gabby; Gabby, this is Evan. We met in Vegas last weekend," Callie explained.

"Pleasure meeting you." Evan's eyes nearly burned a hole through Gabby's cleavage.

"Likewise. I love your new single," said Gabrielle.

"Thank you. They're predicting it will hit the top ten any day now. Grab another drink, girls, enjoy yourselves. The caterer has some killer crab cakes, too, so don't be shy. We're going to play the video in a bit." Evan resumed his conversation with the group of admirers.

Jealousy gushed through Callie. That was it? That's all he had to say to her? He treated her like she was his sister! Why hadn't he bothered to introduce her? Who were these other girls? He was cordial but nothing more—aloof, even. Was he embarrassed by her? Did he not want anyone to know they had been intimate? True, they weren't a couple, but she expected more from Evan. She was used to having his undivided interest and it irked her she did not.

"Everyone, can I have your attention, please!" shouted a balding man with horn-rimmed glasses. He stood in the middle of the living room and clanked a fork against his glass. "Most of you know who I am but for those of you who don't, I'm Evan's longtime manager, Gary Benson. I've been with Evan through thick and thin and we've definitely had our differences at times—" Gary paused purposely and several people laughed. "—but I'm proud to say not only is Evan a trusted friend, he's a talented and loyal client who deserves every ounce of his success. I've just been informed that 'Keep It Sexy' has officially cracked the top ten. Sorry, Evan, I hate to break that to you!" Another round of laughter was followed by clapping and congratulatory whistles. "So, without further ado, allow me to present to you the official music video of our new hit, and here's to Evan shooting all the way to number one!" With a press of the remote, the lights dimmed and the flat screen flipped on.

Evan was breathtaking; on-screen he looked almost as good as he did in person. The man didn't have a bad angle and it was doubtful he had ever taken a rotten picture in his life. Callie kept waiting for her part to air but it never did. Perhaps they were going to play two versions? The lights came back on as the crowd shrieked their approval. Callie looked perplexedly at Gabby and spotted Jeremy Granger in the kitchen.

"Hi, Jeremy, nice work, but what happened to the footage we shot?" she asked.

Jeremy swallowed a mouthful of shrimp tempura. "I had to cut it. You looked phenomenal and I wanted to keep you but it was his label's call. They just thought it was better to keep the focus on Evan. Nothing personal, mind you."

"Of course not, I understand. You win some, you lose some, right?" She slugged her champagne. "Excuse me; I have to go to the ladies' room."

Hunched over the bathroom sink was a lanky brunette with a

rolled-up twenty jammed in her nostril. She snorted a rail of white powder before looking up and offering Callie the bill. "Want some?"

"No thanks; I'm not in the mood." She stomped out and found Gabby perched on the leather couch in the living room. "Gabby, do you mind if we go? This night has been awful."

"Sure, we don't have to stay. I'm fine with calling it an early night," Gabby said. "What happened to your part in the video?"

Callie shook her head. "They didn't want me in it."

"I'm sorry, hon. That happened to me before, too. Happens to the best of us. Come on, let's get out of here."

She was grateful Gabby was easygoing. They dashed without saying a word to anyone.

17

[Chase] Female, early 20s, must have long brunette or au-
burn hair. Sexy and beautiful but the kind of girl you can
bring home to Mom . . . Guest Star, RECURRING

Callie scribbled the casting office's address on a manila enve-
lope and stuffed it with a headshot and résumé. She scrolled farther
down the computer screen.

Must have martial arts experience.

Damn it. That detail had escaped her. She scrolled down the page
until she found another casting to intrigue her.

[Lisa] (21–26) Open ethnicity, pretty, athletic figure, dark
hair. A sensitive, sincere young woman who falls for the

bad boy every time. No tattoos, WE REALLY MEAN IT! . . .
LEAD

She rubbed the tattoo on her inner wrist: a shooting star next to her father's initials.

That eliminated Lisa, too. Playing a Goody Two-shoes was never much fun, anyway. She reached the end of the attachment and growled in frustration. The castings were weak; even bimbo roles were scarce. Three weeks had passed since her call-back and she hadn't heard a word. Not a good sign. She slammed the laptop shut and picked up the latest issue of *Got It!* from the coffee table. As a general rule, she didn't read tabloids unless she was getting a pedicure or having her hair styled, but Candice was addicted to them. One of the headlines caught her attention: "Sexy Singer Romancing Nude Model." Page twenty featured a candid photo of Evan kissing a pretty blonde, along with an accompanying article:

> Evan Marquardt sure knows how to pick 'em! The "Keep It Sexy" crooner is always surrounded by lovely ladies but his favorite flavor of the month is Rachel O'Connor, 19, soon to be seen nude in the November issue of *Coquette* magazine. The tantalizing twosome have been spotted at various Hollywood hot spots and our cameras caught them canoodling on a recent shopping trip to Robertson Boulevard. Hey, kids—keep it PG!

Rachel O'Connor—the name didn't ring a bell but her face was familiar. The Nordic features and creamy skin . . . Where had they met? Recognition hit her with the force of a Mack truck—the *Coquette* shoot! That's how she knew Rachel! She felt woozy as her brain processed this new twist. Evan was banging that frigid bitch?! How was that possible? Why on God's green earth would he want *her*? And *Coquette*—didn't they have better taste? What a train wreck of a human being! Callie slammed the magazine on the floor and lit a cigarette. Smoking was a habit she had picked up when she started working at Harry's. It hadn't developed into a full-blown addiction—or so she told herself—but she consumed two packs a week, sometimes three. She toked and blew the smoke out through her nostrils. Evan's new romance was a slash in her skin and *Coquette* was the salt.

The door flew open and Candice charged through. Her eye makeup was smeared from crying. "I hate casting directors! I hope their balls rot off from syphilis! Guess what happened? Take a wild, off-the-wall guess. Starr Talent arranged an audition for me as the lead in a movie—one of those cheesy horror films. I didn't think much of it, but I went. And, holy fuck, was I ever *on*. I owned it. Well, I never heard back from them so I just called Doug to see what was up. Get this: Daniel called him to complain how rude I supposedly was. That I wasn't on time and my arrogance was, quote, 'offensive.' I was only thirty minutes late, maybe fifty. And since when is it a crime to be confident? So I'm a little cocky, sue me. He said he never wants me in his casting office again. Can you believe the nerve? It's not my fault he's an uptight fag. I need a Xanax." Candice popped two pills and offered the bottle to Callie; she swallowed one. Why not? Nothing like a little benzodiazepine to sweeten life's lemons.

"Was the audition for *Nympho Cheerleaders Attack!* by any chance?" asked Callie.

"Yes, that's the name of it. How did you know?"

"I told you about it, remember? That's the movie I had a call-back for."

"You did? Sorry, it must have slipped my memory, I've had so much shit on the brain. Daniel actually told Doug I was unprofessional. Can you believe that? *Me,* unprofessional? I don't understand; no one's ever said that to me before. How can I really be that awful?"

"You've always been aggressive, Candy. Sometimes it rubs people the wrong way."

She wiped inky mascara from her cheeks with a tissue. "Look, I'm no moron; I know I'm an acquired taste. But banning me from setting foot in his casting office? People are so mean. This town is full of nothing but a bunch of pricks with tampons shoved up their asses. Fuck it; it doesn't matter anyhow since casting's completed."

Callie's heart pummeled. "They're done casting? Are you sure?"

"That's what Daniel told Doug today. He said they found the female leads. I guess you didn't book it, either." A look of relief passed across Candice's flushed face.

"Thanks for stating the obvious. Who did they settle on?"

"Didn't ask, don't care. First I couldn't get my call-back rescheduled and now this. I can't catch a goddamned break. What a bullshit industry." Candice rummaged through the fridge and bit into a chocolate bar. "*Coquette* is throwing a big party tonight and they're paying me to stand around in nothing but body paint. Five hundred bucks to be part of the scenery. Do you want to come?"

"I don't want anything to do with that magazine," sniped Callie.

"Oh, come on, don't be so bitter, Cal."

The pot calling the kettle black! "I *am* bitter! I can't believe they chose Rachel over me. Have you ever met her? She's a mess."

"I've never heard of her before. But as long as she photographs well, they don't care how fucked up she is. Besides, do you realize how many tits they see on a monthly basis? Millions. The girls who get turned down the first time are often accepted the second or third time around. I just had dumb luck." Candice had flown to L.A. to shoot her pictorial in January, a week after mailing *Coquette* nude Polaroids during her senior year at Michigan State. During her stay in L.A., she met Lars Lindquist at a nightclub and never returned to college.

"All the same, I'll pass. I'm not in the mood."

"What's wrong with you? Something else is bothering you, I can tell. You look royally pissed."

"Have you read your new *Got It!*? Here, take a look at this."

Candice scanned the article and jeered, "What a loser! Another L.A. scumbag. Argh, men."

"Why didn't it occur to me he was just another player?"

"Mama, it's called being blinded by the cock. Trust me, I know *all* about it. I should teach seminars, for crying out loud."

"It was stupid of me. What a fool I am. I actually thought I was different—that I was special. Arrrh! I need some fresh air before my head explodes. Want to go for a jog?"

Candice's jaw dropped. "Why don't you just wait for Miss Xani to kick in?"

"Nah, I need to clean my lungs out. I've smoked too much this past week."

"Xanax cures world hunger in my book. Anyway, I don't have time. My nail appointment is in an hour. Go clear your head and I'll catch you later."

Callie laced up her Adidas and whizzed along Franklin past La Brea. *Don't let this bring you down,* she thought, each syllable under-lined by the pounding of the pavement. *I'm too good for Evan and that dumb movie.* Sweat seeped down her forehead and stung her eyes. *Fuck them all!* She headed back east and grabbed a bottle of

Evian at the corner gas station. A voice mail awaited her when she returned to her apartment.

"This is Wilder Productions calling for Callie Lambert. Please give us a call back as soon as possible. We'd like to offer her the role of Layla in the movie *Nympho Cheerleaders Attack!* . . ."

18

Virginia DiPrizio inhaled the smell of percolating coffee in her kitchen and sighed. She hadn't heard from her daughter in weeks. What had Cal been up to? Hopefully the craziness of L.A. wasn't getting the best of her. She was a smart girl but too impulsive—how could she pack her whole life up and move cross-country to a place known only for crime, earthquakes, and liberal weirdos? And to a city she had never even visited! It was completely irrational—ludicrous—giving up a steady job working for Dr. Ryder in search of fame and fortune. The sooner she learned that, the better. It was only a matter of time before she came to her senses and returned to Michigan. She poured Coffee-mate in her mug until her joe turned beige. The phone rang, startling her.

"I was just thinking about you, Cal. Have you decided to come home yet?" said Virginia, cradling the receiver in her shoulder.

"Gee, Mom, it's good to hear from you, too," Callie said evenly.

"Oh, stop; you know I'm happy to hear from you. I never know when to call you, what with our schedules and the time difference."

"I have good news, Mom. Are you sitting down?"

Virginia planted her sizable rear in a dining room chair. "I am now. What kind of news? You've come to your senses and are moving back home?"

"Not quite; it's far more exciting than that. I just got off the phone with Wilder Productions. I'm going to be in a movie!"

"Wilder Productions? Is that pornographic? There was a report on the news last week about how prevalent pornography is in Los Angeles. I'd drop dead of a heart attack if you got sucked into that."

"Mom, it's nothing like that. It's mainstream. Not only am I a *lead* but I booked it on my own! I won't have to give any commission to an agency."

"Well, that's good," Virginia said cautiously. "How did you manage it?"

"Tyler gets the castings from a friend and e-mails them to me. The director really likes my take on the character and thinks my comedic chops are impressive," Callie gushed.

"I could have told him that; you've been a ham since you could talk. This is progress, I'm glad. I was getting a little worried things would never move along for you. What's the name of the movie?"

Callie hesitated; she wasn't ready for her mother to pick apart the project just yet. "They haven't settled on a name," she lied. "It's a horror film and it will be a lot of fun. I'm so excited, I can't even tell you! I can hardly believe it."

"Tony! Listen to this—Callie is going to be in a movie. One of the lead actresses," Virginia said excitedly.

"Like, a *movie* movie? She gettin' paid for it?" said Tony.

"How much are they paying you? Doesn't an agent or lawyer have to negotiate that stuff?" Virginia said.

"The pay is a scale rate. It's a low-budget feature which means the money isn't great, but the exposure will be awesome."

"Just so long as they're not trying to rip you off, I guess that's all right. Beggars can't be choosers."

Callie winced and changed the subject. "How are you and Tony?"

"We're hanging in there," said Virginia. "Tony's retirement party is next Friday and on Saturday we're leaving for the Bahamas with his sister and her husband. I've lost twelve pounds since you've seen me and can finally fit into my old swimsuit. First time I've been able to squeeze into a size ten in years. You should see me—I'm almost as svelte as my old self! Like Candice, only taller. How is she, anyway? That girl always had the best figure. I saw her mother today at the grocery store with a new BMW, a 600 series. Boy, is it something else."

"Candice is well. She's been living with me temporarily until she finds a new place."

"But you live in a studio apartment," Virginia said incredulously.

"It's a little tight, but we manage. She's gone half the time, anyway."

"You two must be sleeping on top of each other! With the price you pay for that shoe box, you could rent a mansion here in Troy."

"I have to get ready for work, Mom," said Callie exhaustedly. "I'll talk to you later. Have fun on your trip if I don't speak to you before you leave." She bitterly wished she hadn't phoned her mother. What a downer! Why was she riddled with cynicism? Why couldn't she congratulate her? She always praised Candice's beauty and admired her family's wealth but ignored her own daughter's merits. Grandma Esme was full of adoration and encouragement—why couldn't her mother be? It was as though she delighted in sapping the energy from a beautiful opportunity. Dad would have approved, wouldn't he? She was told they shared a similar optimistic attitude and liked to think he would have been proud of her, but there was no way to be sure.

The calendar on her fridge was filled with chicken-scratch: an improvisation class, an eyebrow waxing, a wardrobe fitting, and a read-through with the cast at the Knoxley Theatre. She had forgotten to inquire which actress landed the part of Kiki, Layla's nemesis, and now she dialed Gabby's number. But what if Gabby hadn't booked the part? It would come off as boastful, insensitive. She hung up before the call connected.

Four o'clock—Harry's in an hour. She made a mental reminder to notify Adam of the dates for her upcoming surgery. The nervousness over Dr. Coop's scalpel was diminished by the concept of a bump-free silhouette in time for her big-screen debut. Filming wasn't slated to begin until early October, leaving plenty of time to heal. Her tonsils had to come out, she'd say, and a week or more of recuperation was required. Doctor's orders. Most likely, management wouldn't give her a hard time, but if they did, she'd find another job. She pulled a Harry's Hamlet polo over her head and braced herself for another long shift in hell.

The Knoxley was packed with unfamiliar faces; Tom and the Wilder brothers were the only people Callie recognized.

"There's our Layla!" piped Will, scooping a forkful of rice onto his plate. "Help yourself to all this food I picked up—burritos, quesadillas, tamales, good stuff. We're going to get started in a minute. It's great having you on board."

Callie cracked open a bottle of water. "Thanks, it's great being here."

Tom leapt onstage and stuck his fingers in his mouth. His high-pitched whistle quieted the chatter. "Boys and girls, listen up! I requested a meeting with my actors so everyone could familiarize themselves with the story and their characters. We're going to read the script aloud in its entirety and cover any questions at the end. Who doesn't have a copy?" Tom paused as a door slammed. The clicking of heels echoed in the theater as Gabrielle rushed down the aisle. All heads cranked to see who had caused the interruption.

"I'm so sorry I'm late, Tom," Gabby said, and plopped down next to Callie.

"No problem, babe, we actually started a little early. This is Gabrielle, everyone, better known as Kiki, the resident bad girl of *NCA!*" Tom ogled Gabby from the roots of her hair down to her peep-toe sandals. "And don't let those sexpot looks fool you—her comedic chops are razor-sharp. With a little guidance, in fact, I think I may have a modern-day Carole Lombard on my hands."

She blushed as Tom's assistant handed her a script.

"I'm so happy to see you!" Callie whispered.

Gabrielle returned Callie's smile and patted her knee. Not only was Gabby a proverbial face—she could offer acting advice and give pointers, too. She downplayed her experience ("I'm just eye candy. I provide the scenery and occasionally they throw me a bone and let me toss out a few lines," she had explained) but wasn't a novice—she had been on many a film and television set over the past six years. Her take on Kiki was high-camp and dripped with saucy gusto.

The plot of *Nympho Cheerleaders Attack!* was farcical at best. It revolved around a cheerleading squad, headed by Gabrielle. When her popularity becomes threatened by Layla, the new coed on campus, she stops at nothing to destroy her competition. Brainwashing her fellow cheerleaders into becoming sex-crazed, bloodthirsty demons is second nature to Kiki. She loves nothing more than killing her rivals after bedding them, male and female alike. In Layla she physically and mentally meets her match. But the star of the show was the naked flesh. A bevy of blood and exposed breasts—*Nympho Cheerleaders Attack!* was a fantasy for the quintessential straight male.

Dawn, a petite brunette, raised her hand. "Is this going straight to DVD?"

"We've been promised big-screen debuts in L.A. and New York. Depending on how it fares at the box office, it may go to other cities after opening weekend. We're going to reach out to as many film festivals as possible. Screamfest, Shriekfest, maybe even Toronto and Sundance. It shouldn't be difficult with Sal's huge fan base. As soon as he signed on, we knew this movie was going places. It's got legs," said Will. Sal Saunders was a horror movie legend with forty-plus years in the industry. The Wilders hoped his portrayal of Hamsburg, the crotchety college dean, would lend the film commercial viability.

"We've got something special, here, folks; the horror genre couldn't be any bigger at this time and I for one am thrilled. Simply put, one can't go wrong with beautiful, bare-assed women filling the screen. Gabrielle and Callie, my two main minxes, you're going to look better than a teenage boy's wet dream. Trust me—the audience will be eating from the palm of your hand. Celluloid will fly! That goes for all you girls." Tom surveyed his bored-looking supporting actresses. With his dark facial and body hair, he resembled a wolf.

"Is this supposed to be like one of those B-grade films?" asked a girl with a platinum rocker do. She shooed a fly from her pinto beans.

"Not *like*, Nicole; it *is*. I wrote this after downing a twelve-pack during a Russ Meyer marathon," said Tom.

"Where are we filming?"

"Boyle Heights. The building is a former insane asylum, rundown and completely filthy. When we scouted the property, I found straitjackets and patient documents, even dirty needles. It's delicious how creepy this place is."

Nicole scratched her head and exchanged uneasy looks with Brittany.

So, what do you think of this craptastic masterpiece?" Callie said to Gabby. They walked to their cars on La Cienega.

"It's a job and it's money and God knows I need it," said Gabby. "Who knows, maybe it will even be a hit. There's certainly an audience for it."

"Tom was staring so hard at you, I thought he was going to foam at the mouth."

"I'm used to it. Trust me, without these air bags, I wouldn't get any attention. Why I ever let Justin talk me into getting them so big, I'll never know. I guess I should be grateful; I'd never have booked a single thing without them." Gabrielle fiddled with her keychain and the lights of her white SLK blinked in the distance.

"You've got talent, Gabby. I really believe that. Comedic roles are right up your alley. You didn't book the part just because of your boobs."

"Thanks. Either way, it's fine with me. I'm not one to take myself too seriously. When you lose your sense of humor, things go downhill awfully fast." With a wave, Gabrielle zoomed off into the night.

20

The nurse inserted an IV into Callie's arm. The anesthesia quickly took effect and she felt euphoric, limp as a rag doll.

"Okay, darlin', count backwards for me, starting with twenty," said the nurse. "Twenty, nineteen, eight . . ." Callie drifted into unconsciousness and woke up two hours later with her nose in a cast. Breathing was tricky; what the hell was up her nose? She gasped for air. "Breathe through your mouth. You have packing up your nose," she heard a woman say. Nauseated and disoriented, she tossed in her gurney.

Candice was in the waiting room when they wheeled her out. "Hey, there, mama. Let's get you home and propped up in bed."

"Can't you just gimme a pill?" Callie slurred. Her reflection was unrecognizable to her. *I look like a rotten banana. When am I going to be normal again?* She hadn't expected to feel so dreadful. Yellow and purple discolorations surrounded her eyes and crusty clumps of blood filled her nostrils like raisins. On day two, Dr. Coop removed the packing, each strip of gauze coming out of her nostril like a never-ending handkerchief from a clown's pocket. On day seven, the cast was taken off.

"The refinement is subtle yet drastic at the same time," Dr. Coop said proudly. "Very elegant, even with mild swelling."

"I feel like a new woman." She couldn't put down the handheld mirror; the former asymmetrical, bony bridge was replaced with a graceful slope.

"If I ever need my beak fixed, I'm paying Dr. Coop a visit," said Candice as she drew Callie a bath. She made a convincing Florence Nightingale, aided by her mother's twenty years as a registered nurse. "I can't believe how natural it looks, and after such a short time span, too. Looks like you'll be ready for your close-up in no time."

"I hope so. With all the nudity, though, no one's going to be looking at my nose."

"That's so true. Doesn't it worry you? It would me. The movie could destroy your chances of ever doing mainstream projects. No one will take you seriously. Call me crazy, but it makes me kind of glad I didn't get the part."

"You were spread-eagled in a world-famous magazine," Callie said. "How's that any different?"

"*Coquette* is legendary, a global institution. It's not the same thing at all."

"I can't believe you, Candice. That's so hypocritical!" Who, after all, had shed a pail of tears over the movie in question only days ago?

"We disagree, I guess. Let's change the subject, I don't want to argue."

"Fine by me."

"Lars is taking me out tonight. Don't give me that look; I know what I'm doing. It's only dinner and we've decided to still be friends. I've got to bolt and go shop for an outfit."

"How's the apartment hunt going?" Callie asked as she stepped into the tub. A month and a half had gone by without any mention of Candice looking for new lodgings.

"I'm looking at a place in Beverly Hills next week. A big one-bedroom, one bath. Don't worry, movie star. I'll be out of your hair soon."

Callie sank as deep in the water as she could without submerging her head. As comforting as the water felt, it was difficult to relax—she was too distracted with her issues with Candice, and called Grandma Esme on speakerphone to voice her concerns. "Her laziness is on my nerves, Grandma. And it's so odd that she resents me for the movie instead of being supportive. Maybe she's just used to always getting her way. I don't know what to make of it; she's never acted like this before."

"Jealousy is an ugly thing, honey. She'll come around, don't worry over it. You've got a big gimmick coming up and don't need anyone bringing you down." For a seventy-five-year-old, Esme was remarkably modern and nonjudgmental. If filming *Nympho Cheerleaders Attack!* made her granddaughter happy, then she was all for it, too.

The flipside of her downtime was a treat—cozying up in bed with a tub of Häagen-Dazs, surfing the Web, watching TMC . . . surgery had its perks. Harry's was anxious for her return. Ten days seemed a long time to recover from tonsillitis, Adam griped, but Callie held her ground; she was in no shape to be seen. To her delight, Bedroom Eyes resurfaced, beckoning her via text. *I miss you. Meet me at my place?* Every fiber in her body craved him, despite his involvement with Rachel. That voice, that skin, those eyes . . . he was completely irresistible. But with her jacked-up appearance, she'd just as soon let the Queen of England see her before Evan. Oh, well. She responded with one word: *Busy.* How often does a singer with the top song in the country get blown off? Let his balls turn blue, she thought. He'll just dial his backup lay, whoever that was. Rachel must be out of town or on her period. Or maybe they broke up. . . .

To get through the boredom of her convalescence, Callie scoured the gossip blogs for an update on the lovebirds (though she'd never admit it to anyone). *Evan and Rachel: It's Love . . . How Evan and Rachel "Keep It Sexy" . . . Evan and I Have Sex 8 Times a Day! . . .* Blah, blah, blah. Callie's face deepened in color with every spicy detail until she felt crazed with envy. Damn that bare-assed trollop! Why couldn't there be any reference of a split or a hint of trouble? Finally, hours after searching, a negative headline: *Nude Pin-Up's Steamy and ILLEGAL Past Revealed!*

Ah-ha!

> Aleksandra Gordeeva, madam to the stars, reveals in this
> exclusive interview how she supplied Hollywood heavy-
> weights with beautiful starlets for over a decade, includ-
> ing nude model Rachel O'Connor.

The exposé was accompanied by a picture of Aleksandra, a heavy, frizzy-haired woman slathered in neon makeup, surrounded by four pretty girls. One of the girls resembled Rachel, but it was the honey-blonde with a protruding chest that caught Callie's attention. Unquestionably, it was Gabrielle.

> "My girls go for twenty thousand dollars for one single
> night," Aleksandra, swelling with pride, says in broken

English. "Some more, some less. If girl has title, even better. More credits she has, more money she make. Rachel no exception; she make big money when she work for me. Directors, CEOs, you name it. They pay top dollar for my girls, cream of crop, all models and actress. You be shocked how many escort in Los Angeles. City is tough for young girl on her own. Cost lots if you want to live good. And who does not want to live good? If girl is beautiful, there is much, much money to make."

Callie's jaw dropped. *Gabby was a high-rent hooker?* That couldn't be! She was too sweet, too smart to be a lay-for-pay. But why, then, was she pictured with the madam? She couldn't have made much from her sporadic acting and modeling gigs. And she never mentioned having another occupation. It would explain the night of the charity gala, too. It was all too coincidental. . . .

Beep!

Her phone jolted her back to reality. Another text from Evan. *Come to my album release party in Bel Air on Oct 1st. I'd love to see you, baby.*

Hmmm . . . what could be the harm in attending a little soiree? By then, she'd be in fine shape. Tyler could accompany her and do her makeup beforehand—he always made her look like a million bucks. She could toy with Evan, play hard to get, and flirt with other men. Hopefully he'd react—although he didn't come off as the jealous type. He was too collected to display a case of ruffled feathers so easily. If Rachel O'Hooker was there, even better; the girl could use a lesson on the meaning of class. A little friendly competition never hurt a fly.

21

The Mediterranean-style mansion, at twenty thousand square feet, was more hotel than home. Callie had never been to a Bel Air residence and the enormity of wealth was unlike anything she had ever witnessed. The guest list was small—fewer than three hundred people—and security was tight. IDs were required to enter the gated street.

"Gee, do you think they could have built this place a little bigger?" Tyler said. "I've never seen so much marble in my life."

The mansion was crammed with Choo-heeled guests, some famous, all wealthy. A Picasso hung in the dining room, a Basquiat in the master, and a Monet in one of the nine bathrooms. Evan's new CD thumped from the speakers. Callie and Tyler were admiring a Greek statue when someone wrapped an arm around her hip.

"Glad to see you could make it," Evan said. He pulled back when Callie stiffened.

"Hey, you. Congratulations on everything," she said coolly. Was that a look of disappointment on his face? His smile was easygoing but he looked confused by her detachment.

"Thanks. First number one I've ever had."

"How exciting. This place is unbelievable. Who owns it?"

"Byron Bernstein, president of Urban Records. Speaking of exciting, I heard about your movie. That's fantastic! Gary, my manager, was telling me about it yesterday. He and Tom Johannesburg go way back."

Tyler cleared his throat.

"I'm sorry, Ty," she said. "Evan, meet my friend Tyler. Tyler, Evan."

"Pleasure," cooed Tyler.

"Likewise. The film sounds like one wild ride and I'm sure you're more than capable of playing a naughty cheerleader." Evan's eyes glinted wickedly.

"The premise of the film is pretty ridiculous, but it is the lead," Callie said offhandedly. "I couldn't turn it down. It's bound to appeal to the average American male, what with all the gore."

"And don't forget the tits. This movie's got more knockers than a Beverly Hills plastic surgeon's office in spring," added Tyler.

Evan laughed. "How can you not love that? I'll definitely check it out. You, by the way, Callie, look gorgeous. Something's different about you."

"How so?" She blinked.

"I can't put my finger on it . . . did you cut your hair?"

She shook her head.

"Color it, perhaps?"

"Nope. Wrong again."

"Hmmm . . . I give up. Not that it's any of my business. I guess I'm being nosy."

Tyler giggled and Callie flashed him a look of annoyance. "So, where's your date this evening?" she said.

"No date whatsoever; I'm flying solo. Plenty of friends and colleagues are here. That's enough to keep me entertained."

"I didn't know if you were still with Rachel . . . ," Callie said.

"Rachel? She's not even here. Rachel and I are *not* an item, contrary to all the BS that's printed. She's a fun girl—*was* a fun girl. Up until she started giving these silly interviews and feeding the fire." He swigged his gin and tonic.

"The tabloids love to exaggerate," offered Callie.

"Not exaggerate—just flat-out lie. But what am I going to do? The nature of the beast. *Excusez-moi*—I have to make my rounds. Catch you two in a bit." Callie followed him with her eyes.

"Oh, boy. Skank's got it bad," Tyler said.

"Is it that obvious?"

"You light up like a Christmas tree around him. It couldn't be any more obvious if you tattooed it across your forehead. Trying to act all cool, like you don't care. Please, I can read you like a crystal ball." A waiter moseyed by with a platter of gourmet sliders and Tyler snatched three.

"And here I thought he was tied down with Rachel."

"The way you were telling it, they were altar-bound any minute. See, didn't I tell you not to believe all that trash?"

She nodded. "God, Ty, I feel so stupid for reading those gossip columns and even worse for believing it."

"You're obsessing. Remember, he's not looking for a girlfriend. I don't want you working your vadge up for nothing. He's definitely a tall glass of water, I'll give you that. Too bad he doesn't bat for my team." He bit into a burger. "Yum. I don't know what all they put in these things but it's definitely more than Kobe beef. Must be laced with crack and it's on a one-way straight to my thighs. So, when is Candice moving out?"

"Supposedly in a few days."

"That's good. One less thing you'll have weighing on your mind. That girl is trouble. I've never been a fan."

"She's definitely a lot of work."

"Candice majors, minors, and marinates in drama. She's too much, even for me, and that's saying a lot. Relationships shouldn't be that difficult. Ooh, look—there goes a tray of caviar. And five different kinds, too. Nothing better than that, especially when someone else is footing the bill. Come on, let's go grab a plate. Who knows when we'll ever be in a place this grand again."

"Y OU ungrateful, useless bitch. I showed you the ropes and this is the thanks I get?" Gabrielle said. She lay crumpled on the damp, concrete floor of the locker room, her wrists and ankles bound. One side of her head was sliced to reveal brain matter; blood flowed out of the wound, trickling down her neck and chest. Her hair, once immaculately highlighted, hung in thick red clumps. A slashed navy sweater stretched across her breasts like cobwebs and allowed her nipples to poke through the few remaining threads.

"You played me for a fool, Kiki, thinking I'd be your little puppet. Well, guess what? This puppet doesn't like to be played! Cayden College is about to have one less cunt on campus." Callie, beads of perspiration rolling off her body, towered over Gabby with a blood-caked knife in hand. She raised the weapon to Gabby's throat.

"Cut!" Tom said. "I need more blood. Where's Patrick? More blood, please!"

Patrick, the head of special effects, scurried on set and doused Gabby with red liquid. "More, more, more," Tom said. "Keep going. Don't be shy, Pat. I want her soaked. More on her left breast . . . now we're talking. Give the audience what they pay to see. Tits and gore equals higher ticket sales. And what makes everyone happy, Patrick?"

"Dough," Patrick said, and gave Gabrielle another bloody squirt. "Lots of dough."

"Lots of dough," Tom repeated. "Damn fucking straight. No one likes an empty theater." As crazy as Tom Johannesburg was for women, Diablos, and rare rib-eyes washed down with Blue Label, everything fell a distant second to his love of money. He spent it almost as quickly as he made it and was equally adept at both. The fifty-odd films he had directed and/or produced from 1971 on afforded him homes in Saint Barts, the Pacific Palisades, and South Beach, not to mention maintenance for three ex-wives and five children. The formula for making Tom tick was as simple as it was expensive. "Gabby, baby, how are we doing?"

"Can I get some water? I feel light-headed," she said.

"Of course. Let's take five, people." Tom placed a bottle of water to her lips and watched her gulp away.

Callie took a seat off-camera. She had been on set for ten hours but was more exhilarated than exhausted. Portraying Layla was the most fun she'd ever had on the clock.

"If he gets any friendlier, she's going to be gargling his balls," hissed Nicole. She sat next to Callie, her pierced upper lip curled in a snarl. "Must be nice being the pet." Tom's attentive demeanor left little doubt how he felt for his leading blonde. Gabrielle responded passively to his coddling; she wasn't overtly friendly but she wasn't shooing him away, either. But Callie didn't see how their interaction affected anyone else, and was protective toward her costar.

"Do you even know Gabby?" said Callie. "She's a really nice girl."

"Yeah, I bet. She's so nice, I bet she sucked off the entire production staff. Why would anyone give *her* one of the leads?"

"Gee, let me think," Callie quipped. "Maybe because she's gorgeous and funny and perfect for the part? Just a thought."

"She's, like, gross. I mean, just look at her; if one of those titty sacks pop, we'll all drown to death. Like, for real, that's enough silicone to flood Staples Center. How can anyone take her seriously?"

"The film is called *Nympho Cheerleaders Attack!* Why would *any* of us take it seriously?"

Nicole rolled her eyes and twisted the stud in her lip. "I guess. So, who's your agent?"

"I'm looking for a new one. You?"

"DNA. I've been with them for two years, ever since I moved here from Canada."

"Any good?"

"They're not bad but not great. I call them TNA—just another mediocre agency peddling tits and ass. Ever notice how they all go by initials? What, is a name with over, like, three syllables too complicated or something?"

"I need quiet on set!" Tom yelled, and glared at Nicole. She clamped her mouth shut. Will and Wendell huddled in a corner talking in hushed tones to an important-looking tall man with graying hair, and waved at Callie to join them.

"I want you to meet Paul Angers, the owner of PA Talent. We've been friends since college. He's been in this business almost as long as me, but not quite," Will said.

"I've got you beat by ten years, Wilder," joked Paul. He gave

Callie a firm handshake and summed her up with shrewd eyes. "I just checked the dailies. You have some fine comedic chops, young lady. I'm impressed. What other projects would I know you from?"

"This is my first acting gig, not counting a commercial I did back in Detroit. I've been in L.A. for four months," she said.

"Really, now? Interesting. I hail from Kalamazoo. Lots of good Midwestern stock here in L.A. We're not all farmers, contrary to what everyone here thinks, and you're definitely not just a pretty face, and I'd know, too. I see more than my share. You can actually act. That's a rarity. Here's my card; schedule something with my secretary and we can talk shop. I know you're busy with the film, but whenever you get a chance—"

"I think tomorrow is clear," she said.

"Can't do Friday. I'll be in meetings all day. Just give Ursula a call and we'll figure it out. Bring whatever headshots you have, too."

"Callie, here, nails every scene in one take. All of the girls are very good, but she's got something extra. Same with Gabby, the blonde," said Will.

"Blondes are no good to me. All the ripe parts up for grabs are for brunettes, early twenties. Exotic but relatable, like Callie. Keep spinning your magic, young lady, and stay in touch." Paul and the Wilders walked off together.

She wanted to call Ursula that very second, but there was no way of knowing her filming schedule days in advance. She'd have to wait, and patience wasn't her strong suit. Chill, she told herself. Paul was interested and that was the important thing. He had seen her footage and knew she was capable; that was one foot in the door. She'd get the other foot in soon enough.

"Ahhhhhhhh!" Callie shrieked. Her eyes darted around the bedroom in search of an exit but she was trapped. Flames engulfed her bed and smoke clogged her lungs. Like kernels over a screaming hot burner, the fire crackled. A scream rose above the inferno; the masculine voice was eerily familiar and wailed like a siren. But where was it coming from? Not only was her vision obscured beyond farther than a foot, but her limbs went limp as well. She listened helplessly, petrified. *"Help me, Callie! Help me! I need you. . . ."*

Callie shot up in bed. Her body, drenched in sweat, trembled as though she were a junkie quitting cold turkey. Minutes passed before she realized it had just been a nightmare, she wasn't in any danger. The sky, though dreary from the morning marine layer, was clear of smoke. She took a huge breath and flopped back on the pillows. It was October 28—her father's birthday. Strange to think he'd now be a middle-aged man, no longer the youthful, raven-haired father of her childhood. All day she moped in pajamas, teeth grimy and hair uncombed. Why bother changing when she wasn't needed on set? Wasn't there a friend who understood death, someone with whom she could share her angst? She dialed Gabrielle's number.

"I'm just a wreck today, Gabby," she said between sniffles. "I miss my dad so much. I really wish he was here. He would have been fifty today."

Gabby was apologetic, her voice soothing as a lozenge. "Believe me, I know grief. Justin's been gone for only a third of the time your father has but it feels like an eternity."

"It really does. Funny, it's the simple stuff I remember so well, even at five years old. Like when he bought me a Mickey Mouse raft and we went over to our neighbor's pool."

"It's always the little things, isn't it? I miss the way Justin's lips quivered ever so slightly when he snored. Silly, random things like that. I've been on antidepressants for years. Seroquel, Lexapro, Zoloft, you name it."

"Who's your therapist?"

"He's a psychiatrist. Stuart Holtsclaw. He pays house calls, too, and he doesn't charge an arm and a leg. Why don't I give you his number?"

Callie jotted his information down and thanked her. "I should be happy right now, shouldn't I? But sometimes I get into these funks I just can't shake."

"We all need help sometimes, it's only natural. Without your health, mental or physical, you have nothing. *Nothing.* You've never talked to a professional about your father?"

"Never. My mom isn't a fan of modern medicine. She's the type who holds it all in and doesn't like to admit there's a problem. Like, if you don't talk about it or acknowledge it, it must not exist. Real healthy, huh?"

"My mother is the same way. But at some point, you have to address the issue at hand. You're a big girl; you can decide what's in your best interest."

"I'm going to give him a call."

"Do that. On a different note, I'd like your opinion on something totally unrelated." Gabby suddenly switched her mother-hen tone to that of a small child.

"Go ahead, shoot. This subject is too depressing, anyway."

"Tom *really* likes me."

"Gabby, I hate to break it to you, but that's not exactly a news flash. Astronauts floating in space can see that," Callie said.

"Well, he's doing something about it. Tonight is the world premiere of *Blow It Up,* the action film he directed. It's expected to be a monster hit and he wants me to be his date. Do you think it would make things on set too awkward? I can just hear the cattiness now; Nicole and the others already think I slept with the entire western hemisphere for the part. Imagine how awful they'll be when they find this out."

"Who cares what they think? It's not your fault you make them insecure. What are you going to do when he tries to crawl up your skirt?" Callie said.

"I thought about that. He's a nice guy and he's been very sweet to me. . . ." Her voice trailed off.

"He also has a history of bedding his actresses, it's a well-known fact. I sure am glad he hasn't hit on me yet; he's so hairy and gross. But if you can tolerate him slobbering over you all night, I bet the premiere will be fun."

"I think so, too. There will be oodles of press, and I'll be right there on the director's arm. I'm thinking a pale pink dress with chandelier earrings. Should I wear my hair up or down?" asked Gabby.

"Definitely down; it's too pretty to put up. You look great in pastels, too. I've never been to a premiere before but it sounds über-glamorous."

"They're exciting. I've been to several, but never with the director. All right, I have to run. I'll tell you how everything goes. Definitely give Dr. Holtsclaw a call. He's quirky, just to warn you, but what doctor isn't? He's helped me out a great deal and I doubt you're half as screwed up as I once was."

Callie carefully blew her nose—the tip was still numb from surgery—and made an appointment with Dr. Holtsclaw. He couldn't meet until the following week, but it was better late than never.

24

"Close your eyes for me," said Ming Lee, the key makeup artist, and lined Callie's eyes with metallic shadow. "I'm going buck-wild with your makeup today. Layla's going to look especially special for her close-up."

Callie held a copy of *USA Today* and flipped to her favorite section, D. Prominently featured on the cover were Gabrielle, Tom, and the two lead actors from *Blow It Up*. Gabby, resplendent in a strapless gown and fur stole, beamed next to her director. His thick arm circled her waist.

"Is that Tom and Gabby?" asked Ming. She stopped swirling her makeup brush to examine the picture. "Wow, she looks gorgeous. She's got a body for days. Check out those boobs, holy smokes! I wear a 36C and she makes me feel flat-chested."

"Try standing next to Gabby with a 34B; I'm a two-by-four," quipped Callie.

"Haha. Man, is Tom ever caught up in her. I caught them making out the other day."

"You did? Where?" Callie exclaimed.

"In his trailer. The door was cracked open and I could see them in a lip-lock. Not just any little peck but a full-on tonsil hockey session. Romances always start on set, don't they? Every set I've ever worked on, there's been hook-ups; actors banging other actors or directors or crew members. Between you and me, I can't imagine letting that man touch me. He's so unattractive and hairy. But, he's got beaucoup bucks, so on second thought, if I were a hot, young thing . . ." She warbled a throaty laugh.

"I wonder why she didn't mention that to me when we talked yesterday," Callie said.

"She seems like a very private person. Maybe she doesn't want to advertise certain things, even to her friends."

"Maybe . . ."

Larry, the production assistant, strolled through the room and handed Callie a sheet of paper. "We have your schedule figured out for the next few days. You're off Tuesday." He looked at the newspaper and whistled.

"We were just talking about them," Ming said. "They've got a little hanky-panky going on."

"You think?" Larry said sarcastically. "We all figure they've been knocking boots for a while. Tom is one lucky guy, I gotta hand it to him. He must have had a bomb-ass time last night 'cause he didn't make it to bed, unfortunately for us, so proceed with caution, Callie. Just a friendly warning. Hey, Sal, how's it going?"

"Hunky-dory, thank you." Sal Saunders took a seat in the

makeup chair next to Callie. A mixture of Old Spice and BO plugged her nostrils. His face was dehydrated and gaunt from forty years of smoking. Except for a shock of snow-white hair, he looked identical to his film characters that Callie remembered watching as a child.

"You're good to go, sweetie," chirped Ming.

Callie hopped to her feet and approached Sal. Her palms were clammy. "Mr. Saunders, I'm honored to be working with you. I've been a fan ever since *Hollow and Haunted*."

"You're Layla, I presume?" Sal said. His slate eyes pierced through her with laser-beam intensity.

"Yes. We have a scene together today."

"I'm aware of that. So, you're the one they call 'One-Take Callie,' eh? That's good to hear. I hate wasting time."

"I do, too. Fortunately, memorizing lines comes easy for me. I could really use your advice about a scene, what with all your experience—"

"But more than that," Sal said, "I hate babble. Excuse me. I'd prefer silence while I prepare." He closed his eyes as Dotty, his personal makeup artist, applied foundation.

Callie turned on her heel. "What an asshole," she said under her breath. An hour later, she met up with him again to film the first of their five scenes together. Although distant when the cameras weren't rolling, Sal sprang to life when he heard "action." He exuded devilish charm as Hamburg and kept the crew entertained with his knack for physical comedy. Even Tom, who stomped around like a stormy cloud, lightened up from Sal's performance—if only momentarily. When Tom wasn't shouting for silence, he was barking orders at anyone within a foot radius.

"Craig, tape these wires down for me! This is the second goddamned time I've tripped over them. And where in the blazes is the cappuccino I asked for yesterday? Christ almighty, people, work with me." Tom rubbed his bloodshot eyes and turned to Callie. "Now, you, young lady. Your big monologue is next up, the heaviest scene in the whole film. How do you feel about it? Prepared?"

Callie had gone over the dramatic scene countless times but hadn't mastered crying on cue, a glitch that made her doubt her abilities as an actress. "I've got it down," she said. Liar.

"Good girl. Can't wait to see what you've come up with," Tom said.

Two hours and twenty takes later, Callie's eyes remained dry as the Sahara. Try as she did, she couldn't muster any tears. She wondered when Tom would start screaming profanities. He sat in his director's chair and nibbled the tip of his thumb, waiting for her performance to happen. Callie finally threw her hands up. "I'm sorry, Tom—I don't know what's wrong with me. I can't do it."

"Don't be so hard on yourself," he said. "It's not an easy scene. I rewrote it a million times and almost axed it entirely. Do you want to break?"

"No . . . I don't know . . . I guess I just don't have it in me," Callie moaned.

"Malarkey. Don't be goddamned ridiculous. You can do it. I'm positive on that, otherwise I wouldn't have hired you. Hmmm . . . Let's try this." He crouched next to Callie on set and lowered his voice. "Layla is upset because every single person in her life has double-crossed her. There's no one for her to turn to and she feels lost. Utterly *alone*. Tell me about a time when you felt most alone and scared and vulnerable, when you wondered how in hell you'd make it out alive and in one piece. Think about that . . . a friend or pet or family member who's no longer with you. You will never see your loved one again on this earth. They're never going to touch or hug or kiss you. Ever. Just think about that for a few, let it soak in.

Tell me when you're ready, but don't feel the need to rush it. Just take your time, let it soak in. . . ."

Callie thought of her father and suddenly her eyes poured. Finally! She did her scene. And another take. And another. And another until she couldn't shed any more tears and her body felt weak from dehydration.

"And, cut!" Tom said. "I got what I need. Well done, Cal. That last take was especially spot-on. All right, boys and girls, it's three A.M. and it's a wrap."

Callie wiped her eyes and blew her nose; emotionally, she was spent. Home had never sounded so good. She bumped into Tom on the way to her car.

"Say, Callie, before I forget," he said, "I've got a good friend who can help you work on your acting. One of the best coaches around. Her name's Deirdre."

"Deirdre Coleman?"

"That would be her. I'll buzz her and see if she can give you some pointers. You're good, don't get me wrong, but with a little coaching, you'll be brilliant."

"Thank you, Tom. I really appreciate that." It was easier obtaining a one-on-one with the pope than booking a session with Deirdre Cole. Coaching three decades' worth of Oscar-winning actors made her the most sought-after teacher in town. Callie had auditioned for her class several months ago—and was turned down flat. ("Not bad, but you're too green," said Deirdre. "And your tone is nasally. Come back after you've worked with a voice coach and have some credits under your belt.")

"You're welcome," he said. "Now, go and get some rest. I for one am fucking beat."

25

Callie staggered into her apartment building. Her weary expression turned into one of puzzlement as she approached number 10; music and a jumble of voices were audible before her key entered the lock. Candice was splayed on the floor along with two people Callie had never seen before, all of them glassy-eyed. Cocaine was piled on a glass platter—a treasured Christmas gift from Grandma Esme—and plastic cups with cigarette butts littered the place while hip-hop boomed from an iPod.

"Hi, Cal, I didn't know you'd be home so soon," Candice said nonchalantly.

"It's three thirty in the morning, Candice! What do you mean you didn't think I'd be home so soon? Who are these people and what are they doing in my apartment?" She marched over a gangly-bodied man and flipped off the music.

"I just thought I'd invite a few of my friends over. We came back 'cause all the clubs closed. This is Ian and his brother, Ted. Don't worry, I'll clean up. Sit down and party with us." Candice scraped a line of coke with her credit card.

"I just had a long day on the set, I'm dog-tired, and I want my apartment back! You don't get it, do you, Candice? You live here rent-free, raid the refrigerator without offering to buy food, bring strangers into my home without asking me, and, to top it off, do blow off my grandmother's china!" Callie's face and neck were crimson.

"Callie, let me explain. It's not what—"

"Explain what?! How you're a mess? How you blow off auditions and piss off casting directors because you'd rather get wasted? I've had it with you using me. Not anymore, the party's over. Pack your shit. That goes for all of you—get the hell out of here. *Now!*"

Ian and Ted rose to their feet and left, but Candice remained. Tears filled her eyes. "Callie," she said, "you can't really mean that. . . ."

"I really do, believe me. I love you, but I can't help you anymore. This is the last straw. Leave, and take your shit with you," Callie said.

Candice scooped up an armful of shoes and garments and dumped them in a garbage bag. "I'm missing some stuff. I left some dirty clothes in the hamper, I think. Will you call me if you find anything?"

Callie nodded but avoided eye contact. Candice stumbled out the door.

Paul Angers's Hollywood office was just five minutes from Callie's apartment. She didn't want to risk being so much as one second late and arrived a half hour before their scheduled time. The office was bare bones in decoration; two chairs and a steel coffee table sat forlornly in the middle of the room. A few framed movie posters—clients of his, Callie presumed—hung on the otherwise barren walls. Ursula presided behind a desk, her frame easily dwarfing the hefty piece. Her diminutive, high-pitched Southern drawl stood in sharp contrast to her size.

"Hello, there. You must be Mr. Angers's one thirty, Miss Callie Lambert," said Ursula.

"Yes, I'm a bit early."

"Now, there's somethin' I don't hear every day. That's a rarity in this town, usually everyone is runnin' behind. I'll tell Mr. Angers you're here." Ursula cradled the receiver in her shoulder while her immaculately manicured nails clicked away on the keyboard. "Mr. Angers, Miss Lambert is here . . . yes, sir. Of course, I'll tell her. He'll be right with you, sugar. Make yourself at home."

"Thank you."

Paul emerged from a room behind Ursula's post. "Come on in, Callie. Have a seat anywhere you like. Glad to see you brought your headshots. I'll take a look at them in a bit. So, how's *Nympho Cheerleaders* treating you?"

"I'm having a ball letting my inner diva rip. The only thing I'm nervous about are those sex scenes."

"Ah, yes, there's a racy exchange between you and the other girl. What's her name? The blonde . . ."

"Gabby. She's a friend of mine, so I'm hoping that will make it easier."

"I'm sure the crew will be the first ones on set and the last ones to leave," Paul chuckled. "Even though the subject matter is fluff, the script is a well-written satire and you get the whole tongue-in-cheek tone, too, which says a lot about you as an actor. You have a natural aptitude, and finding a pretty girl who understands comedy isn't easy, believe it or not. So, tell me—what do you want?" Paul leaned back in his swivel chair, hands pressed together.

"I want an agent who believes in me as much as I believe in myself," she said in steely earnestness.

"Bold and to the point. I like that. The Wilders think very highly of you and if you're on their side, you're golden. The only reason I stopped by that day was because you really impressed Will and he thought I should have a look. I was an agent at Metro for twenty years before I opened my own agency eight years ago, so believe me, I've seen a lot of actors but not very many talented ones. The thing I like most about running a boutique agency is I get to focus on each client as an individual; that's why my roster is made up of less than sixty. Let's have a look at your headshots. Hmmm . . ." He leafed through her photos, the corners of his mouth bent downward. "When were these taken?"

"Six months ago. No good?"

"No good," he echoed. "They look very amateur. I have some recommendations for photographers and they're not too pricey, either."

"What about my comp card? I've been using it for modeling for over a year."

"The comp isn't bad. In fact, this one could work as a headshot." He pointed to a three-quarter-length photo of Callie attired in a white tee and jeans. "I like it because you look fresh but still sexy. You're not trying too hard. You remind me of a young Raquel Welch—only a friendly version."

"But I don't want to look like *anyone*. I just want to be me."

Paul rested his elbows on his desk. "Relax. I don't think you're trying to be anything you're not. I like your spunk, though. So many kids come to Hollywood thinking they're the next Marilyn or Jimmy Dean and I find it sad. The truth is they never will be. It cannot be done and you know why? Because there can only be one. Individuality cannot be duplicated."

"What types of actors do you represent?" asked Callie.

"An eclectic mix—character types, some leading men, and way too many Ethels and not enough Lucys. No one like you, and I've been hunting for a leading lady." He grabbed a stack of headshots. "There's this girl, Gretchen, who has a similar look but she's shorter and British. Taylor, here, just booked a Spielberg film. She's only sixteen, moved here from Florida last month. Josh, this fellow, has been a regular on *Son of the Hamptons* for three years."

Paul's frankness appealed to her similar straightforward nature. He wasn't another Doug Starr peddling five hundred look-alikes. And—most important—he had faith in her abilities.

"Paul, you've found yourself a new client."

26

The breeze carried the tangy smell of molasses through the air. Meat sizzled on the grill; the flames licked hunks of beef and ears of corn. Diego's Catering made Callie's mouth water. She hadn't had barbecue, her favorite, since living in Michigan. For four straight weeks she'd religiously maintained a diet of steamed vegetables and grilled chicken. The camera added ten pounds and looking as svelte as possible was the number one goal. With all of her nude scenes safely behind her, though, she saw no reason to continue torturing herself. Happily indulging her appetite, she gorged on carbs and red meat until the seams of her jeans were about to burst.

"Gabby, bite her neck. Ooh, yes, just like that. . . . Throw your hair back, Callie. . . . And again! Don't look so strained, you should be in ecstasy—this goddess-of-a-woman is devouring you. Hair! I need hair on set. Bigger, tease the fuck out of it. . . . More, more . . . Give me I-just-fucked-the-shit-out-of-you-for-two-hours-straight sex hair, damn it! That's more like it. . . . Terrific . . ."

She thought of her sex scene earlier in the day and blushed. Callie was as nervous as Gabrielle was comfortable, but then it wasn't the first time she had had simulated sex; *Wicked Seduction*, a late-night cable movie, had given her plenty of experience. Love scenes were as easy for Gabby as reciting the Lord's Prayer and Callie was relieved the script called for Kiki to seduce Layla instead of the other way around. It was enough just worrying how her naked body was positioned for the camera. Who would have thought a sex scene had to be so perfectly choreographed? Tilt your head farther back; don't hold your knees so close to your body—it creates an unflattering shadow across your stomach and blocks your breasts; tear her panties off *before* she kisses you, not after. . . . So many dos and don'ts to remember! One page of script took five hours to perfect. And yet, despite all the technicalities, Callie was aroused. Gabrielle's sizzling kisses and bold sexuality would excite a ninety-year-old impotent gay man. Callie had never been intimate with a woman, behind closed doors or otherwise. A peck on the lips was as far as she had ever gone.

Six grueling hours later, the girls kicked back in Gabrielle's trailer and ate lunch.

"I saw you in *USA Today*; you looked amazing," said Callie, gnawing on a spare rib.

"I was shocked they ran that picture! My parents called when they saw it. They seemed proud of me, for once. Finally, their daughter gets a write-up in something mainstream and respectable," Gabby said dryly. "Tom and I had a lovely time. It's amazing the number of people he's connected to; he knows *everyone*! And he's so generous, too. On the way there, I mentioned I was a little cold, so he told his driver to pull over—we were right by the Grove. He actually went into Barneys and came out five minutes later with a mink stole! Can you believe that? *Mink.* He insisted I wear it—wouldn't take no for an answer. No one's ever done anything like that for me before."

"Did you spend the night?"

"Yes, and every night since. He says he's in love with me."

Callie swallowed. "What did you say to that?"

"I didn't know what to say. He's so good to me, naturally I care about him. He's not exactly the most handsome man, like Justin. But what he lacks in the looks department he makes up for in personality. He keeps me in stitches most of the time. There's never a dull moment, which is great, because I hate monotony as well." She lowered her tone. "Plus, he's hung like a horse. We had sex four times last night, I kid you not. The libido on that man! He wears me out and I'm twenty years his junior."

The visual of a naked Tom Johannesburg sporting a hard-on induced Callie's gag reflex. "So are you two exclusive?"

Gabby nodded. "As a matter of fact, my lease expires at the end of the month and he wants me to move in with him."

"Talk about a whirlwind, Gabby. You've only known each other for a few weeks!"

"Tom doesn't know the meaning of slow. When he knows what he wants, he pushes the pedal to the metal. Actually, I want to come clean about something. The night of the premiere wasn't the first time I'd gone out with him. In fact, it wasn't the first time I'd slept with him, either; we met several months ago."

"Before auditioning for *NCA!*?"

"Yes. A mutual friend set us up. In the past, sometimes I've . . . well, I guess you could say . . ." Gabrielle clamped her mouth shut.

"Sometimes you've what?" prodded Callie.

"I haven't always made the most morally sound decisions. Heaven knows I've never pretended to be a saint and I'm not proud of some of my choices, but I've always done my best to survive and—above all—be a good person. I'll leave it at that."

"Gabby, I've never judged you; you don't owe me any explanations. Who am I to play God?"

"That's one of your traits I really admire." Gabrielle tugged on a strand of hair. "I've always gone off instinct and my gut is telling me to go for it."

"Like that Cobain lyric in 'Polly': 'It amazes me, the will of instinct.'"

"Instinct is so powerful, isn't it? I know this is all sudden, but it's awfully nice to be taken care of. He's the first male in Hollywood to tell me I have more to offer than a mountain of cleavage. Although I'm sure that's what attracted him in the first place."

"He hooked me up with an acting coach I've been dying to get in front of. My first class is next week. His connections are out of this world."

"It's a fantastic perk, of course. But truthfully, it's not the only reason I'm with him. It's the little things he does, too."

"Such as?"

A flush spread over Gabby's cheeks. "Such as the way he tickles my arms at night because he knows it puts me to sleep. He always opens the car door for me and makes sure I'm comfortable. 'Angel,' he'll say—he's always calling me angel—'is this too much air on you? Let me know.' There's this unexpected soft side and I love it."

"I never would have guessed: Tom the Teddy Bear."

"Few would. See, that's exactly what I need—a man who's crazy about me and worships the soil I walk on."

"I wish Evan felt that way about me," Callie sighed. "But he's so busy promoting the album, we haven't talked lately."

"His schedule is unbelievably hectic. Yesterday there was a picture of him performing in Sydney and just the day before in Rome. Speaking of Italy, that's where Tom is shooting his next movie and he has a part for me, too. Nothing major by any means—just two scenes and ten lines—but it's a big-budget thriller."

"Must be nice. Does he need a brunette? I have the perfect girl in mind." Callie pushed the jealousy to the back of her mind.

"I'll see what I can do," Gabby laughed. "It's hard to believe this wraps tomorrow. I hate it when a project comes to an end. I like the routine of looking over my lines in the makeup chair every day and joking with the crew."

"It's like one big family. Oh, well—back to the grind, slinging hash," Callie sighed. "Low-budget doesn't pay the rent, unfortunately."

Being desired—by a chart-topping singer, a holier-than-thou casting director, or anyone whose opinion mattered—was addictive and Callie was jonesing for her next fix.

27

"Dr. Stuart James Holtsclaw, celebrity psychiatrist. You must be Kelly."

"*Callie*. Come in, Doctor."

Dr. Holtsclaw placed his faded luggage-brown briefcase on the dinette and removed his sports coat. Salt-and-pepper hair provided contrast against his turquoise eyes. ("The bluest peepers my patients have ever seen," he loved to brag.) For being well into his fifties, he moved with the agility of a man half his age.

"We're going to patch you up, don't worry," he chirped. "Let's get right down to it. First off, I have to ask: You're not suicidal, are you?"

"No. Just depressed."

"How long do these bleak periods last?"

"A day or two. I go for weeks feeling fine then fall in a funk. My mom is the same way, only worse, and she doesn't believe in medication, either. I'd come home from school and find her in bed with the blinds drawn."

"And your father?"

"He died of a brain aneurysm when I was five. I had a nightmare about him last week. On his fiftieth birthday, no less. All day, I didn't leave the house or brush my teeth."

"Interesting . . ." He scribbled notes in a leather-bound notebook. "Sounds like you were quite a sight. Tell me more. Growing up without a father, did you get into trouble with boys?"

"Was I promiscuous, you mean?"

"Exactly."

Callie chewed her nails. "I've never believed in saving myself for marriage but I don't spend my nights getting gang-banged, either. I've had a few boyfriends . . . ten, maybe. But none of them added up to much. Maybe I just set too many expectations and then I'm let down. I don't know . . . I'm definitely scared of getting too close to someone."

"Why do you think that is?"

"Because I'm afraid he'll disappear. It's much easier to keep my heart under lock and key. But there's this one guy I met. . . . He's special. We get along really well and the sex is *so* hot. But his career takes him all over the world and I don't see him much. Besides, he's got so many women panting at his feet, why would he want to be with me?"

"Maybe falling in love scares him, too." Dr. Holtsclaw pushed his pen against the cleft in his chin.

"I didn't look at it that way."

"It frightens the bejesus out of most people, kiddo. One of the reasons I've remained a bachelor. Tell me about this movie you're in. How's it going?"

"It was great while it lasted, but now that it's over, I feel rotten," she grumbled. "Once again, I'm an unemployed actress. Back to the real world: waiting tables. Asking a bunch of grumps how they want their eggs cooked."

"It's common for depression to hit after a high note. The life of an actor—it ain't a picnic. One of my clients—I can't name names, but she's on the cover of this month's *Cosmo*—went through a time when she was unemployed for two years. She couldn't land a gig to save her life. Ebb and flow, that's what this industry is all about. It seems to me you're a perfect candidate for antidepressants. Have you ever been on any before?"

Callie shook her head. "Never."

"Let's try Wellbutrin," he said cheerfully. "The side effects are low—you may be a little speedy at first but it won't make you gain weight. We'll start off on seventy-five milligrams, once in the morning. Are you sleeping well?"

"It depends. I've always been a light sleeper and it's hard for me to shut my brain off. I'm always bouncing from one thought to another."

"So it's difficult to relax? Are you anxious?"

"Sometimes, yes. I've had a few panic attacks before and I thought I was going to pass out. Have you ever had any? They're the *worst*."

"I've never experienced them myself. What brought about these panic attacks?"

"The first one I remember having was ten years ago. It was right after my mom and I got into a fight—a really nasty one. We didn't speak to each other for two days. My head was spinning and spinning until I couldn't breathe and I was hyperventilating. I had another one before a photo shoot. Nerves, I guess." She scratched the back of her neck, a tic that manifested when she felt uncomfortable.

"And sometimes they've come out of the blue. I could be at Starbucks when one will suddenly hit. Stupid, isn't it?"

"Criminy, no. A lot of people suffer from anxiety. I'll call in some Xanax. That will take the edge away and ward off panic. And I'll throw in some Ambien, too, for when you have insomnia. What's your diet and exercise routine?"

"I do cardio and sometimes yoga or Pilates. I'm trying to eat healthier, too, but being from the Midwest, it can be challenging. People don't eat the same there as they do here in California."

"You're preaching to the choir, kiddo. This boy's born and raised in Chicago. They love their Fanta and anything with dairy and red meat—real nutritious. Try incorporating lots of fish into your diet, especially salmon."

"Ugh. I can't stomach salmon, but I like white fish. And I love shrimp cocktail."

"Stay away from shrimp, they're not good for you—high in cholesterol." He pulled a pack of smokes out of his shirt pocket and stuffed an unfiltered Camel between his lips. "All right, kiddo, nice meeting you. Any friend of Gabrielle Manx is okay with me."

She handed him a two-hundred-dollar check and walked him to the door. "How long have you known Gabby?"

"Oh, let's see now—four or five years. That girl's been through hell, what with her husband offing himself."

Callie's eyes bugged. "He committed suicide? She never went into detail but said it was a 'freak accident.'"

"It was freaky, all right. She found him hanging in the closet when she got home from work. She's a tough cookie, a real survivor. And she's so easy on the eyes, I'd treat her free of charge—but don't tell anyone." He winked and lit his cigarette.

Callie was surprised Dr. Holtsclaw would reveal such personal info about Gabby; maybe it was an innocent slip or he was just overly trusting. "My lips are sealed," she said.

"I'll call you in a few days to see how you're doing and we can schedule a follow-up. Be well." Smoke curled over his head as he jaunted down the hall. An engine thundered and the doctor peeled off in his canary yellow Corvette.

"Cal, I wish you'd pick up. This is ridiculous. We haven't talked in months and I have so much to tell you. . . . Fine, have it your way. I'm going home for Christmas tomorrow and I was wondering if you were, too. I'll be there a week and I'm already tearing my hair out from boredom. We need to get together. You can tell my brothers all about your movie—you know what big Sal Saunders fans they are. It's not the same without you. Call me, okay? Stop being a snot."

She deleted Candice's message. Yes, she was returning to her home state for a visit, but she had no intention of spending it with Candice. Mending the fence wasn't high on her list of priorities, despite the holiday season; she was still steaming from their spat and angry at herself for not talking things out rationally. Losing her cool didn't happen very often and when it did, it took people by surprise. *Pop!* Like a can of soda. Once the fizz settled, it was business as usual.

Grandma Esme prepared for Callie's visit by baking and broiling until her kitchen overflowed with goodies. "My granddaughter is coming home for Christmas," she told anyone and everyone who listened. "I'm just tickled! I thought for sure she'd stay put in California—her boss doesn't give her much time off and you know how miserable the weather is this time of year. But she told me, 'Grandma, clear a spot for me. I'm staying at Mom's a few days and with you for two.' You could have knocked me over with a feather."

Callie spent her last night in Los Angeles at Gabrielle's. Tom had driven to Carmel earlier in the day for a visit with his eldest son and Gabby opted to stay in her new home. "I have something to show you," she said excitedly over the phone. "It's going to knock your socks off! We'll have an old-fashioned sleepover and I'll drop you off at LAX in the morning."

The Johannesburg–Manx residence was situated atop a cliff in the Pacific Palisades and was as sprawling as it was private. The garage housed an eclectic collection of Ferraris. The driveway was circular and the pool Olympic. A lion made of marble teetered on the edge of a spewing fountain. Gabby buzzed Callie through the gate.

"It's so good to see you! Come in, I have a fire going. It's awfully chilly tonight, even for December. I'm making Baileys and coffee." A bichon frise snuggled in her arms and three more bounced at her feet. (Tom was an enthusiastic collector of the white fluff balls and bred them as a hobby.) She offered Callie a steaming beverage and with a swoop of her lithe, bronzed limb, dangled her hand in front of her. An eight-carat, Asscher-cut diamond mounted in platinum nestled on her finger.

"Gabby! Look at that ring!" Callie grabbed Gabrielle's hand for closer inspection.

"Tom proposed last night. I've never seen a stone so clean and sparkly." Gabby cranked the volume on the stereo. Christmas carols danced from the speakers.

"Neither have I. It's larger than my apartment!"

"He does like everything big." She laughed, gesticulating toward her chest. "We were having dinner at Spago and I went to the restroom after our plates were cleared. When I came back, there was a Cartier box on the table. It wasn't the most romantic proposal but I'll tell you, I've never been so surprised in my life! I swear, I must have looked like I was catching flies. We haven't even talked about a date yet but I'd be honored if you'd be one of my bridesmaids."

"Of course! Count me in."

"I'm thinking of having the ceremony here. The setting is so beautiful and intimate. It's not like Tom and I are novices at this. Between the two of us, there are five previous marriages."

"*Five?*"

Gabby blushed. "Years before I met Justin, I was married for about, oh, ten minutes or so. *Big* mistake. I was only eighteen. Anyway, enough about me. How are you?"

"I would be much better with a Texas-sized diamond. My agent says this time of year is extremely slow, so I'm just trying to roll with it." She plopped next to Gabby on the plush rug facing the fireplace. Wall-to-wall mahogany bookshelves and etched ceiling beams lent the feeling of an Aspen resort.

"He's not exaggerating. The holidays are *painfully* slow. This town practically shuts down from November until January. If it weren't for Tom's new movie, I wouldn't have worked at all last month." Gabby took a swig from her mug. "The Wilders came over last week and guess what? They're ecstatic with *NCA!* so far. We watched a rough cut and you're dynamite, Callie. Your performance blows everyone else's out of the water, mine especially. Sherri Finstad is in charge of PR and from what the brothers tell me, she's quite the hustler. They say she's going to land some primo photo shoots and interviews for the release in September."

Callie frowned. "September? That seems so far away."

"Who cares if it's two years from now? Don't you see? This is going to be bigger than anyone ever thought! Except for Tom, of course, who knew it the moment he conceived the idea. And which two girls are going to get the most coverage? Why, the blonde and brunette lead, naturally! The ones who show the goods always get the most press." Gabrielle bounced on her knees as she spoke; her fervor was palpable.

"You really think so? That would be something."

"*NCA!* is Tom's baby, and if he has any say, we're taking this to the moon. I can really feel something cooking, mark my words. Everything is lining up perfectly; it's almost too good to be true! For the first time in years, I'm really happy. Okay, present time." She swiped a package tucked underneath the blinking tree.

"I have something for you, too. Nothing extravagant, but it's the thought that counts." She handed Gabby a tissue-paper-stuffed bag.

"Mmmm," Gabrielle breathed, inspecting the soaps and candles. "Gingerbread, my favorite. Reminds me of when my mother baked cookies as a kid. Go ahead, open yours."

Callie tore at the gold wrapping to discover a white Chanel clutch nestled in the box. "Oh my God! Gabby, I, um, I can't . . ." she stammered.

"Yes, you can; I insist. This has been a good year for me and I want you to have it. Do you like it?"

"*Like it,* are you kidding? Do fish swim? I don't know what to say, Gabby. . . ."

"Merry Christmas, hon. Thank you for being there for me. This coming year is going to be unlike any other." They clinked their mugs together.

"For only Baileys, this really packs a punch," said Callie, slurping.

"A splash of vanilla-flavored vodka, too." Gabrielle winked. "Let's do a shot of peppermint schnapps. We have a lot to celebrate."

Several rounds later, the girls struggled to remain steady on their feet.

"I'm drunk," laughed Gabby. She rolled on her back. The fire illuminated her cupid's bow and the cheekbones she inherited from Native American ancestors glowed. Callie admired her features and felt a tingle in her groin. She had been attracted to Gabby since their first meeting—she couldn't understand anyone not being attracted to her, Gabby was pure sex on heels. Spending as much time together as they had—long, sweaty hours, naked on set—intensified Callie's curiosity. It was months since she had been intimate with anyone and she craved human touch, and alcohol only fueled her desire. She crawled between Gabby's parted legs and loomed over her, tigerlike. Gabby leaned forward and their lips met in a scorching kiss. "Have you ever been with a woman before?" Gabby whispered.

Callie shook her head. "Never."

"You should try it. It's a lot more fun than doing it with a guy. Girls know how to make each other feel good. I've been told I'm pretty talented. Here, lean back and I'll show you what I mean."

"Umm, okay . . ."

Gabby rolled Callie on her back and removed her pants. "You're so wet! You should have told me and we could have done this sooner. I've always liked you, you know, Callie. Watch, I'll make you wetter still." Her tongue explored voraciously.

"Ooooh, nibble it more," Callie begged, gripping Gabby's head. Her eyes rolled in the back of her head. No man had ever devoured her so well, not even Bedroom Eyes. Her moans cut through the chorus of "O, Holy Night." "Don't stop, Gabby . . . Ohhhhh, God . . ."

29

Virginia waved her fork and exclaimed, "These are the best crab cakes I've ever had."

"Humph," grunted Tony. "The steak is great. Better than Ponderosa."

Callie warily eyed her plate of rubbery chicken. "Yeah, Ruby Tuesday has some killer food."

"Your mother says you were in a movie, some horror thing. You still workin' on that?"

"Tony, you haven't been listening. She finished that in October," said Virginia. "What is it about exactly, Callie?"

"A college cheerleading team. It all goes haywire when the new girl—me—arrives on campus."

Virginia's face contorted. "That doesn't sound like much of a movie to me. Not that I know anything about moviemaking."

"My friend saw a rough cut and said I'm really good, Mom. The producers think it will do well. The horror genre is huge, you know."

"Well, if things don't work out, you can always go back to being a dental assistant—a *real* job with a dependable salary. It's a shame you're wasting all that training. Dr. Ryder was a good man to work for, too. He told me you can come back anytime."

"But I wasn't happy, Mom. I'm in this business for the long haul and I'm definitely not moving back *here*."

Virginia rolled her eyes. "I figured you'd say as much but you can't say I didn't try."

"I'd rather be shackled to a sizzling radiator." Callie sampled her rubbery fare and grimaced. "Have you heard of Tom Johannesburg?"

"Isn't that the guy who came up with *Blow It Up* and *Firecracker Jones*? He knows how to make one hell of an action movie." Tony sawed off a chunk of sirloin and swallowed it.

Callie nodded. "He's had a lot of hits. He wrote and directed *NCA!*"

"What's *NCA!*?" Virginia asked.

"Um . . . it's the name of the movie." Callie took a deep breath and plunged ahead. "It stands for *Nympho Cheerleaders Attack!*"

"Whoa!" bellowed Tony. "Now *that's* something I wanna see."

Virginia elbowed him in his doughy belly. "You cannot be serious, Callie! What kind of name is that? Jesus Christ! You told me it wasn't porno!" Her fawn-brown bouffant bounced with every syllable.

"That's why I haven't mentioned it, because I knew what your reaction would be. Yes, there's nudity, but no, it's not pornographic. Sex sells, Mom, face it."

"I've said it before and I'll say it again: Hollywood is the devil's playground. People will do anything to make a buck."

"Those are Jews for ya," muttered Tony.

"You're selling yourself short, Cal. Mark my words: you will regret being a part of such trash. How is anyone going to take you seriously if you go through life flashing your cans?"

"We just view things differently, Mom. I'm comfortable with my body and don't see anything wrong with it."

"Well, there *is*! How can you say that? What am I going to tell my sister and friends and the Board of Directors of Midwestern Society?" Her shortness of breath was audible and she struggled to control her wheezing. "Listen to me! I'm completely flustered."

"Easy, Ginnie." Tony rubbed her back.

"I get so easily winded these days, I swear."

"Just 'cause you let things upset you. Let's not spoil your appetite, now; talk about somethin' else."

"Yes, let's change the subject, shall we?" Virginia speared a piece of imitation crab. "What's the problem with you and Candice? I ran into her yesterday at the Somerset Mall and she said you two aren't talking anymore. She can't figure out why you're so mad at her."

"It's too complicated to get into right now. How is she, anyway?"

"I didn't think she looked as pretty as she normally does—"

"Looked worn out to me," interjected Tony.

"Her face was drawn and she seemed jittery," Virginia continued. "She's dating a new guy who made a fortune in real estate. She said to tell you hi and that she really misses you. Call her, Callie. It's silly to let such a long friendship go to waste. Life is too short and you two are like sisters."

Callie sipped her Chardonnay.

"What, nothing to say? Well, you always were stubborn as a bull, just like your father." She whipped out a compact and reapplied her lipstick.

"You always say that. What other traits do we have in common?" Callie said earnestly.

Virginia rubbed her rouged lips together. "Your metabolism. It's just not human. And your talent for mimicry, although you're by far more sarcastic than he ever was."

A baby's wail in an adjacent booth caused Callie's shoulders to stiffen; the cries sliced through the commotion at the bar—balding men in Red Wings jerseys and wrinkled khakis hollered at the hockey game on TV while their Ogilvie-permed wives stuffed greasy potato skins in their mouths. "God help me," Callie mumbled.

"Did you say somethin', Cal?" said Tony.

"Nope, it was probably your stomach."

"Must have been." He unbuttoned the top of his Wranglers and rubbed his flab. "What time am I droppin' you off at your grandma's tomorrow?"

"Whenever. One or two?"

"How 'bout noon, 'cause I bowl at one."

"Even better."

"I'd take you, but the annual Women of Troy brunch is taking place and I can't miss it," Virginia said.

"It's okay, Mom. No biggie." She counted down the hours until she'd be in the company of Esme. If she was going to be in the Midwest, she'd rather be with her grandmother than with anyone else.

Esme pressed her spatula against the bread; the pan hissed from the pressure and Callie's mouth watered. No one made a grilled cheese like her grandmother. As simple a sandwich as it was, she used a secret ingredient to make it out-of-this-world scrumptious. (Grandma Esme liked to say it was "love.") Callie took full advantage of her culinary skills while in town.

"I forgot what a home-cooked meal tastes like, Grandma. As you know, I burn cornflakes," Callie said between large bites.

Esme set a glass of milk on the table and untied her KISS ME I'M GREEK apron. "Honey, eat up all you can. You look a little thin to me."

"I've always been thin."

"Just like your father, that's true." Esme's velvety eyes turned wistful. She and her son had been extraordinarily close, especially after her husband died when Alex was just twelve. The all-encompassing love for her only child was challenged when he married Virginia Novak; Esme was less than thrilled. Virginia, she thought, wasn't right for her son; she was too flighty, finicky, and—worse—in the middle of going through a divorce. But Alex was smitten and proposed marriage. The birth of Callie Catherine Lambert seemed to bridge the gap between the two Mrs. Lamberts. "How was your visit with your mother?"

Callie shrugged. "Same old, same old. Tony was obnoxious, as usual."

"He may not be the most sophisticated man or have a sense of—how do I say it, propriety?—but he seems to make her happy."

"For some reason, he does. I wish she wasn't so judgmental. Candice's mom is so chill and I wish mine could be that way."

"We can choose our friends but we cannot choose our family." Esme had a knack for phrasing things diplomatically. She patted Callie's shoulder reassuringly and gazed at her with loving eyes before a sudden look of shock passed across her face. "Oh, my goodness! Look at me, young lady. You did something to your nose!"

Callie grinned self-consciously. "Nothing major, Grandma, don't worry."

"It's smaller, I can tell. When on earth did you do this and why? There was nothing wrong with it to begin with!"

"A few months ago I had a doctor shave the bump down. Just a minor little tweak, that's all. It photographs better this way."

"Well, dear, I guess you know what they like out there. People in show business love messing with their bodies, don't they? Pushing things up, pulling things out, taking tissue out of their butts and putting it in their boobs—or whatever it is those surgeons do. It's a whole different universe out there. I don't understand it, but I'm old, I guess. Go relax, honey, while I clean up."

Callie flopped on the faded floral couch and flipped on *Holly-wood Hotspot*. "Grandma! Quick, come in here!" Esme scurried over, as fast as a seventy-year-old woman could scurry.

"Director Tom Johannesburg has been released from jail after posting fifty thousand dollars' bail," said the reporter. "His fiancée, actress Gabrielle Manx, called nine-one-one yesterday after a domestic dispute reportedly turned violent. Friends and colleagues of Johannesburg, who met Manx after directing her in an upcoming film, are shocked by the incident and say it's completely out of character. . . ." Mouth agape, Callie watched the footage of Tom's recent film premiere. With the smiling Gabrielle at his side, they appeared to be the quintessential loving couple.

"That's my friend who was in the movie with me. I can't believe it . . . ," Callie mumbled, reaching for her phone. She was sent to Gabby's voice mail.

"You mentioned her. My, she's lovely. What's she doing with a jerk like him? I'd rather you stay single for the rest of your life than be with a woman-beater. Why, if Grandpa ever so much as laid a finger on me, one of his legs would be broken by my father and the other by me!" Esme shook her head in disgust.

Fury raced through Callie's loins. Tom was a passionate, unpredictable man—she had borne witness to his temper, though never aimed at her directly—but to physically abuse his would-be wife? And someone as sweet and docile as Gabby? The show's announcer interrupted her musings.

"Next up: ten things you didn't know about America's hottest new singer burning up the music charts. Our own Kristin Klapp talks exclusively with Evan Marquardt, a one-on-one interview you can't miss."

There was Bedroom Eyes, looking yummy as ever. She was moist with lust. Would calling him look needy? What if he ignored her?

Ugh, rejection! She wanted *him* to call *her*. But desire knew no pride. She texted: *Watching Hollywood Hotspot . . . lookin' good!* Ten minutes later, her phone rang.

"I'm searching for a sexy brunette with a warm smile and a tight ass. Can you suggest anyone?" asked a familiar voice in a British lilt.

Callie bit her lower lip. "You're in luck. What are you up to, stranger?"

"Six foot two, about one hundred and ninety pounds."

"My, aren't we the jokester this afternoon."

"Actually, it's midnight here in London."

"London? So that's where you've been hiding out!"

"How I wish. I've been flying all over the place like a loon. Just yesterday I got back from Berlin where I recorded a remix of 'Keep It Sexy.' I'm staying put for a few weeks."

"Sounds exciting, I'm jealous. I'm visiting my family in Michigan. It's so gloomy and depressing, you'd hate it. But it's only for two more nights and then back to L.A."

"What are your New Year's plans?"

"None." She was scheduled at Harry's on New Year's Eve.

"Perfect! You can spend it with me. I'll tell my assistant to take care of the arrangements. It's an easy hop from Metro to Heathrow."

Her heart thundered like a mare at the Kentucky Derby. "You're serious?"

"Of course I am. And it would be extremely rude of you to refuse me, now, wouldn't it? Pack your bags. You and me in London, baby."

Heathrow bustled, swarming with travelers like locusts. Callie didn't mind—German, Chinese, all of the foreign dialects at every corner of the airport were exciting. Thank God she'd heeded her mother's advice on getting a passport last year. ("You never know when you'll need to travel out of the country," Virginia had warned.) She stretched her legs with long strides. Man, did it ever feel good to walk. The things she took for granted. Not that she was exactly cramped on the plane; Evan had purchased a first-class ticket for her. No wonder celebrities didn't mind flying so much—what a breeze! With an unlimited supply of top-shelf liquor and movies— plus enough room to give her apartment a run for its money— she'd gladly fly over the Atlantic regularly, too. She walked past a suited elderly man at baggage claim and did a double-take; he held a sign that read CALLIE LAMBERT and hauled her luggage to a waiting town car.

"Where are we going?" she asked. She loosened her ponytail and fluffed her limp hair. It was early in the morning in London but her body told her it was close to midnight on the West Coast.

"Knightsbridge, madam," the man said. "About a half hour's drive, unless we get caught in unforeseen traffic." They pulled up to a slick fifty-story building next to Hyde Park and were buzzed into the building by a security guard. Callie rode a private elevator to the penthouse, and Evan, ensconced in a dark terry cloth robe, greeted her at the door with a hard kiss.

"Good to see you," he murmured. "But I thought you were going to be naked."

"Well, I could be very soon . . . ," she said, wrapping her arms around him.

He tugged at her jeans and dragged her to his bedroom. As tired as she was, she easily found energy to make love. Planet Earth could be on the brink of combusting into a raging inferno, crumbling skyscrapers amid mass hysteria, and she'd have no difficulty being aroused by Evan. His smell, so musky and masculine, was a shot of espresso to her groin.

"Fuck, I love the way you feel," she moaned as he entered her. If only her past lovers could have been as skilled as Bedroom Eyes. He touched and teased her in a way no one else had—with the possible exception of Gabrielle. Callie had a flashback of their night in front of the fireplace when Gabby's tongue swirled up and down her body. She was gifted, yes, but it was different. There wasn't anything comparable to the feeling of a man, especially one like Evan. His brawniness complemented her femininity and she melted in his skilled hands like a pat of Land O'Lakes.

They lay pressed against one another in a clammy heap and Callie drifted into slumber. She woke to the smell of sautéeing garlic. Evan stood over the stove with a wooden spoon in one hand and a bottle of olive oil in the other.

"Whatever you're making smells delicious," she said. Rich, gorgeous, great in bed—*and* able to cook? She sat at the breakfast bar with her knees to her chest and pulled her oversized T-shirt over her thighs.

"This is an amazing pesto pasta dish my mother taught me. I make it all the time for Riley. You'll love it."

She took in his three-bedroom flat; with the carpeted floors and walnut walls, it possessed an intimacy his L.A. home lacked. Framed personal photographs adorned the tabletops and baby grand piano.

"How often do you see your son?" she asked.

"As often as possible, usually a few times a week when I'm in London. His mother can be a difficult one to deal with, though."

"What does she do?" asked Callie.

"Thanks to my child support, Claudia does nothing, now," he said evenly. "But she used to be one of my backup singers."

"How long were you two together?"

"For three years. We split when Riley was two." He swirled the spoon around the pan with brash strokes.

"That must have been really tough. My longest relationship was eight months. I realized I was too young for a steady relationship. Besides the fact that Brian was as dull as dirt." She paused to open a bottle of water he placed in front of her. "Do you want more kids?"

"Wow, I didn't know I was scheduled for an interview today." She averted her eyes and chugged her water.

"I didn't mean for that to sound as dicky as it did. I guess I'm still trying to unwind from my warp-speed schedule and am a tad uptight. Although you're a fantastic stress reliever." He winked.

"No worries," she said quickly. "I'm just curious because I'm an only child and always wanted a brother or sister. It was pretty lonely growing up, especially when my dad passed away. I didn't have many playmates; my mother was paranoid about allowing me to play at other kids' houses. She said you could never trust the parents."

"Good that she was protective," he said encouragingly.

"But looking back, it was strange. My mother has always been a control freak and as much as she monitored my comings and goings, she was so busy pulling two jobs and dealing with her own issues that I never felt I got enough attention."

"Is that why you wanted to become an actress? You wanted the praise you felt she never gave you?" He stared at her thoughtfully, head cocked.

"I never thought about it that way. Maybe so," she said after a pause, lowering her eyes.

Evan approached her and softly kissed her forehead. Their eyes locked before Callie nervously jumped out of the chair. "So, is this feast almost ready? It smells delicious."

He slid a steaming bowl of pasta in front of her. "Eat up. I'm glad you're here with me, Cal. Welcome to London."

Greedily, she slurped the tasty noodles. "Evan, you know what I want to do? I'd love to grab a beer at an authentic pub, one with lots of history."

"I can arrange that," he said. "There's a slew of old pubs on Fleet Street, we can go there, if you like. I didn't know you were the beer sort."

She raised one eyebrow. "You forget I'm from Michigan, so, yes, I enjoy a beer from time to time."

"Brilliant! A girl who likes variety—that's A-OK in my book. Lunatic groupies never bother me at pubs like they do other places, so that sounds perfect. Finish your pasta and we'll cab it."

Callie bundled a cashmere scarf around her neck and inhaled the brisk air. London was, while still biting, far less cold and wet than Michigan. And how refreshing not to breathe the smog of Los Angeles! As she walked through the doors of Ye Old Cock Tavern, she considered informing Adam she wouldn't be working New Year's Eve but decided against it. What was the point? He'd most likely can her, with or without an excuse, and she didn't much mind. The only thing that mattered was spending her days and nights with Evan in, of all places, the UK. Harry's Hamlet was thousands of miles away, mentally and physically.

"This is great. Now I really feel like I'm in England," Callie said. She sat at a heavy wooden table while he ordered two pints from the bartender. The dozen patrons were buried in their Boddingtons and fish-and-chips and didn't so much as even glance Evan's way. "I have a question for you. It seems out of the blue but I've always been curious. . . ." She sipped the frothy lager.

"I'm all ears," replied Evan lightheartedly.

"That girl, Rachel O'Connor. If you weren't dating her and you didn't want to deal with the paparazzi, why were you seen at nightclubs together? And shopping on Robertson Boulevard, of all places?"

"Look, Rachel and I dated a little—although it's *hardly* what she made it out to be in those awful interviews she gave. She's pretty, young, Miss November. . . . Come on, Callie—I am a man, after all. But she always wanted to go where she knew she'd get photographed, which is really what ended it for me. A publicity whore is obnoxious. Why does she bother you so much?" He propped his elbows on the table.

"Because when I met her, she was a frigid, partied-out bitch," said Callie. "I couldn't understand why, of all the girls panting at your feet, you liked *her*."

"Rachel was wild—a true party girl. I couldn't keep up with her, to be honest. This is rather amusing, actually; I never pegged you as the jealous type. It's kind of cute." His bright eyes glinted.

"*Jealous*? Please. You deserve better, that's all, and she seems so trashy. Is it true she was a hooker?"

He laughed. "I don't know, but I wouldn't be surprised. She was a good time. It was noncommittal, totally casual."

"Like you and me?" She regretted blurting the words as soon as she uttered them. Evan stared at her with an intensity that turned her already rosy cheeks a shade darker.

"I don't recall ever inviting Rachel to visit me in another country." He grasped her face with both hands and kissed her. She responded by clenching the back of his hair and stroking her tongue against his.

"Someone get these birds a bloody room!" shouted a man.

They pawed and nibbled a minute longer before leaving. Raw sex beckoned.

32

Life with Evan was one spontaneous romp after another, like unwrapping a shiny, sugary treat every minute. She'd ask for a dish of ice cream and he'd offer her a chocolate-sprinkle-covered waffle cone of dulce de leche. Unending invites to private parties besieged them. "Dinner at Supperclub tonight, doll? Or would you prefer Italian? If so, I'll ring up Cecconi's and make sure they save us a seat. I've got first-row tickets to see Elton John, as well. I personally don't care, it's all the same to me, so take your pick." He meant it. Every day with Bedroom Eyes was a Saturday night. If they missed the opening of a new club or a music mogul's cocktail party, they made up for it by going to an event more magnificent the following evening. Heavy on glamour, high on octane, Callie was smitten with the excitement.

Prancing around with her famous tour guide had its pitfalls;

Evan rarely went unnoticed and it often wasn't possible to squire around his American visitor without assistance. Bodyguards accompanied the couple but Evan found them cumbersome. He liked as little fuss as possible, an unpretentious attribute that appealed to Callie. The scenario was typical; a romantic dinner at a chic eatery or table service at the nightclub-of-the-moment—in the VIP section with the best view in the house, of course—before, inevitably, a group of fans discovered his presence. They gawked and pointed and salivated if Evan so much as raised a napkin to his mouth. He was gracious—even after security had to shoo over-zealous women away—but explained, when pushed, "If I'm with my girl, I'm off the clock."

Callie tagged closely behind a bodyguard as they exited Sketch. The burly man, calm and impenetrable, pushed through the camera-infested mob. Flashes illuminated the inky sky and made it difficult to see farther than a foot ahead. "And you think L.A. is worse?" she yelled into Evan's ear.

"By far!" Evan shouted back, and took her hand in his. "The Brits are tame in comparison."

"Evan! Keep it sexy with my sister and me! We want to have your babies!" shouted a stout woman with pocked skin. Callie shot her a demonic look.

The first taste of the nasty side of celebrity came when Callie saw her face thrown in the daily tabloids. *Marquardt and Mystery Brunette Elope* read one headline; *Identity of Evan's New Girl Revealed!* proclaimed another. The interest was unsettling. Like any performer, she enjoyed attention, but it wasn't the adulation she had envisioned, and it certainly wasn't on her terms. Messages from friends—mostly acquaintances—who caught her on entertainment shows and blogs clogged her voice mail, including one from her mother.

"Your phone doesn't work overseas, I'm guessing. I didn't know you were in London, why didn't you tell me? Tony and I were watching *Hollywood Hotspot* and all of a sudden, there you were! I couldn't believe it. They showed a clip of you leaving a party with that singer, Edmond or Edwin, something like that. My girlfriends called to tell me they saw it, too; *everyone's* talking about it here. It's kind of exciting, I have to admit. Anyhow, the reporter said there's a rumor you're going to be in *Coquette* and I'm wondering what this is all about. As usual, you've left me in the dark. . . ."

Paul Angers had given Callie the news a few days into the New Year: *Coquette* wanted her and Gabrielle for a pictorial *and* the cover—thirty thousand apiece with the signing of the contract and an additional thirty after completing a weeklong photo shoot in February. The issue was slated to coincide with the theatrical release of *Nympho Cheerleaders Attack!* in September. The paperwork was faxed to Evan's and, before her signature was dry, Callie rang Gabrielle to revel in the news.

"Didn't I tell you Sherri Finstad would work her magic?" Gabby said.

"You did, but I'm still shocked! The first thing I'm doing when I get back to L.A. is look for a new apartment. Moving out of the Valley will feel better than sex!"

Gabby laughed. "I got your message, by the way. Thanks for worrying about me but everything's fine."

"Did Tom really hit you?"

"No, no, things totally got blown out of proportion and I overreacted. I'm not pressing any charges. It was silly of me to call the cops in the first place."

"But, Gabby—"

"I'm busy moving forward with the wedding. I've forgotten how much work it is to plan one! May eighth, so save the date."

"But if he really did hit you—"

"Trust me, Callie," she said sternly, "I'm *fine*. I'm a big girl, you know, I can take care of myself. The press made it out to look much worse than it actually was, so let's just drop it, okay?"

"Fine. Subject dropped," she said with frustration.

"Let's focus on the positive: you're having the time of your life with Evan, we're shooting the cover of *Coquette* in a few weeks, I'm getting married, and before you know it, the movie will be out. This year is really starting off with a bang!"

Callie grimaced at Gabby's choice of words. "It certainly is."

33

"Are you going to just stare at it or are you going to open it?" Evan teased. He snuggled with Callie underneath the blankets of his California king. Chinese takeout containers littered his-and-her end tables as *Goodfellas,* his favorite movie, played on television. A robin's egg blue box was perched on top of her stomach. The trademark color was unmistakable.

"Tiffany!" she gasped, untying the silky white ribbon. "Oooooh . . . Are these emeralds?" She sat up in bed and inspected the baubles.

"And diamonds. What do you think?"

"They're the most beautiful earrings I've ever seen. Just gorgeous. And my birthstone, too."

"I know. Why do you think I chose them? Congratulations on *Coquette,* baby." He leaned in for a kiss and she planted a giant smooch on his lips. "Go ahead, put them on. . . . Yes, I'd say I definitely made the right choice." His eyes twinkled with satisfaction while she made the chandeliers dance by swinging her head from side to side. A somber thought struck her—what did this mean? Was he her boyfriend? Only boyfriends and husbands gave presents like this. Were they an exclusive item, a monogamous couple? They hadn't discussed the exact nature of their relationship in the ten days she'd spent with him. She knew without a shadow of a doubt she could be a faithful partner but wasn't so sure about Evan. . . .

"What's the matter?" he asked. "Since when did jewels make a girl so sad?"

"I don't want to leave tomorrow; I want to stay with you."

"Then stay. We'll reschedule your flight."

She shook her head regretfully. "I can't. Paul has a few auditions lined up for me later this week. I have to get back to the real world."

"Since when is L.A. the real world? Come on, stay with me a few more days. Go back at the end of the week." She hesitated and his eyes bored into hers with a conviction he hadn't displayed before. "Look," he said, "I want to be with you. I *only* want to be with you."

"Do you know how long I've waited to hear you say that?" she whispered.

"Really, now? You've always played it pretty cool. A relationship hasn't been at the top of my list for a while. I didn't think I had time for it, or that I was even ready. I can't lie; it will be challenging with my schedule. This is the longest I've spent without a microphone in front of my face in eight months. Constant meetings with managers, interviewers, being hounded by the press, hopping from one plane to another—it's all made me crave something *real*, something private I don't have to share with the whole fucking universe. I finally realized a chunk was missing."

"And what was it?"

"You, silly."

Callie's saucer eyes moistened and Evan continued. "You make me feel sane. Balanced. You're not chasing me for a cut like the rest of them. You don't want your ten or twenty percent, you're not looking to sell a picture or quote for a quick buck. Los Angeles hasn't tarnished you yet and I hope it never will. There are thousands of Rachels out there—probably millions—but I've yet to meet another Callie Lambert." Evan rolled on top of her and nuzzled her neck like a manic gorilla. She giggled and pushed him back.

"Seriously, though. No one has *ever* told me what you've just said or been half as exciting or generous. I've wanted you all to myself the first second I laid eyes on you on set," she said.

"I'll confess I only wanted in between your legs at that point."

"I figured as much. Do you realize how long it had been since I had sex? Six months! I felt like a cat in heat—a horny, howling pussy. I tried and tried to convince myself I didn't want anything more, either, but I could never get you out of my head. Not for long, anyway."

"I have that effect on people—I spread through your subconscious like a mad rash. So, this means you're going to keep me company a little while longer? I won't be able to make it to L.A. for at least a month—the European leg of my tour kicks off at the end of January. And I've decided I want to introduce you to Riley; he'll adore you. I implore you to stay."

"I love it when you beg," she purred, and dialed a number on Evan's phone. "Paul? I won't be home in time to make those auditions. Yeah, I know, but something came up and I need to stay in London a few more days. No, nothing's wrong. Yes, I'm positive. Everything's fine. In fact, things couldn't be more perfect."

34

House music pumped in the makeup room as Callie relaxed in a chair. Tyler painted her face in between sporadically dancing. "I love this song!" he cried. He stood still long enough to apply a liberal dose of liquid liner. "Makes me want to dance all night and party my tuchus off." Callie offered him her flute of bubbly but he declined. "If I drink, I'll get sloppy and you'll look like Helen Keller got ahold of you. But I'll take you up on it when I'm done."

It was noon on a Monday and they were at *Coquette*'s Westside studio for the beginning of their five-day shoot. The company pulled out all the stops for their two cover girls—Dom, anything and everything to snack on, assistants at their beck and call ("Are those chocolate-covered strawberries you requested up to par, Callie?" a gofer asked. "If not, I'll run out and grab something else.") and whomever they desired for hair and makeup. Tyler, of course, was a no-brainer for Callie, but she wasn't well acquainted with any hairstylists. At Gabrielle's suggestion, she chose a Baton Rouge–bred cutie named Tessa. She was amazed with Tessa's ability to create spectacular waves that put the *b* in bounce.

"Don't blink," Tyler ordered. "Your lashes need to dry. I'm off to piss." He returned with a grimace covering his boyish face.

"You look like you just sucked off a lemon," noted Callie.

"There's a huge, hairy guy wandering around," he said. "Is he the director who got arrested? The one engaged to the hooker?"

Callie scowled. "Gabby's not a hooker, Ty. Maybe she fell on hard times in the past, but that doesn't mean she's a bad person or we should judge her."

"Sheesh, skank, calm your pussy before you sweat off your paint. I'm not trying to be nasty—just calling a spade a spade. This town is full of pay-for-play, guys and girls alike. Nothing new here. Gotta do what you gotta do."

"I'm just amazed she took him back," sighed Callie.

"Happens all the time. I'll tell you what it is—bitches love a rocked-out bank account. I don't care how loaded or famous a guy is—no amount of money could make me stay with someone crazy. I wig out if a guy wants to spank me, let alone beats my ass. You wouldn't think it to look at me, but this one likes it vanilla. Nice and easy, thank you very much. Throw some rose petals on the bed and I'm happy."

A sudden rap at the door made Tyler jump. It was Tom with his favorite bichon frise, Bardot, cradled in his arms. "Why, if it isn't my Layla!" he said.

Callie eyed him coldly. "Hello."

"Heavens to Betsy, is that thing even real?" Tyler scratched the dog's head. "She looks like a stuffed animal."

"Bardot, here, is my baby. She treats me better than any of my own kids," Tom said. "Thought I'd stop in to say hi. How's it going, Callie? You nervous?"

"Not really."

"Good. No reason to be. You're a regular pro. You know the drill and you're in great hands. Hank is one of the best. He's getting some fantastic shots of my lady love right now. Smokes, look at those Bambi eyes on you! Fantastic."

Callie ignored the compliment.

"She's going to give every straight male from here to Maine a Matterhorn-size erection," said Tyler.

"Absolutely. I've always said, if you're going to do it, do it big. All right, I'm going back on set. Nice seeing you, kid. Keep up the great work." The moment Tom turned his back Callie rolled her eyes.

"That dickhead thinks he can schmooze me," she huffed.

"Then he obviously doesn't know you very well. You were cold as death but I've seen you much worse." Tyler surveyed his handiwork. Come-hither, heavy-lidded peepers were his specialty. "Tell me what you think. Should we go smokier?"

"A little, and can you wing it up more in the outer crease? You know how I love a good cat eye. I wish you could do my makeup every day, Ty."

He smudged the charcoal shadow with deft strokes. "And I wish I could find a husband built like Mr. Universe with a château in the south of France, but that's not going to happen, either. There, I'd say you're fully skankified." He wiped his brushes clean and took a swig of bubbly. "Have you told your mother yet about *Coquette*?"

"No need to. She found out from the press."

"Oh, snap! She must have had an absolute cow."

"Actually, I think she's warming up to the fact that I just happen to make a living wearing fewer clothes than most people. Not that she's given me her seal of approval, exactly, but she wasn't nearly as pissed as I thought she'd be."

"That's progress, at least. Your mother is as uptight as they come. What's going on with Evan? When's that hot piece back in town?"

Callie groaned dreamily. "Another two weeks. He's playing Athens tonight."

"How grand is his place in London?"

"Beautiful but not what you'd expect. It's much smaller than I would have guessed, especially after seeing his house in the Hills. To tell you the truth, I actually like it a lot more. After a few weeks there, it felt like home. You know, I can see myself living there, Ty. That's how much I adore him."

"*What?* Someone call a doctor! This coming from Miss I-Don't-Want-a-Man, who was only about career this and career that?"

"I know, I know. It's not like we've said the three magic words yet. . . ."

"The three magic words? You mean Dolce and Gabbana?" said a straight-faced Tyler. "Try to go slow, Cal—no reason to rush it. Rome wasn't built in a day. Lordy, there's plenty of dick on this earth to get wet over without drowning in the first pool of cum that floats your boat."

Callie smacked her lips. "But what a fabulous pool it is."

"To be honest, I'm a little jealous Bedroom Eyes has seen so much of you lately. You've been neglecting your gay. One of my clients—this Brazilian singer I made up for the Grammys—invited me to her birthday at the Abbey tonight. Why don't we go?"

"Tonight? Geez, I don't know. It's going to be a long week and I want to be fresh."

Tyler stamped his foot and shoved a hand on his hip. "It's not like I'm asking you to swallow a bottle of Patrón. We'll socialize for a few hours, get a little loosey-goosey, and then you can go home to ride your Great King—or whatever it is you do when Evan isn't around."

Callie reluctantly gave in. "My call time isn't until ten, anyway."

"Exactly. Geez Louise, I wonder how much longer Gabby's going to be? Marge told me to have you done by one and it's two."

"I'll go see what's going on. My legs are about to fall asleep from sitting." Callie wandered the halls in search of Marge, the creative director. She located the manly, bespectacled woman snacking at the craft service station.

"Hey, sugar pop," said Marge. "Another hour, tops. Have you tried these? Fucking incredible, this Belgian chocolate." She licked her fingers and reached for another.

The butterflies flapping in Callie's stomach made food repellent. Naked shoots—stills or otherwise—caused her anxiety, regardless of the number of times she had disrobed for the camera. "I don't have much of an appetite."

"Go relax, then, take it easy. It won't be much longer."

The animated sounds coming from around the corner intrigued Callie.

"*Amaaaazing!* You've got it down, Gabby, hold that. Absolute dynamite!"

She tiptoed to the set.

Gabrielle was on her back, draped across a beanbag chair like a serpent. Her sun-kissed complexion, dewier than usual, perfectly offset her caramel hair. Dressed in nothing but a pair of knee socks, she effortlessly twisted her sinewy body.

"Unbelievable! Phenomenal, Gabby," cooed Hank. "You're breaking my camera, I tell ya. Breaking it!"

Gabby bit the tip of her index finger and gazed at the lens with saucy eyes. Tom stood off to the side, bouncing on the balls of his feet and swelling with pride. "She should stick her tits out more, don't you think, Hank?" he said. On cue, Gabby thrust her breasts out farther. Hank's flash couldn't keep up.

Jealousy sprang through Callie. How was it possible to hold a candle to someone as ravishing and poised as Gabrielle? It was pointless to even try—impossible. The mere thought made her woozy. Gabby was flawless, the kind of woman every red-blooded male lost his marbles over. She probably even oozed sex straining on the toilet. *I feel like a Gremlin.* Callie braced herself against the wall and tried to silence her panic. *Cigarettes. I need a cigarette. No, I don't. Cigarettes are for losers.* She had been nicotine-free since leaving for London and intended to stay that way. She flitted off to the dressing room and chomped a Xanax. *Gulp. Thanks, Doc.* Wellbutrin had helped her depression—especially since Dr. Holtsclaw increased her dosage to 450 milligrams—but it was Sister Xani who really revved her engine. Within twenty minutes' time, her ragged nerves were smoothed straight. Combined with alcohol . . . oh my. She chased Sister with another shot of Dom. What a rockin' buzz. *Heaven.* Much better than a bump or two of blow; blow was chintzy and only provoked anxiety. An hour passed and Callie, stretched across the chaise, felt as pliable as Gumby. She forgot about Gabrielle's unattainable perfection and nodded off.

"This is just what the doctor ordered." Tyler looked approvingly at his surroundings. "Men, music, and mojitos! My kind of night."

A girl with long, jet-black hair boogied up to the bar with her two male companions and ordered a round of drinks. Callie squinted and tried to get a better view; could it be Candice? No. This girl was too thin to be Candice. But her exaggerated gestures and swishy walk were all too familiar.

"Who on earth are you looking at?" asked Tyler.

"That girl over there reminds me of Candice, don't you think?"

"I can't make out her face very well, but that's definitely not Candice's build. And from what I remember of her—granted I haven't seen her in a while—she had really thick, wavy hair. That girl's mane is hanging like a greasy, sopping-wet noodle."

"You're right. But her mannerisms . . ." Callie's voice trailed off.

"I'm going to use the little boys' room," Tyler said. "Catch you in a minute." He traipsed off just as the ebony-haired girl turned into full view. It *was* Candice. Only it wasn't the same person Callie remembered. Even in minimal lighting, Candice's under-eye circles were visible and her lackluster complexion and sunken cheeks were gasp-inducing. Sadness boomed like a cannon through Callie's heart. In spite of their fallout, she loved her longtime "sister" and dearly missed her fiery spirit, energy, and hyena cackle. All of those intimate talks late at night when neither could sleep . . . Did Candice feel the same? Or would she be rebuffed? Callie swallowed hard and approached her.

"Oh, my God! *Callie!*" Candice threw her lank arms around Callie's neck. "What are you doing here? Why haven't you called me? I've missed you *so* much."

"I know. I've missed you, too, Candy."

"I'm so sorry for everything. You've always been good to me and I fucked it all up. I was such a louse, a total douche bag. Things haven't been going so great lately, Cal." Tears welled in Candice's tired, cobalt eyes.

"No?"

Candice shook her head and tried to control her trembling lip. "No."

"I'm sorry to hear that. I want to hear about everything."

"We were just about to leave to go to Mickey's. Can we get together soon to talk? Preferably in a place where we can hear each other."

"Please, let's. I have so much to tell you," said Callie.

"Same here, girl. God, same here."

35

Paul Angers rolled his chair over to a file cabinet and flipped through Callie's folder. "Can you get more headshots printed? I'm all out of your close-up, that beauty shot everyone goes crazy over."

"Sure thing. Any word from Sandy Gillick's office about that sitcom?" said Callie.

"I put in a call to her this morning but she was busy. I'll call her again at the end of the day. When I spoke with her last week, she said how impressed she was with you but the network was undecided if they were going to go with an unknown or a name. Let's keep our fingers crossed. On another note, I was thinking that this would be a good time to invest in a publicist, Callie. Even though *NCA!* isn't a big-budget extravaganza, it's bound to get some attention because of Sal Saunders's huge fan base. *Coquette* will obviously give you a big push, too, and a publicist could really work with those two credits. Judging from the Polaroids, your shots look unbelievable."

"Not too shabby for a kid from the cornfields, huh?"

"Not in the least. And the ones where you're straddling Gabrielle—oh, boy. Those are guaranteed to cause a stir."

"Yeah, I'm sure it'll be a hit with the Walmart-shopping soccer moms of America."

"Definitely with their husbands, that's for sure," Paul snickered. "You had an offer today for a film about a girl who works at a sex shop. She trades places with a vibrator for the day and it's called—you ready for this—*The Bionic Dildo.*"

Callie's mouth dropped. "Paul, you're lying!"

"I kid you not."

"See? This is what worries me. Crap like *The Bionic Dildo* is the best I'm going to get from now on."

"Then we'll keep declining until you're offered something that deserves you. Remember, there's no pressure to jump at the first thing that comes your way. I know you don't want to cruise down T and A Drive forever, but you've got a little money in the bank and you're generating buzz—not exactly a desperate predicament. If this is the best you get when you hit thirty-five, then it's time to worry." Paul scribbled on a legal pad. "Here is a number you should call."

"Kat Killian," she read. "I've heard of her."

"She's quite abrasive, I'll warn you, but it clearly works for her because the woman's been in PR for years. She's worked with a few clients of mine."

"Okay, can you call her for me?" She glanced at the Cartier Roadster adorning her wrist. It was, to date, her biggest splurge, and worth every penny. "Crap. I'm running late, Paul, I've got to get going."

"Nice watch. A gift from that handsome singer you're involved with?"

"Nope. I bought this myself. But, he did get me *these*." She angled her head and showcased the bling dripping from her lobes.

"He's got great taste."

"Doesn't he? I'll drop off the eight-by-tens by the end of the week, Paul."

"Good girl. Hopefully we'll have some news from Sandy in a few hours."

"Fingers crossed! Catch you later." She scurried out of the office with such vigor, Ursula's papers fluttered off her desk. Bedroom Eyes was due to land in Van Nuys by private plane any minute. After a monthlong absence! She missed him so much, she could taste the salt from his skin. Little idiosyncrasies tugged at her heartstrings— the way he ran his hand through his hair while deep in thought, back to front; listening to his gentle breathing when she woke in the middle of the night . . . *Just another hour or so . . .* She was combing the aisles at Bristol Farms in search of his favorite Bordeaux when her BlackBerry rang.

"Hey there, sexy lady," Evan purred.

Callie squealed. "Finally! I've been thinking about you nonstop. Are you home yet?"

"En route. Meet me at my place in a half hour?"

"Perfect. I'm right down the street on the Strip."

Twenty-two minutes later she folded her body in his arms. He inhaled her scent and cupped his hands around her waist, drawing her close. "You smell so good," he raved, "like a sugared, buttery peach."

"Take your clothes off," she ordered.

"So dominant and feisty today. I love that." He removed the cotton tee from his tanned, chiseled chest. Callie unbuttoned his jeans and, dropping to her knees, devoured him.

"God, have I ever missed you," she said, coming up for air.

He tugged her hair at the crown. "Mmmm, the feeling is mutual. Now, get down on all fours like a good girl."

Her moans cut through the air like a machete. "I feel like a new woman," she sighed after their fervent romp.

"Good, baby. You felt amazing, just fucking brilliant. I could stay inside you for days. What would you care to do tonight?"

"As long as I'm with you, I don't care."

He smiled his signature, sexy grin. "I love that about you. Gary's having a few people over for drinks, really low-key. Why don't we go to his place?"

"Cool—mellow sounds perfect. Gabby and I are scheduled for the interview portion of *Coquette* tomorrow morning at nine and I want to be fresh. I'm going with her afterwards to see her wedding planner."

"She's still going through with it, is she?"

"Yeah, full throttle. Says she was really pissed off and overreacted and that she never should have involved the cops. I don't know—I mean if she's happy . . ."

"Gary's known Tom for years, back when he was married to his first wife, and he's never heard of any domestic violence issues. No charges, no rumors, nothing. Maybe Gabby has a hotheaded side you don't know of. Behind closed doors, anything is possible."

A dozen people—a middle-aged man and a group of barely twenty-something girls—mingled at Gary Benson's Los Feliz mansion. The girls eyed Callie with a mixture of awe and scorn and stared at Bedroom Eyes as if he were a walking strip of bacon. She felt his phone vibrate in his pocket. "I better take this call, doll. You know Gary. Make yourself at home."

"Callie! Nice seeing you again, babe." He kissed her cheek and his thick frames brushed against her nose. "I want you to meet Irina. She moved here from Ukraine last week." A bleached blonde, breasts five cup sizes too large for her wispy frame, stroked his shoulder with her acrylic nails. Her teeth were as crooked as a rickety fence on an abandoned farm. *Wow. She should have spent her money on veneers instead of implants.*

"Good to meet you!" Irina gushed in broken English. She twirled her three-foot-long extensions and batted her chunky false lashes. "Is true you have movie coming out?"

"In a few months, yes," said Callie.

"And you going to be in *Coquette*?"

"Mmm-hmm."

"Irina, here, wants to be a model and actress. Imagine that—moving to Los Angeles to break into show business. Novel idea, right?" His beady eyes twinkled as he patted Irina's perky bottom.

"What you say? You being bad man?"

"No, cupcake—not till later. Why don't you talk to Callie while I fix you a drink. Vodka tonic?"

"What you having, Callie? I have what you have," said Irina.

"Vodka tonic sounds perfect," said Callie.

"You got it. Be right back, ladies."

Irina fixed her puppy-dog gaze on Callie. "My dream is be in *Coquette*. Since I was baby! You think I have right look for magazine?"

"Without a doubt."

"Really? I meet Yves Rousseau last night at party but was too skeered to speak. I sweat, I clam up, I was so ner-vuss. I did not know how to be. How you think I should be? What advice you have for me?"

Callie mulled the question before answering, "Just be yourself. You can't go wrong with that."

"*Really?* I do not know how. Everyone tell me to have blond hair and *big* boobs. What you think?" She pulled her twins out of her top.

"Ummm . . ." *Your surgeon shouldn't have free-poured the silicone; it's not 1999.* "I think it's definitely the look you were going for."

Irina's dimples popped. "Thank you. I—" She was startled by the blast of the TV. Gary, his round face ashen and panic-stricken, shut off the music and cranked the volume of the flat screen.

Another peroxide-drenched girl shouted, "Hey, Gary, turn that down, will ya? I wanna hear some of Evan's music!"

"Shut up," Gary snapped. Evan flew to his side.

"Anything?" asked the singer.

"Not yet." Gary flipped through the channels. "It hasn't hit."

Callie tapped Evan's shoulder. "What's wrong?" He shifted his eyes. "Come on, Evan, you're scaring me. What happened?"

"We just received a call. Something really bad happened. . . ." He shook his head in disbelief, his face swathed in shock. "There was a murder tonight. Really brutal, a horrible thing . . ."

"Someone we know?" she demanded. "Who?" His silence made her heart rate soar. "*Who*, Evan? Tell me!"

"Gabrielle Manx."

36

Sleep dodged Callie the nights following Gabby's death. Even Ambien failed to induce grogginess. Every day brought new details of the murder, each one more horrific than the last.

Marta, the Guatemalan housekeeper, had arrived at the Johannesburg residence late in the afternoon—usually she was there by 10 A.M. but her son's doctor appointment held her up. *Buzzzz.* She rang the doorbell once, twice, three times. No answer. Not a peep. Not even a bark from Bardot and crew. This was peculiar, Marta told the police. She came by every other day and "Miss Gabriella" always greeted her. Her employers were certainly home—she peered through the garage window and saw the familiar white Mercedes and five Ferraris neatly lined up. But why wasn't anyone answering? Perhaps the side door off the kitchen was open—Gabrielle sometimes left it unlocked. Marta jiggled the door handle. Bingo.

"Miss Gabriella? Mr. Toe-mahs?" Marta called. Not a peep. The silence was deafening, she remembered—ominous—and the hairs on the back of her neck stood erect. Normally she was greeted by the dogs, but they were nowhere to be seen. She tried to calm herself by taking slow, methodical breaths but the air was stagnant and thick. She made her way up the sprawling staircase. A wail was audible as she reached the top. "Miss Gabriella? Is that you?" The crying became louder as she inched toward the master bedroom. The door was cracked and Marta entered. In a corner next to the four-poster bed was Tom Johannesburg, crumpled on the floor like a smashed paper bag. Normally an imposing figure, he appeared dwarfed—frail even, she thought. His body trembled with sobs.

"I loved her so much," he choked.

"What do you mean, Mr. Toe-mahs? Where is Miss Gabriella?"

"You don't understand. She was my angel. I loved her so much. . . ." He rubbed his bloated, flushed face.

A tumble of dark hair peeked from underneath the bed frame. "At first I did not think it could be her," Marta explained. "From across the room, the hair looked brunette and Miss Gabriella was very fair. But when I got closer, I could see her hair was dark from all the blood." Gabrielle's neck bore a heinous gunshot wound; her lip was swollen and her eyes were closed shut. Marta touched her cold, bare leg—"I do not know what for, I knew she was dead"—before fleeing, screaming in her native tongue until she reached the neighbors' to call for help. The police didn't have to coerce a confession from Tom—he flooded them with details, babbling on, often incoherently.

"I came home late and she started bitching at me," he jabbered. "I was feeling pretty good; I had a few cocktails in me and didn't want to deal with any bullshit. She kept busting my balls, accusing me of fucking some other actress. I told her she was crazy. She wouldn't shut up about it, kept saying 'I'm no fool, asshole, I know what you've been up to.' She pulled off her ring and pelted me with it so I slapped her. That motherfucking rock cost me more than my goddamned Enzo! And she actually had the fucking nerve to throw it at me! Said she was leaving me and I begged her not to go. *Begged.* I'm Tom Johannesburg, you understand? I beg for *no one.* 'You leave me,' I said, 'and I'll ruin you. You'll never work in this town again! You can bet your sweet tits you'll never get one more goddamned role *ever.*' But she wouldn't listen. And then I grabbed my gun from my closet and I guess it went off. . . ."

"How many times did you fire your gun, Mr. Johannesburg?" asked the detective.

"I don't know. I can't say—it's all a haze. I didn't plan it, you see? I didn't want any of this to happen. It's been a nightmare. A colossal, fucked-up nightmare."

"Once? Twice? How many times did you shoot Miss Manx?"

"Maybe a few. I can't remember. But I'm not a monster! I'm not a fucking monster. . . ."

Gabrielle Manx was the biggest story in the country.

Manx Murder Tape Found

Gorgeous Gabby Loved Orgies!!!

Minxy Manx's $50K Nightmare: Her Plastic Surgeon Reveals All
Sexy Actress Faked Her Death!

The headlines sickened Callie almost as much as her friend's brutal demise. Gary Benson had an inside track and provided Evan and Callie with the details—knowing someone who could separate the truth from the lies was somewhat comforting. Based on her own brief experience with the press, she was well aware how inaccurate the headlines could be, but that didn't make them any less hurtful. Long-lost acquaintances emerged from Gabby's past, eager to give

interviews to anyone who'd listen—high school chums, her ortho-
dontist and personal trainer, even a self-proclaimed feng shui guru.
But it was the press conference held by Dr. Holtsclaw that enraged
Callie the most. A day after Gabby's death, dressed in a sleek suit
that perfectly matched his eyes, Dr. Holtsclaw stood on the lawn of
his Bel Air home surrounded by microphones and newsmen.

"Gabrielle Manx wasn't just a patient of mine—she was also a
trusted friend," he began. "As stunning as she was on the outside,
she was even lovelier on the inside. She had so much to look forward to—especially the upcoming release of *Nympho Cheerleaders
Attack!*, a film she stars in alongside her best friend, who, coinci-
dentally, is another of my patients. Her tragic and gruesome passing is a reminder of how truly sick people are. As a psychiatrist
who not only specializes in treating celebrities but people from all
walks of life, I urge you to seek professional help if you think you
may suffer from a mental imbalance." He phoned Callie after his
televised performance. "Hey, kiddo. I called in your Wellbutrin
refill today. By the way, did you happen to catch me on TV?"

"I did," Callie said icily.

"What did you think? Wasn't it great? I even gave your little
movie a plug."

"Who the hell do you think you are? How dare you use me!"

"No, no. You don't understand—"

"No, *you* don't understand. I don't sell out my friends whether
they're alive or in the morgue. You're nothing but a licensed Hollywood fame whore and it's disgusting. And you're fired, too."

"Come again? I don't follow."

"I'm firing you. Since you have so many celebrity connections,
why don't you ring up the Donald? I'm sure he can explain it to
you." *Click.*

37

The press pounced on the Gabby–Callie connection. Paparazzi loitered outside Hollywood Tower, the complex she'd recently moved to, and unidentified callers blew her phone up at all hours. How did they gain access to her number? She wanted nothing to do with them. Paul spent half his day fielding interview requests from tabloids and news networks and beseeched her to meet with a publicist. ("You need someone to rein in all this commotion. I've had twenty calls from the press this morning alone.") She took his advice and scheduled an appointment with Kat.

The bedlam was Kat Killian's wet dream. She had been wedded to the trade of publicity for twenty years; she breathed it, ate it, slept with it. Her deep, wide-set eyes flashed at the mention of both the famous and infamous alike. John Wayne Bobbitt whet her palate as much as any A-list entertainer. "I'm an equal opportunist," she

loved to say. "Fame is fame." Two dozen framed photographs covered the walls of her Beverly Hills office; Kat backstage at Madi-
son Square Garden with Madonna; Kat beaming next to Ellen
DeGeneres at the Emmys; Kat with Wayne Newton at a charity
event, her pale, bony arm binding his shoulder . . . If the woman
could mainline the sweat of celebrities, she would.

"Everyone wants you, Callie. *Coquette* and the movie make you
kind of interesting, but throw in the Manx murder association and
you've got a whole new ball game. People are *slobbering* with curiosity. It's a completely whacked, unique situation." Kat's voice crackled with excitement.

"The main thing I want to stress is this: I'm not interested in
exploiting Gabrielle. Enough people are doing that and I'm not
selling out my friend," Callie said firmly.

"Look, not to sound callous, but you're running around in your
birthday suit with the lead actress who was murdered by the director she was engaged to. You can't write this stuff! Is it a horrible
tragedy? Of course it is, but in terms of timing, it couldn't be any
better. I have clients who'd chop their balls off for this kind of
ammo."

Callie squirmed in the stiff, two-thousand-dollar Armani Casa
chair. Kat's point, though crude, was spot-on. The publicity machine
was charging ahead full throttle; the Manx–Lambert pictorial was
scheduled for mass consumption in May, days after Callie's twenty-
fourth birthday and months ahead of schedule—and *NCA!* was set
to hit theaters the week after that. Both the studio and magazine
had no desire to let free promotion go to waste (why not capitalize
on that poor girl's slaughter?), with or without the cooperation of
the lone surviving lead actress.

"I understand the twisted irony of it all, Kat. I'm not stupid. But
everyone wants to make a buck off Gabby's death—"

"A much bigger profit than they ever anticipated, no less," Kat interjected.

"No doubt. I get this business is about making money, but—"

"I can get you on *The View* and *Today,* no problem. I'm seriously connected with NBC and CBS. And print, of course—lots of men's magazines. Not just nudes, you know, but bra-and-panty stuff, too."

"I want to move away from all that before I get typecast as 'the nympho bimbo.' Just the thought is depressing."

"It's all in your hands. The sky's the limit as to how far you want to ride the wave. Reality shows, book deals. Only grant interviews if they pay. CNN doesn't pay a dime, so don't bother. I just had a thought—you could start your own line of lingerie and specialize in kinky cheerleader outfits. Ooooh, yes! I like that idea. Leather and rubber uniforms, pom-poms that double as both a whip *and* a French tickler . . . We can really spin this into something lucrative. You said Paul Angers is your agent. What kind of offers is he taking?"

"Mostly tabloids. Yesterday I went to Ralph's and had a pap chase me around, asking what it was like to have sex with a dead blonde with DDDs. It's sick, the sensationalism of it. The only reasons I posed for *Coquette* were (*a*), for the money and (*b*), because they turned me down the first time. Scoring the cover was the ultimate 'fuck you.' But the murder has made it all so high-profile, more than I ever thought possible, I wish I hadn't been a part of it," she sputtered, half in frustration, half in anger, all in gloom.

"I can see your point, but it is what it is. You can either take control of it or let *it* control you." Kat snatched the beeping cell phone off her desk and texted a reply at sonic speed.

Callie smoothed her ponytail, deep in thought. "What do you charge?"

"Three thousand."

"Three thousand a year?"

Kat screeched. "I'll pretend I didn't just hear that. No, a *month*. Most of my clients pay five grand and above but I like you and think you have a lot of commercial potential."

What a deal, Callie thought sarcastically. "I'll think it over. I have another appointment to get to. Thanks for your time."

"Pleasure's all mine. I'll walk you out."

An autographed photo of Bedroom Eyes caught Callie's eye. "How do you know Evan Marquardt?"

"We met at *The Tonight Show*; he was booked the same day as one of my clients. What a sweetheart. Holy shit! It totally slipped my mind—aren't you two dating?" Kat pressed the elevator button.

"We're just friends." She and Evan had made a pact not to publicly discuss the nature of their relationship.

"That's the oldest answer in the book—it's so old, I invented it! Come on, level with me. If you are, that's fantastic, it's one more angle we could—"

"Friends, Kat. *Friends*." She'd be better off proclaiming their love to *The New York Times* than confiding in Kat.

Kat stroked her chin with a long, pointed nail. "Let's pretend I believe you. You can be 'just friends' and still court the press. Go out together where you know you'll be photographed—that's the bare minimum nowadays. Play it coy but definitely play it up. You're sitting on a gold mine."

Callie stepped into the elevator. "That's not really my style."

"We'll work on that. Our first day together and I'll have you re-wired. Think about it. You can always change your mind."

Slam!

The doors banged shut and Callie exhaled. The thought of Kat combing through her private life, looking for every angle to exploit it, was hive-inducing. What a bloodsucker! Callie tried to erase the varmit from her memory. Tyler would be at her apartment in a half hour and she still had to pick up a prescription. A handful of paparazzi loitered in the parking lot when she emerged from the drugstore. She figured they'd been trailing her for some time.

"Hey, Callie, lookin' good, girl. Watcha got there? Some happy pills?"

"C'mon, when you gonna talk to us? We won't bite, honest."

"I bet you're holdin' out till the movie comes out, aren't ya? Waitin' for a big payday."

She scurried past the cameras and jumped in her Mustang, head held high and jaw clenched. *Ugh. Illiterate trash.* No wonder Fellini named them after mosquitoes. What bottom-feeders. They tailed her as she cruised home. She dashed inside her building as quickly as possible, minutes before Tyler arrived.

"Did you know there are paparazzi outside your complex?" he asked as he rushed over to the window and whipped off his Carreras.

Callie rolled her eyes and plopped on the sofa. "Don't even get me started. They're pests. What do they want from me? I don't get it. I have nothing to say to them."

"You butter their bread, Cal. That's how it works. Scandal puts food on their table. Most of Hollywood would give their left titty for this attention. I know I would."

"Not me. I have nothing to say to them. They want to get me going, egging me on, asking the dumbest questions. As far as I'm concerned, they can shove it."

"Skank, let's be honest—this case reads juicier than Jackie Collins. Hot women, murder, money, sex . . . It's human nature to want to know more about Gabby and that bastard Tom. Especially for folks who have no life. Remember how bored we used to be back in Michigan? Imagine what that's like twenty-four/seven. Saps with nothing better to do than stuff their faces with frozen pizza and watch the boob tube. They want to read about all the spice their sad selves lack."

"I know. But count me out of this circus. I just left a meeting with the piranha of all publicists and she couldn't be any happier. She's foaming at the mouth and wants to take it all the way to the bank. Poor Gabby. I guess she didn't value herself much. She sold herself short and now the press is raking her over the coals. She's the victim in this mess but you'd never know it, would you? It's all backwards."

"It sure is. But it will quiet down. It's probably wise to distance yourself from the hoopla so it doesn't overshadow everything you do from here on out. Here, let's smoke a bowl." He pulled a pipe out of his messenger bag and fired up. "Everything she ever did is getting dug up, all the filth. If the press finds out she swallowed an Ex-Lax the night she died, it'll make the front page. She seemed like a really nice person, too. Sure, she had her demons, but who doesn't?"

"Can we change the subject?"

"Fine by me. Your apartment is really cute, practically a mansion compared to your old studio. And the dining room table goes well with all of the curved archways and moldings."

"Supposedly this unit once belonged to Humphrey Bogart. It obviously needs more decoration but it's coming together. A little knickknack here, a lick of paint there . . ."

"Rome wasn't built in a day," Tyler chirped.

"Speaking of which, Candice and her boyfriend get back from Europe tonight. We're having a heart-to-heart soon."

"Candice? Lord. She's fucked you before and she'll do it again. That bitch is sneaky like that."

"She's not in a good place, Ty. When we ran into her at the Abbey, she looked so sickly, it broke my heart."

"She sure did—a hemorrhoidal ass looked better than her. But it's not your fault and there's no reason for getting sucked down her spiral. She did this to herself. You can't change her—Candice has to do that for herself. Loyalty is your strong suit, skank, but also your weakness." Tyler's insight often belied his twenty-six years.

Callie shrugged. "She needs me and I can't turn my back on her. And she apologized. . . ."

"Just watch out, girl. You have enough on your plate without a so-called friend taking advantage of you again."

"Let's just relax and forget the bullshit." She toked on the pipe and propped her feet on the coffee table. *Ahhhh . . .* For the first time in eight days, the tautness in her shoulders dissipated and her mind lacked constipation. Hooray for modern medicine.

38

"Ooh, get a load of these." Candice scooped up a pair of patent platforms from the display table. "Come to me, my sweet."

"Don't you have a similar pair?" Callie said.

Candice's face fell. "One can *never* have enough. Where's the saleslady? The help is never around when you need them. Excuse me, ma'am, do you work here? No? Well, who does, then? Earth to customer service! Can a customer get some goddamn help around here?" The size of her pupils rivaled that of the moon.

"Be nice," said Callie. "I'm sure someone will be around in a minute. Why are you so on-edge?"

"Because of Jon," she huffed. "It's all his fault. We've been fighting nonstop and it's wearing me thin. He bitches, 'you spend too much money, you don't stay home enough, you party too much.' Blah, blah, blah. Spare me, Dad. Excuse me that I'm young and hot and like to have a good time! The first and last time I ever date a guy twenty years older than me, I'll tell you that. They're way too controlling. It really chaps my ass. And he's gotten so cheap lately. I saw this sick Fendi coat while we were in Milan and you'd think I asked for keys to a new Maybach."

A saleswoman approached Candice. "Would you like to try these on?"

"No need. I'll take a pair in a seven." She dropped the shoes in the woman's hand and examined a flashy green sandal. "This color is so you, Cal. It goes great with your hair."

"How much?"

"Twelve hundred."

"Um, no," Callie balked. "They're more your style."

"You're so right. My name may as well be etched on the soles. Good call. Ma'am, I'll take these, too."

"Perfect," said the saleswoman. "I'll put them up front. My name is Tina if I can get you anything else."

Callie dangled a pair of black slingbacks. "Tina, may I try these on in an eight, please?"

"Certainly. I'll be right back." Tina disappeared to the stock room.

"Yeah, Candy, the service here is just dreadful," Callie teased.

"Whatever," Candice snorted. "Not a soul in sight a minute ago. You'd think they'd be better staffed at Saks. Do you need to go to the bathroom?"

"Nah, I went before I got here. Candy, level with me—ever since I picked you up you've been fidgety and pissy. And you look awfully tired, too."

"What are you trying to say, Cal—that I look beat? Just say it and get it out in the open. Go ahead, I can take it."

Callie hesitated. Candice was a tough cookie, but there was no pleasant way of revealing she resembled a bowl of Alpo warmed over. "I'm worried, that's all. You're not yourself. What's wrong?"

"It's all the Diet Pepsi I've been slamming. I should stay away from caffeine, makes me jittery."

Callie arched one eyebrow suspiciously.

"I'm fine; don't worry about me, mama. We'll talk about things later. Right now I just want to have fun and shop. I'm off to pee, be back in five."

Callie sighed as she watched her friend's high-speed strut. Adderall, coke, meth, diet pills . . . what was it? With Candice, it could be all of the above. Sure, Callie was occasionally fond of powdering her nose or munching a pill—it was L.A.; who *didn't* party? Perhaps it was something innocent—Wellbutrin had originally made her speedy and decreased her appetite. . . . But, no—that couldn't be it. The remote look in Candice's eyes wasn't from a steady dose of antidepressants. And it certainly wouldn't be the first time she'd gone off the deep end, either. The summer after graduation, just before Callie entered her senior year of high school, the Boyd family stuck their daughter in a Floridian clinic. One month and twelve thousand dollars later, Candice was back to her familiar antics. To the annoyance of her parents, she had met a boy in rehab and moved with him to Miami. Again, they intervened and threw her in another detox program, this time all the way in the boonies of Alabama for three months. Things were on the upswing when she was accepted to Michigan State. But after a few years boredom set in and then came *Coquette* and California and Lars. . . .

Candice returned twenty minutes later. "This place is Hag Central," she hissed. "I came out of the stall and this old battleax gave me the nastiest look, like I was trying to swipe away her Depends or something. Why can't people just *chill the fuck out*?" Her nostrils were wet with a ring of white residue.

"You have a little bit of, um, stuff on you. . . ." Callie wiped the crusty deposit off Candice's nose.

"Thanks," Candice muttered. "Let's go pay for our stuff."

Tina processed Callie's purchase speedily, but when she swiped Candice's card—once, twice, three times—she said, "I'm sorry, miss, but it's declined."

"Impossible, try it again."

Tina did, without any luck. "Do you have another card?"

"There's plenty of room on this card," Candice snapped.

"It won't go through, Miss Boyd."

"Hold on, let me call my boyfriend. . . . Hey, Jon. I'm trying to cash out at Saks and your Visa isn't working. . . . *What?!* What do you mean you *canceled* it? I'm not in the mood for a joke, this isn't funny . . . but I really need these shoes, Jon! . . . You're sick of *my* shit? I'm sick of *your* shit! . . . Oh, yeah? That suits me just fine, you jackass. I don't need your goddamned money!" Candice shuffled through her wallet and threw a different card on the counter. At last, the exchange was complete.

"Why don't we go relax somewhere before you blow a gasket?" Callie suggested as they retrieved her car from the valet.

"Awesome. I sure could use a stiffy. The Four Seasons?"

"Sure."

They grabbed a table on the patio off the hotel's lounge. Candice stirred a scotch and water and, hands trembling, lit a menthol. "I can't believe I'm smoking."

"I can't believe I'm not," Callie said wryly, and nursed her iced tea. "Ever since I quit that dump, Harry's, I haven't had the desire."

"Wish I could say the same thing. Can you believe Jon cut me off? I mean, what the fuck? How embarrassing! Like I'm trash, having to beg like some sort of street urchin. Fuck that. Not me, pal. Nope. I need to get something off my chest. I've been thinking about this for a while. . . ." She took a long drag and flicked her ash on the ground. "I think I'm hanging up my hat. I'm done with this business. Done. I can't do it anymore. I'm treading water, just spinning my wheels and accomplishing nothing except spending money and making enemies. The last thing I booked was a fitness infomercial eight months ago. Back when I actually had some muscle tone. And I'll confess—I didn't even film the spot. They sent me home when I got there. How *sad* is that?"

"What was the problem?"

"I showed up a little wasted. Yes, it's true. Actually, not a little—a *lot*. I was high as a kite. Not that I haven't been high most of the time for the past six months, but apparently I was super obnoxious and . . . well, you've seen me like that, so you can imagine. I'm so ashamed of myself, I haven't told anyone this. What would people say? 'Gee, what a loser that Boyd broad is.' But you know how small this city is and word gets around quick. Starr dumped me, told me I'm too much of a liability. One more ding in my pristine reputation, right? My parents would be mortified. Anyway, my name is muck here so I think I'm going back to Michigan."

"Candice, I know it hasn't been a walk in the park, but please think this over more."

"I have. I've been thinking about it hard-core for the past few months."

"And you want to throw in the towel?"

"Callie, I'm twenty-five years old and have *shit* to my name. Every man I meet is an asshole, my contract with *Coquette* is up, and I'm basically unemployable. My folks are sick of me wasting their money and want me to get my act together. Do you know how many times I have to listen to them brag about my brothers? Not that they've done much with their lives, but the way my parents talk, you'd think they both cured AIDS. It's beyond annoying."

"But it's when you give up that things take a turn for the better. Look at Gabrielle—she said she was done, too, then booked a lead in a film."

"She also got shot by the director," Candice added.

"Seriously, now—"

"I *am* serious."

"I am, too," Callie said sternly. "You're not a quitter. You can't give up! You've always wanted to be in show business—you couldn't be a Michigan kind of girl if you tried. You call it the 'Mid*worst*' for a reason. How about this: no men, no partying, no staying out all night. Lay off the blow. Take a little break and focus on getting healthy."

"A sabbatical, so to speak?"

"Exactly. And then when you're ready, you'll find new representation and start fresh."

"Maybe I should go away for a few weeks and come back nice and rested. . . . Not another rehab but maybe a spa to clear my mind, sweat out all the toxins . . ."

"And then come back ready to kick ass like you always do." Callie felt as though she were giving an R-rated pep talk to a group of Brownies.

"Hmmm . . . Swear off sex and drugs and booze for a while, concentrate on getting my life in order and come back recharged. . . . That sounds like a plan. You're right, Callie. I've never let anyone spit me out. *I* do the spitting, goddamn it!" She ground her cigarette in the ashtray and pulled a wad of cash from her Speedy bag. "Here's something I should have given you a while ago."

Callie counted the bills. "Six hundred bucks?"

"Five hundred for the rent, plus interest."

"Candice, don't worry about it, I—"

"Take it and shut up. Before I change my mind and spend it on more overpriced stilts." Her eyes glowed with devilishness. "I'm fully aware what a royal pain in the ass I am and I'm sorry. To be honest, I was so jealous when you booked that movie—*livid*. That should have been *my* part! At least, that's what I thought at the time, but then I realized what an atrocious actress I am and you deserve everything you have. I'll never be unsupportive like that again. Promise."

"I'm just glad you're back in my life." She squeezed Candice's hand affectionately and Candice returned the gesture.

"Come on, mama; let's get out of here. It's time for this bitch to dry out. Waitress? Check, please."

39

"I just can't believe it, Esme. You barely have a speck of gray!" Tessa, Callie's hairdresser, exclaimed. She deftly trimmed Esme's short curls into shape.

"And no dye, either," Esme said. "All natural. My mother was the same way. Hopefully my granddaughter inherited those genes." Callie beamed from her parallel chair and chuckled to herself. At seventy-five, Esme gave fifty-year-old women a run for their money. In her prime, she had resembled Gina Lollobrigida and even now she still managed to turn heads.

"Tell me about this movie premiere you're going to tonight," Tessa said. "You must be excited."

"Heavens, yes. This is all new for me. Callie called me up and said, 'Grandma, pack your bags, I'm flying you out to L.A., and bring something fancy because you're going to be on a red carpet.' So naturally I said, 'Honey, I'll be there with bells on my toes.'"

There wasn't anyone Callie would rather have at her side on her big night; it was a no-brainer, one that angered Virginia.

"You can only bring *one* guest?" her mother asked during a typical remote phone conversation.

"Yes, only one," Callie lied, "and Grandma begged me to take her." Callie omitted that Paul Angers and Tyler were attending, too. *Maybe I'm just being selfish,* she thought. After all, just because she and her mother didn't see eye to eye didn't mean she couldn't be proud of her accomplishments, did it? The glamour of a Hollywood shindig would definitely impress Virginia. A novel idea rocked Callie's brain and for the first time she realized something they both shared—a love of glamour. Neither woman left the house without lipstick or gloss, coiffed hair, and a handbag that coordinated with the day's outfit. Still, Callie couldn't bring herself to invite her.

"I cannot believe Esme is going to see a film with the word 'nympho' in it. She'll have a heart attack! Why on earth can't you bring more people? You're the star of the movie, for Christ's sake. Can't you tell them to give you two more tickets?"

The disappointment in Virginia's tone twisted Callie's heartstrings. "I—I don't know, Mom. I mean, maybe I can—"

"It's not every day my daughter has a movie premiere to attend. Those things aren't exactly common here in Michigan, remember? Or maybe you've forgotten where you came from."

Callie's neck flushed. "The producers call the shots, Mom, not me. And besides, you hate gory movies."

"Hold on—Tony's trying to say something. What did you say, Tony? Speak louder, I can't hear you. Yes, I'll tell her. He says to make sure you get Sal Saunders's autograph and tell him he loved his performance in *Kill Me, Kate*."

"Okay." Ugh, Tony—what a tacky pain in the ass.

"And before I forget, one of those tabloids—I forget which one—claims you and Evan are trying for a baby. Claire and I lunched yesterday and she brought it with her. I thought you didn't want children? And out of wedlock, at that!"

"That's a bunch of bull, Mom. I've told you, those magazines are silly. He's too busy working to think about much else."

Bedroom Eyes was resting from his European tour before embarking on the U.S. leg. In less than a year, he had gone from being a well-known entertainer in Europe—the UK, Sweden, France, Germany, only a handful of countries. Now, around the globe, and especially in the United States, it was full-throttle Evan-mania.

Callie whipped out her phone. "Grandma, I'm stepping outside a minute."

"Go ahead, dear."

She rang Evan and was ready to hang up but he picked up on the sixth ring.

"Greetings, you gorgeous little slut."

She giggled and combed her fingers through her flat-ironed locks. "Look who's talking. Thanks to you, I may not be able to wear my new mini tonight, my arms and legs are so bruised from you banging me all over your kitchen."

"Mmm, that was amazing, wasn't it? You're making me hard all over again. How wet are you?"

"Like a sink." His sex-drenched voice made her shiver in the eighty-degree heat and her nipples poked through her cotton ombré tank. "Right now I'm thinking about giving you a tongue bath."

"Come over. I'm just lying by the pool."

"I unfortunately can't, baby. My grandmother and I are getting ready for tonight."

"Ahh, that's right; Grandma Esme's in town."

"She's more excited about this thing than I am. Definitely not your typical senior citizen. Are we still on for tomorrow?"

"Absolutely; looking forward to it. Hopefully I won't disappoint her with my cooking."

"It won't take much to impress her, Evan, she already adores you. I've talked about you quite a bit."

"Oh, really? I'm a popular subject, am I?"

"Indeed you are," purred Callie. "She knows everything."

"She knows I ravaged you all over the kitchen I'm using to make her dinner?"

"Well, maybe not *everything,* but close. Anyway, I had a minute and just wanted to say hi."

"You're sweet, doll. Have fun tonight and knock 'em dead, my little nympho."

40

Callie felt as though a swamp was housed underneath her Hervé Léger sheath. *So sweaty.* Thank God she could still wear the bandage dress—the hem skimmed her thighs, barely concealing her love bruises. Cross, uncross, cross, uncross—her legs wouldn't keep still as the limo slowed to a crawl next to the Majestic Crest Theatre. Damn it, when were those two milligrams of Xanax going to kick in?

"Skankazoid, you okay?" Tyler whispered. He was a picture of leisure in his sleek Marc Jacobs sports coat. "You're squirming more than a virgin on her wedding night."

"Just a little nervous, that's all." The chauffeur opened her door. She tried to count the number of reporters clustering around the front of the theater. Eighty? Definitely. One hundred? Possibly. She swallowed. *Here goes nothing.*

Paul led her to the front of the press line. "I just got a text from Sherri Finstad and she's running late, unfortunately. Looks like you'll have to do this alone, which I'm not too crazy about."

"No worries, Paul," she said, smoothing her dress.

"Just do what you do best. You look like a million bucks, so just work it. I'll be waiting for you off to the side with Tyler and your grandma. Remember, you don't have to answer any questions you're not comfortable with."

"I know."

"See now, this is a time when you could really use your own publicist to direct—"

"Paul, listen to me: I'll be fine. I can handle myself, trust me. Coy is my middle name." She reassured him with a smile and placed a well-heeled stiletto on the red carpet. Channeling Naomi Campbell, she paused dramatically for the assembled photographers, stomach sucked in, hands on hips.

"Hold that pose, Callie . . . Nice!"

"Give me a smile, Callie-girl!"

"Over here! Look over your shoulder with that sexy pout!"

"Blow me a kiss. Yeah, just like that. Again!"

"Show us the back of your dress!"

They barked so many requests, she couldn't comprehend them all. Or maybe it was the Xanax kicking in. About damned time. *Screw it. I'll pose however I want and they can keep up.* Berry-slicked lips pursed, she flirted and shimmied while the cameras flashed. They couldn't get enough of her and she devoured their attention like an Animal Style Double-Double burger. Having so many people—strangers—focus completely on her, zealously shouting her name, was exalting. Best of all, it was on her terms—she was in control of the commotion instead of the other way around.

A gaggle of journalists waited for her as she strutted farther down the carpet. A scrawny woman with veiny hands shoved a microphone under Callie's chin; she had never been interviewed live and her legs tensed with apprehension. She took comfort in towering over the ultra-short woman.

"There's been much written lately about the other star of the film, the late Gabrielle Manx. I understand you two were friends; how difficult has her murder been for you?"

"It's been hard," Callie said cautiously, tucking her hair behind her ear. "With the movie finally out, I hope people can see what a talented actress Gabby was—she was never the bimbo the press has made her out to be."

"With a name like *Nympho Cheerleaders Attack!,* bad acting is the first thing that jumps to my mind, but the reviews have been shockingly decent. How does that feel?" the woman continued.

Callie beamed. "Fabulous! Everyone wants to feel appreciated, right?"

"There have been reports that Gabrielle slept with her alleged murderer, director Tom Johannesburg, the very first night they met. Can you confirm this?"

"I have no idea and it's none of anyone's business," sniffed Callie.

"Gabrielle was a call girl. True or false?"

"Absolutely false." She prayed the woman would trip in her faux leather heels and sprain her ankle.

"Are you and Evan Marquardt tying the knot? Are you engaged yet?" asked a man standing next to a video camera emblazoned with the *Hollywood Hotspot* logo.

"No and no."

"Ms. Lambert, Corey Cox here with *Rise and Shine L.A.* Critics are comparing this to a much bloodier version of camp classics like *Valley of the Dolls* and *Showgirls.* What do you think about that?"

"That's really cool. I'm a fan of Jacqueline Susann and Joe Eszterhas." Her lazy Midwest accent was audible as her senses slackened from the pills. *Mmmmm. Like molten honey.* Cruising through her bloodstream at a leisurely twenty.

"It doesn't bother you?"

"Why should it? I knew what I was getting into. The name of the film says it all, doesn't it? We're not exactly trying to be *Doctor Zhivago.*"

"Tom Johannesburg makes movies that demean women. How do you defend this statement?"

"I don't," she quipped. "It is what it is."

"Victory for Vaginas, the feminist organization, has taken issue with the movie and your *Coquette* pictorial. They say, quote, you're a disgrace to the female race. Would you like to comment?"

Callie rolled her eyes.

"*The Detroit Free Press* remarked you look anorexic. Are you?"

"No," she said, "but in the words of Kate Moss: 'Nothing tastes as good as skinny feels.'" *I'm a saucy bitch.*

"What's next for you, Callie? More sexploitation flicks?"

She shrugged her shoulders. "We'll see. I'd like to have a diverse career. I don't exactly want to get pegged as a naked lesbian horror slut my whole life, know what I mean?"

"Is this film too much for your average moviegoer? The sex, the violence, the nudity?"

"That's for the audience to decide," she said with a flutter of her lashes.

"Do you plan on appearing in more pornography or have you hung up your G-string?"

"Thongs or boy shorts? Boxers or briefs?"

"What do you think about Gabrielle's life story being turned into a movie of the week?"

"Do you hope Johannesburg gets the chair? Or should he rot in jail?"

"Why won't you confirm you're dating Evan Marquardt?"

"You smell delicious! If you came out with your own line of perfume, what would you call it?"

Callie responded to the questions with stony silence and greeted the fans who lined the sidewalks, issues of *Coquette* in their hands. Enthusiasm plastered on her face, she autographed copy after copy. The issue had hit newsstands days earlier and Callie was pleased with the outcome; the cover was of Gabby on her knees, grasping Callie's thigh-high boots and hungrily staring up at the towering brunette.

"You rocked it, girl," Tyler said when Callie joined her group.

Paul excitedly put a hand on her shoulder. "Have I got some news for you. I was just speaking to the Wilders and there's talk of *NCA!* becoming a television series. It's a sequel to the movie, which is perfect since your character is the only one who survives."

She stared at him blankly.

"Yes, yes, I'm serious! Spike is *very* interested."

"They want *me* as a series regular?" said Callie.

"Believe it, my dear. Let's keep our fingers crossed. Toes, too."

Grandma Esme tugged on her granddaughter's arm. Her sable eyes sparkled. "Honey, I can't tell you how happy I am for you. You looked so beautiful out there, so poised and grown-up. If only your father could see you . . . You've made me so proud."

It was the best compliment she had ever received.

41

"This is outstanding, Evan," said Esme. She savored a bite of couscous. "Callie's talked about you so much but she didn't mention you're quite the chef. How wonderful."

"I'm glad you're enjoying it. When you're raised by a single mother, you learn your way around the kitchen. Out of all the gourmet dishes I cook, guess what my son's favorite is: peanut butter and jelly sandwiches! That's all he wants lately. That and cornflakes." Evan emptied the bottle of San Pellegrino into Esme's glass.

"Thank you, dear. Callie went through a similar phase when she was a little girl, too. Macaroni and cheese, morning, noon, and night."

Callie sat on Evan's knee and wrapped her arms around his neck. "Grandma, Evan *loves* my pictorial."

"As he should, honey."

"I picked up a copy the day it came out. Out of a ten, I give it an eleven." Evan winked. She snuggled deep in his lap while he stroked her back. "I especially love the outdoor shot of you lying on your stomach with the 'Calliewood' sign in the background."

"I looked at it yesterday and I must say—not just because she's my granddaughter—Callie's pictures came out better than the other girl's. Not that Gabrielle isn't—wasn't—gorgeous, but God didn't intend breasts to look like beach balls."

"Gabby called them her 'money makers.'" Callie sipped her Syrah. "She didn't think there was anything particularly special about herself. She would have been floored to see people's reaction to her performance."

Evan agreed. "She was one of those rare breeds who was beautiful both inside and out. Gary dined with her and Tom many times and he told her she was on the edge of a major career upswing. Unbelievable how things get nipped in the bud, isn't it?"

Esme shook her head. "Tragic. Absolutely tragic."

"Let me pour some more wine for you ladies."

"Just a splash, Evan. If I have more than two glasses I'll be jitterbugging on the table. Callie, dear, when will you know more about the TV show?"

Evan's blue eyes flashed. "TV show? What's this news?"

"I forgot to tell you!" said Callie. "Paul said there's a major chance *NCA!* could become a series. I should know more in a few weeks."

"Look at you! That's fabulous, doll. I propose a toast: to Callie and your new project. Oh, by the way, *Men's Report* released their annual list for the hottest one hundred women in the world and guess who clocked in at number eighty-eight?"

Callie blushed. "Really? The list came out today?"

"Sure did. I read it online this morning."

"Paul mentioned I'd make the list. He's friends with the editor. It's all about who you know, I guess. It's nothing I earned."

"Don't sell yourself short, babe. That's quite a bragging right," said Bedroom Eyes. "Consider where you were this time last year."

"True. Eighty-eight, huh? Not too shabby for a girl from Michigan." The three clinked their glasses together.

Esme took a hearty sip and smacked her lips. "Well, how about that. My granddaughter is one in-demand commodity."

"You're not embarrassed, Grandma?"

"Embarrassed? Of who, *you*? Never, honey! Admittedly, things are much more risqué than when I was young. And I'll confess I don't see why people have to expose their cans to make something interesting. But that's just the way things are nowadays. You've accomplished so much in such a short amount of time; how could I possibly be embarrassed?"

Callie grinned. Things were finally on track; she had a handsome, über-successful boyfriend and a doting grandmother. A promising career loomed on the horizon—and, just as important, she didn't have to compromise her integrity by selling out her slain friend and hire a bloodsucker like Kat Killian. It was hard imagining back to the time when she waited tables at Harry's. Just a year ago she couldn't book a gig to save her hide! For far too long, every day crept by the same monotonous way: wake up in the cramped apartment, stinking of grease from working the previous night, demoralized from serving cantankerous customers who thought it her duty to be their whipping post—all the while dreaming of a gig to save her from hash-slinging misery. Nothing out of this world, but she could now afford two thousand dollars' rent, a Z4, and a steak at Dan Tana's. And all because of a low-budget celluloid savior with a snicker-inducing title.

"You're flying to New York on Friday for the East Coast premiere, aren't you, doll?" Evan said.

"At the crack of dawn—six A.M. I'm not much of a morning person, as you know."

"No one in L.A. is. It blows my mind when I drive past Starbucks at eleven in the morning and it's packed. You can tell these blokes just rolled out of bed. How long are you gone for?"

"Until Sunday. You're sure you don't want to come with me, Grandma?"

Esme shook her head. "Honey, I've had a ball, but I'm looking forward to trotting around the house in my robe and slippers and sleeping in my own little bed. New York's too fast-paced for this old girl."

42

"Callie Lambert, you've set women back one hundred years!"

"Is it really necessary to portray women as homicidal nympho-maniacs?"

"Ms. Lambert, you're nothing more than a raging opportunist capitalizing on your deceased costar's sexuality! For shame!"

Militant feminists. *Barf.* Callie chuckled to herself; it was more than a little fun rattling their cages while putting forth zero effort. Aside from the half-dozen hecklers, the premiere at the Ziegfeld was a smooth affair, more chill, in fact, than the event in L.A., with fewer reporters and cameras. The familiar fluff questions besieged her (speckled with the occasional solemn query)—not that she expected more from a movie about oversexed cheerleaders. To her disappointment, she recognized only C- and D-list actors and reality show veterans ("Please, skank. Did you really expect Johnny Depp to swing by?" gibed Tyler.) Whatever. She was the girl of the hour and the only actor from *NCA!* who showed. Paul, Will, Wendell, and Sherri accompanied her to dinner at the Waverly Inn afterward.

"I have an interview lined up tomorrow with WABC, and after that it's off to *Letterman*," Sherri said. She reached in her Amaretto sour and snacked on a maraschino cherry. "You'll do fine. Real softball stuff and you'll be done by six. And then Saturday I have a reporter from *The Post* coming to see you. You won't even have to leave your hotel room; I've arranged for him to meet you in your suite. I'll be there, too, of course. So, spill—what are you wearing tomorrow for the show?"

"The dress you're wearing tonight—and don't take this the wrong way, 'cause you look gorgeous—is a little conservative." Will knocked back a shot of Jack.

"Exactly," said Sherri. "We'd like you to wear something a little more va-va-voom. Formfitting, lots of cleavage."

"It's called *Nympho Cheerleaders*, for God's sake," added Wendell.

Callie looked at the dress that clung to her body like a wet T-shirt; *this* was considered conservative?

"Show the goods, get the press, you know the drill," Sherri said.

"Umm . . . how about a low-cut mini dress? I packed a fuchsia Versace."

"Perfect!" said the Wilders in unison.

"Can you hide a push-up bra underneath it?" asked Sherri. "You have nice breasts, but they need just a little . . . help."

"She looks fabulous just the way she is, Sherri," Paul said protectively.

"Of course she does, Paul, I'm not denying that. And I don't want to sound like a bitch—"

"You just are," snickered Will.

"That I am, I'll give you that. But the name of the game is T and A, and I want her spilling out as much as possible. If I had my way, I'd send you out in a bikini. Hey, it's my job to say these things." She shoved another cherry in her mouth and twisted the stem off with her stubby fingers.

"I get it, guys. I'll do my best to prop the girls up," Callie said. Hail, hail, push-up bras! In Los Angeles, her natural B-cups were on par with the rack of a ten-year-old. She had willed them to sprout into monsters during her teenage years but it wasn't meant to be. Breast implants crossed her mind, naturally, especially after working alongside Gabrielle—wouldn't anyone have a complex about their breast size after standing next to Gabrielle?—but the thought of stuffing saline or silicone sacks in her body unnerved her. Besides, why look like every other girl in town?

"So, level with us, Callie," Sherri said with a wink. "What's really going on with you and Evan Marquardt? Pictures don't lie."

"We're friends."

"Just friends? Come on . . ." Sherri propped her elbows on the table and leaned forward. She wiggled her spiny eyebrows.

"Close friends," said Callie.

"How close is close?"

Callie fidgeted with a piece of hair escaping her updo. "Um . . . well . . ."

"Oh, for Pete's sake, just admit it already. He's a great catch; if I nailed him, I'd yell it from the top of the Empire State Building!"

"Sherri, who are you kidding? You do that now as it is," snorted Will. "Doesn't matter how he earns his bread, he could just as well be a handyman for all you care."

Sherri cackled. "Right you are. Hey, my fat ass has to take it where I can get it, unlike our starlet here."

Callie shrugged. "We're both quiet that way, Evan and I. You have to keep some things to yourself."

Sherri scooted her chair closer to Callie and whispered, "Just tell me one thing: Is the sex good?"

"No, not good. *Great*. Eyeball-rolling."

"Mmmmm, I bet. The body on that one is something else. How big is he?"

Callie blushed.

"C'mon, between us girls. I heard he gives a donkey a run for his money."

"Who did you hear that from?" asked Callie.

"A little birdie told me."

Just how many women had Bedroom Eyes bedded, anyway? Callie asked herself. Obviously with his fame and gorgeous looks, the man got around—that was no secret. But he had curtailed his sexual proclivities now that they were together, hadn't he? Maybe they should have a talk just to make sure. . . .

"Ma'am, may I take your order?"

The waiter caught her off-guard. "Um, sure. Let's see . . . how about your truffled mac and cheese?"

"Excellent choice."

The rest of the table ordered and Will loudly cleared his throat, solemnity plaguing his face. "Folks, Wendell and I talked with Spike today. We hate to break this to everyone, what with this beautiful dinner in the Big Apple and all the positive reviews the film's garnering—"

"I was reading *Rolling Stone* on the plane today. Peter Travers gave us a terrific little review," added Wendell.

"He certainly did. We also have a seventy-nine percent rating on *Rotten Tomatoes*. So, with all this exciting stuff happening, we don't mean to burst anyone's bubble. *But*." Will paused dramatically as the waiter reappeared with an expensive-looking bottle of bubbly. "They'd like to see, if at all possible, Miss Callie Lambert—officially one of the sexiest women on the planet and the only character who makes it out alive in one piece—could reprise her role as Layla for the small screen. In fact, they ordered seven episodes without even seeing a pilot. "

"*Seven?*" Callie gasped.

"Lucky number seven, missy, that's correct. They want it to be ready early next year in time for the mid-season replacements. We told Paul about it earlier."

"I only found out an hour ago, Callie, and wanted to surprise you. We'll go over the numbers later in private. It's a nice offer. There's room to negotiate, but I'm pleased." Paul's monstrous grin revealed two chipped teeth, a casualty of his hockey-obsessed youth.

"How does that sound, Layla?" Will said.

"It sounds absolutely unbelievable. I'm shocked—*thrilled*! This is crazy! Wait a minute—this isn't a joke, is it?"

"Not in the least. Believe it, kid. The series focuses on Layla's life after her horrific college years. She wants to be a normal girl, but, of course, she can't because she's not really human. It's quirky, it's sexy, it's perfect for Spike's audience. We're just trying to settle on someone to write the script. Tom isn't exactly turning out much material behind bars these days. At any rate, we're shooting it after Screamfest, which is just around the corner."

"We're a shoo-in for Best Picture," Wendell said.

"Let's not start sucking each others' dicks just yet," said Will. "If you ask me, nothing is a shoo-in. Callie, I can't tell you enough how much we appreciate your contribution to this film. I knew you were our girl as soon as you set foot in that room, and, by God, I was right. You did not disappoint." Will's gleaming silver hair and portly body made him resemble an over-gorged fox.

Callie stepped outside to share the news with Evan. *Pick up, pick up, baby. . . .* She was a victim of voice mail.

Several bottles of Cristal later, Callie collapsed in her bed at the Gramercy Park. She was reminded how much she had enjoyed herself—her head felt like a herd of Clydesdales was stampeding through it—when her BlackBerry rang. It was Tyler.

"Have you lost your mind?" Callie growled. "It's six A.M. here."

"I know, but I'm at an after-party in the Hollywood Hills," he said. Voices of drunken Angelenos filled the background. "It's really private, too, lots of celebs. I just saw Leo and Cameron and—"

"Tyler, please. Can't you tell me about this another time?"

"I thought you'd want to know your man is here."

"So what? You've met him before. Go say hi."

"Well, I just did. But it wasn't the way you'd expect. See, I was looking for a bathroom and stumbled across Evan in one of the bedrooms. He was a little preoccupied."

"What do you mean?"

"I'm trying to phrase this delicately, but here goes: I walked in on Evan with not just *one* girl—he was with *two* girls."

"Doing what?"

"Unless he moonlights as a gynecologist, I'd say they were having a ménage à trois."

She yanked her sleeping mask off and bolted upright. "No! Are you kidding me?"

"I wish. Their bottoms were off and their titties were out. Bad titties, too—round and hard, like grapefruits. I could see the scars on those things before I even entered the room. Just about blinded me."

"Oh, my God," Callie whispered.

"You're telling me. I witnessed things I'd never wish on any gay boy. 'You inbred tramps!' I screamed, 'Get the fuck off my best friend's boyfriend!' Shocked the shit out of them. Must have jumped a mile, easily. He looked at me like I was a ghost, just *shocked*. Naked as a jaybird. I felt beyond awkward so I ran out to call you. Oh my word, this bitch is fired up. Do you want me to go back in? I'm in the mood to kick some serious gonorrhea-infected ass. Just say the word and I—"

"No, no, don't go back in. I've wondered if the rumors were true—I'd heard things, but I didn't want to believe it. . . ."

"Honey, believe it. I'm sorry to be the one to break it to you. He may fuck like a stallion and look like Adonis, but he's a man-whore if ever I saw one."

Evan, that sneaky slut! That smarmy, disgusting sleazebag! To think of him as capable of being a one-woman man. As if! He was constantly surrounded by women, how could she have thought he'd be faithful? "I'm such a fool," she muttered.

"No, Cal, you're not. You're a sweet girl dating a guy who can't keep his pants on. Happens to the best of us."

"You're right, Ty. Thanks for telling me. I have to go." She had to call Evan, and not a minute later; she needed to talk *now*. But he didn't pick up. Not on the second ring and not on the seventh, either.

"Hi, Don Juan, it's Callie, remember me? Your girlfriend. Correction—your former girlfriend. I heard you had a party for three, clothing optional. Funny, I must have lost my invitation. If you like variety so much, why don't you just be a bachelor? You have too much ass on your plate, huh? Well, *doll,* go knock yourself out. I don't need your first-class plane tickets and I don't need your fucking emeralds and I don't need you! *Go fuck yourself!*" She threw her BlackBerry across the room. It slammed against the armoire, busting into pieces, but she was too pissed to care.

43

Unleash your inner tiger.

So read the ad for Bengal, a lounge on the Lower East Side. Callie's imagination swirled while she sat in a chair at the Sally Hershberger Salon. She emerged with the bounciest, sleekest blow-out she'd ever received. She'd extended her stay in New York for another five days—alone time was imperative, totally underrated. Being far away from Evan and the smog-fueled congestion of L.A. was just what the doctor ordered. The farther she hoofed it in the Big Apple, the more an article she'd read in *L.A. Magazine* rang true: the average Southern Californian spent a quarter of their lives behind the wheel. Sad. How nice it was to actually *walk* and be alone with her thoughts! Simple pleasures like ordering a dog at Nathan's and scouring the racks at Cadillac's Castle and Old Hollywood . . . The primary goal, of course, was to clear her lovesick heart—and it wasn't working. Not a single call from Bedroom Eyes did she receive, nor an e-mail. Not even a text. Every pub and person she strolled past reminded her of *him,* whether she was shopping for a blouse ("Made in the UK"), asking a local for directions to the nearest subway (he was a Brit), or sipping a caramel latte at a café in TriBeCa. (The waiter's name? Evan.) Evan, Evan, Evan— all day, all night, Evan! She kicked a pebble with her equestrian boot and strolled past a pub—Riley's. *Sigh.*

What she really needed was old-fashioned, hair-pulling, ass-smacking sex. And, as Candice so eloquently put it, "There's nothing like a new cock to get your mind off an old one." In nearly two years, Evan was the only man she had been with, and it was high time to change that. Sample some ass like one of the boys. And what better place to find a sexy piece than in one of the most eclectic cities in the world?

She dusted her cheekbones with Orgasm and slithered into a new purchase—a slinky, one-shouldered Grecian frock. The winged liner, glossy pucker, epic legs—by the time she slipped into a taxi she was hot-wired for sex.

"Bengal on East Houston," she told the driver. "Between Avenue A and B."

"Gotcha," he said. "Girls' night out?"

She giggled. "Something like that. Everyone's got to let their hair down at some point, right?"

"That's what I'm talkin' 'bout." He clocked the meter. "You gotta live it up, baby. Life's too short."

She had never gone to a bar solo before or with the sole purpose of hooking up. Sure, she'd had her share of one-night stands, but never anything preplanned. This was foreign territory; exotic, dangerous, wanton. First time for everything. She strolled through the ultra-modern establishment and nursed a glass of wine at the bar.

"Vodka soda," said a patron to her left in a thick Eastern European accent. "Pardon me, miss, but you look very familiar." His bee-stung lips and five o'clock shadow caught Callie's attention. And those arms . . . muscles for days, golden and godlike. His dark eyes scaled her body.

"I don't think we've met," Callie said.

"No, I don't think we have, but your face . . . I know you from somewhere. I'm Petru. It's a pleasure. And you are? Wait, don't tell me. Casey, Carrie . . ."

"Close. It's Callie."

"Ah, Callie. Callie Lambert, yes? You were on *Letterman* the other night. What, you look so surprised!"

"I didn't think anyone still watched that show."

"You were promoting that horror movie, the one with the Manx murder girl."

"Guilty as charged." Excluding the film's premiere, it was the first time she'd been recognized in New York.

"You did a great job. The movie looks funny, too."

"Just make sure you down a few beers before you watch it. You're not going to come away enlightened or stimulated."

"Well, maybe not *intellectually,* anyway," he said softly.

She batted her Garbo-esque lashes and sipped her wine.

"I must tell you, as stunning as you were on TV, you're more beautiful in person. What are you drinking?"

"Chardonnay."

"It looks like you need another. Sir? Your best Chardonnay for the lady. So, Doamnă Callie, what are you doing here all by your lonesome?"

"I've been a lazy shopaholic, enjoying some quiet downtime before I go back to L.A.," she said.

"I see. Silly question, but you have a boyfriend in L.A., I'm assuming?"

"Nope. I'm single." Single . . . the word had an odd ring to it. Subconsciously, she arched her back like a feline and Petru stepped closer.

"You have the most gorgeous mouth. Hungry, sexy lips." He ran his index finger across her lower lip. Two rounds of drinks later, they were in the Gramercy's elevator riding up to her room. Petru pulled her hair at the nape and nibbled her neck. "You need a good fucking, don't you, little girl?"

"God, do I ever," she breathed. She pressed her crotch against his and kissed him with abandon. *Mmm, this is just what I need. . . . Fuck you, Evan Marquardt, you're not the only one getting laid.* They tumbled on the couch and feverishly stripped off each other's clothes.

"Go down on me?" she said. Petru had already slipped a condom on and was pawing her breasts.

"Later," he mumbled. A few dozen pumps and moans later, he rolled off of her and propped his back against the cushions.

Ummm . . . Is this a joke? "You can't be serious, Petru."

He wiped a bead of sweat off of his brow. "What?"

"That's it? You're done after three minutes?"

"Don't worry, I'll give you more later. Let me take a nap first."

"Actually, you should probably get going. I have to be up early tomorrow and need some sleep."

"Okay, no problem." He dressed and, in the doorway, leaned in for a kiss. Callie pecked his cheek—barely skimming the skin—and slammed the door.

She stomped to the bathroom and started the shower. *I could have done a better job with my Great King.* The memory of Petru's bedroom skills—rather, the lack thereof—melted away with each pulse of water. What a joke! The biggest dud *ever*. How could a sexy man so seemingly full of bedroom prowess be so lousy? And more, why oh why did Evan have to be such an amazing lover? She decided he had permanently spoiled her; every future paramour would be compared to him. *Damn you!* Rough but sensitive and arduous. The body, the face, the skills . . . all were above reproach. Except that, in the words of Tyler Bragg, he couldn't "keep his pants on."

Her brand-new iPhone rang while she was toweling off. (It was just as well her CrackBerry bit the dust; she'd been meaning to replace it for a while.) It was her mother, frantic.

"Have you heard?" Virginia sobbed.

"Heard what? Mom, what's wrong? Is it Grandma?"

"No, no. It's Candice. Oh, Callie, it's terrible. Her mother just called me in hysterics. She overdosed."

"No!" gasped Callie. "When?"

"A few hours ago. She's at Cedars-Sinai."

"Is she going to be all right?"

"I don't know at this point. None of us do."

"This can't be happening. . . ." Callie's voice rang hollow.

"Poor Lara's fit to be tied, the whole Boyd family is. Candice has really put them through the wringer emotionally and financially."

"I know. She told me she was changing, though. She said she was giving all that up, all the partying. And she really seemed to mean it, too."

"She's an addict, Callie. She can't quit on her own. She needs serious help. God almighty, I just pray she comes out of it and makes a change. Where are you?"

"I'm still in New York but I'm taking the next flight home. I'm so glad you told me, Mom."

"How could I not? I know you had a falling-out—"

"We patched it up."

"I know you did. What I'm saying is, you've had your share of ups and downs, but in the end, you've always been there for her. She's very lucky to have a friend like you. Callie, promise me you'll never do something like this? I couldn't bear it." Virginia's tears prompted Callie to weep, too.

"I promise, Mom. You have my word." She mentally swore off coke then and there; she never wanted to touch the garbage again.

"If I lost my only child, it would be the end of me. We may not be the closest, but we're working on it, aren't we? Aren't we doing better?"

"We're trying, Mom."

"That's all anyone can do—we try our best. By the way, did I tell you how pretty you looked on that talk show? Margaret and Aunt Claire came over and we all watched it together. You looked so classy and grown-up. I said, 'Look at that one. She's mine—that's my daughter.'"

"You did? *Really*?"

"I certainly did. I haven't told you often enough—you know how difficult it is for me to show my soft side—but I really am proud of you. Sure, I'm critical—you say cynical—but I'm proud to have you as my daughter."

Twenty-four years she had searched for her mother's validation, and Virginia's sudden admission knocked the breath out of her. "Mom, that's all I've ever wanted to hear you say. I never felt you thought I was good enough—ever."

"Oh, come now. That's not true. How can you say that?"

"You've never told me this before. I've always felt you wished I was . . . well, someone completely different, actually. Smarter, prettier, more grounded . . ."

"Not at all. I have the best little girl in the world. Any parent would be proud to call you daughter. Listen to me! This whole Candice debacle has me so emotional, I sound like a Hallmark card." Virginia took a deep, wheezy breath. "I love you, kid."

Callie wiped her moist eyes. "I love you, too."

44

Ugh, hospitals—why did every one of them have the smell of ether-soaked gym socks? Candice was tucked deep in the starched sheets, sound asleep. She had never looked more fragile. Her skin rivaled a corpse's coloring. Beautiful, vivacious, voluptuous Candice—no more. Callie placed a plush teddy bear under her friend's frail arm. Her breathing was deep and clear and, within minutes of Callie's arrival, she opened her eyes. "Hey, mama," she said softly. "I thought you were in New York."

"I was, about twelve hours ago."

"You didn't have to come back just to see me. I'm fine, just a little tired."

Callie arched an eyebrow. "Oh, really? Just tired?"

"Exhausted, actually."

"Don't give me that exhaustion BS. It's the most overused excuse in Hollywood. I know what happened, Candy." Callie dabbed lip balm on Candice's cracked lips.

Candice looked away. "Can I have some water?"

Callie handed her a cup and raised her head to sip. "Much better," said Candice after a hearty gulp. "Where were we?"

"Your incident. The fact that you almost died yesterday."

"Oh, yeah. *That*. I've really gotten myself in a pickle this time, Cal. If Jackie hadn't called nine-one-one, I'd be a goner."

"You said you were turning over a new leaf. Remember, at the Four Seasons? You told me you were going to clean up."

"I did." Candice forced a wan smile. "It lasted a few days. Falling off the wagon is unfortunately super easy for me."

"But, Candy—why? I'm trying to understand."

"Because I'm just a big fucking mess. That's what my parents say, anyway. They think if I move back home, I'll be healthy and stable. What they don't realize is that this town has really fucked with my head. My self-worth is in the shitter. Jon broke up with me yesterday. I don't love him like I still love Lars but it's just one more rejection. The straw that broke the camel's back. How dare *he* break up with *me*? I felt lower than I've ever felt in my life. Everything has come at me like a goddamned freight train lately. All I wanted was to get completely blitzed, so Jackie and I scored an eight-ball. Mission accomplished." Candice toyed with the teddy bear's ear, avoiding eye contact. "I guess I went a little far."

"A *little* far?" Callie said. "That's the understatement of the year and you know it."

"I know," Candice whispered sadly. "I didn't do it on purpose, I swear. I wasn't trying to kill myself."

"But you almost did."

"Yeah, that's true; I did. My parents are insisting I go back to Michigan State. They've been cracking that whip for a while now and with this new drama, they really mean business. I only have a year left to earn my degree. I could find a normal job and get back to the real world, as boring as that sounds."

"That doesn't sound like a bad idea, Candy."

"They cut off all my credit cards, too. Rehab or else. Again. Third time's a charm, right?"

"It's okay to need help, you know."

"No, it makes me weak."

"Weak? Hardly. You're the toughest person I know. The baddest broad out there."

"But you told me not to give up, that I'd be doing myself a disservice. It would be a mistake to move back."

"Maybe I was wrong," Callie sighed. "I didn't know it was a matter of life or death, but I should have seen the signs. You've been miserable for a while and look how it's come to a head—with you at Cedars-Sinai."

"And in the most unfashionable duds known to man," Candice added.

"I'll second that; those gowns are hideous. This is a new opportunity for you, Candice—a second chance. Clean up, go to school, get your head on straight. . . . Besides, you can always come back to L.A. It's not like it's going anywhere."

"Not unless a seven-point-oh quake takes it down, which my dad is certain will happen." She rolled her eyes. "You know how those Midworst people think California is nothing but doom and gloom."

A nurse in polka-dot scrubs waddled into the room carrying a massive bouquet of roses. "Miss Boyd, you have a delivery," she said.

Candice looked at the card and squealed.

"Lars, I'm guessing?" Callie said.

"The one and only. Isn't he sweet? God, I love that bastard."

45

"HOW many of these do I have to sign, Paul?" Callie asked. She sat across from his cluttered desk with a stack of papers in front of her and a pen in hand.

Paul shuffled through the documents and handed her a sheet of paper. "Here, all of these," he said. "About ten more. I've highlighted everything."

The contract for the television version of *Nympho Cheerleaders Attack!*—renamed *The Cheerleader Chronicles* for cable television—guaranteed Callie $35,000 per episode, excluding Paul's cut. If Spike chose to order a full season of the series after the seven-episode run, her salary would be renegotiated, and, according to Paul, most likely tripled. Regardless of whether the show was a hit, Callie was over the moon with the agreement. ("Why, in just one episode you'll be earning what you made in a whole year at Dr. Ryder's!" Virginia gasped.)

"Who would have thought a silly sexploitation film would get me this far, eh, Paul?" She jotted her signature in her left-handed chicken scratch.

"It's a win–win deal for the both of us. Oh, Glassman and Gillick called and want to see you on Friday for a casting. They have you in mind for a new Soderbergh project."

"Am I reading for the hooker or the stripper?"

Paul guffawed. "Neither, she's an art dealer."

"I'm impressed. And shocked."

"Young lady, you're branching into mainstream, I'm telling you," Paul said, licking his thumb and flipping a page.

"A celebration is in order, wouldn't you say? Got any plans for tomorrow evening, Paul?"

"Can't say that I do." Paul did precious little for recreation. His life revolved around his clients and Chelsea, his springer spaniel.

"Good! What do you say we do dinner at Nobu in Malibu? My treat."

"Well, now, how can I refuse that?"

"I guarantee I'm the only girl in Los Angeles who offers to not only pay for her own meal but someone else's, too." Callie made a call and spoke to the maître d'; he'd been a friend of Gabrielle's. "Okay, Paul. We're down for nine o'clock."

"Really, now? On a Friday night at nine? How'd you finagle that one?"

"I've got connections, Paul, didn't you know?" she said with a glint.

"I'll say. Nine it is. Looking forward to it."

✻ ✻ ✻

She handed her keys over to the valet and marveled at the cluster of paparazzi on hand; clearly someone famous had arrived but she couldn't see the culprit causing the commotion. Dolce and Gabbana's Masculine—Bedroom Eyes' favorite cologne—hung in the air.

"Hey, look, it's that Manx murder babe," said a mangy paparazzo. Several mosquitoes snapped her picture. "Lookin' good, girl! So, it's date night for you and Evan?"

She was ambushed and her vocal cords froze. Why would he ask that, she wondered? *Is Evan here?* Impossible. What were the odds of that? The timing was too ironic. They hadn't seen or talked to one another in over a month. He had bombarded her with texts—*I miss you, doll; Call me, lover, we need to talk; Where have you been? I don't know why you're ignoring me. Call me, I love you . . .* Screw the lies and excuses; nothing he had to say could take away the sting of being cheated on.

Amidst a detonation of flashbulbs, Evan Marquardt stepped out of a black Bentley driven by Gary. His eyes met Callie's and he smiled—that sexy, sinful grin that always managed to make her clitoris tingle. He shouldered his way through the throng of cameras and steered her inside.

"Ooh, Callie's got a knight in shining armor," taunted a Latina mosquito.

"Why did you two arrive separately?"

"Where've you cats been campin' out? No one's seen ya's together in months!"

They remained silent until safely inside the restaurant.

"Can we talk?" Evan led her down the hallway by the restrooms, away from the hustle and bustle. "Why haven't you answered any of my calls?"

"Sssh!" She jiggled the restroom door handle. "Let's talk in here. . . . Why don't you leave a message like everyone else?"

"Why would I leave a message? You won't even return my fucking texts. You've completely blown me off." His eyes were fixed with a fire she had never witnessed before.

"You have this mixed up," she countered. "*You're* the one who got caught red-handed with your pants down. Why would I want to talk to you, let alone have anything to do with you after what Tyler saw you doing?"

"Baby, let me explain—"

"Explain?! Yes, please do. I want to hear you explain away why you were in bed with two naked sluts. Let's hear it—give me your best shot."

"Look, the party was a little crazy, but don't act like you don't know how after-parties are here in L.A. Give me a break, Callie. We both know you're not some virginal saint."

Her bottom lip quivered. "And I never claimed I was! So, tell me—what really happened in that room? Let me guess—you were innocently partying with two naked girls in the middle of the night but nothing happened. You really expect me to believe that? Really, Evan?"

He looked away and remained mum.

The veins in Callie's neck bulged. "You pig! You lousy, shady slut! I can only imagine what else you've done when I haven't been around. On the road, especially."

"Callie—"

"Save it, Evan. You can have any girl you want—what are you doing with me, then, wasting my time? You want to be a bachelor, knock yourself out. But I really cared for you and I thought the feeling was mutual." *Do not cry. Damn it, girl, hold it together.*

"I do care about you, doll. Listen to me: I'm not perfect and I'm not pretending to be. So I made a mistake—"

"You certainly did. A *big* one!"

"Yes, a big, major mistake. But you and I—we've got something special, you can't deny that. We're alike, two peas in a pod."

"No, Evan," she scolded. "That's where you're wrong. We're not at all the same. In fact, we're built completely opposite. I can be faithful and you cannot. Period."

"Not at all the case, doll. I—"

"You want to tap everything in heels and that's your prerogative; do what you gotta do. But don't expect me to stick around, because I'm not sharing you. Actually, you did me a favor, because the longer you're away, the more I realize I don't want to share myself, either."

"But—"

"And another thing that really chaps me: I gave up lots of auditions—against the advice of my agent, I may add—so I could spend more time with you in London. How *sad* of me. I have far too much going on to pine over Evan Marquardt and his stuck-on-cruise-control cock." She rocketed out of the bathroom, leaving a baffled Bedroom Eyes in her wake. Paul held a seat for her at the bar.

"Are you all right?" he asked. "You look pretty riled up."

"I just ran into an old friend, unfortunately." *Shake it off.* "I'm fine. Let's have a toast."

Am I really fine? . . . Yes, absolutely! Who needs a man to be fulfilled, anyway? I have a bona fide career, moola in the bank, and a solid support system. Why would I want a self-consumed prick to complicate things? I deserve much more than that.

Paul handed her a passion fruit martini. "Here's to you, my dear. To quote that cigarette slogan: 'You've come a long way, baby.'"

"Thank you. Cheers!" Callie flashed her pearly whites and hoisted her glass. "Here's to me."

46

"Skank, pass the sunblock." Tyler slathered lotion on his limbs. "You don't want a charred gay on your hands, especially with all this ink. Not a pretty sight."

"Spare me, then, by all means." Callie waded into the pool. *Ah-hhh . . .* Eighty-two degrees, the perfect temperature. In the August sun, probably closer to ninety. "This is a perfect afternoon."

"It would be nicer if the real estate agent had thrown in some muscled-out pool boys, but, yeah, this will do."

The friends had found the perfect place to share—a rented four-thousand-square-foot hacienda—and moved in earlier in the week. With two of the four bedrooms positioned in complete opposite wings of the house, their Hollywood Hills pad offered a stunning view of the Hollywood sign and the perfect amount of privacy and space. Callie toyed with buying a place—with *The Cheerleader*

Chronicles getting picked up for a twenty-two-episode season, she could afford something magnificent—but her Midwestern frugalness stepped in. Better to stash a sizable chunk for a rainy day. "Save those pennies, honey," cautioned Esme, and she appreciated her grandmother's point. The well could easily become dry; what if she never booked another well-paying role again? Banking on "what if" didn't put food on the table. And even though she rarely admitted it, she was lonely. Ha! Who would have thunk? At the ripe age of twenty-five, she needed more human contact than she did two years ago. In Tyler she found the perfect housemate; he wasn't home often but when he was, the blend was harmonious.

"There was a story I was going to tell you—what on earth was it? . . . ," Tyler said.

"If it's about the Limey, I don't want to hear it."

"Lord, girl, take a pill. What, is Aunt Flo in town?"

"I just don't want to hear about *him*. I don't want to know which track he's working on or how many girls he's schmoozing. I just don't care." She hadn't spoken with Evan in close to a year and she had almost succeeded in convincing herself he was a mere footnote. She loved him, no question—even after he cheated—but she couldn't trust him.

"Mmm-hmm. Right. And I got pounded by David Beckham this morning." Tyler cranked his lounge chair back and covered his face with a fedora. "Anyway, no, it's not about Evan. It's that girl he was with, Rachel. I was at the video store yesterday and saw her on a box cover of breeder porn."

Callie snickered. "I had heard she was doing soft-core, girl–girl fluff, but didn't know if it was just a rumor."

"Definitely not a rumor—I saw it for myself. She was buck naked, a big ol' purple dick in her mouth. I knew you'd get a kick out of that. Guess she got bored with the girly stuff. Can't say I blame her there."

"That mainstream career didn't pan out so well."

"It sure didn't. Oh, well. A girl's gotta eat."

"True." *Ha! I wonder what Evan thinks of that? Oh, Callie, shut up. Change of subject!* She hoisted herself on a boogie board. "I'm flying out to Tucson tomorrow to shoot a spot for the Super Bowl."

"No kidding? And why haven't you told me this before?"

"I just found out this morning."

"Typical entertainment. Gotta love how everything's so organized." He rolled his eyes.

"It's a small part, just one day's work. I'm stranded in the desert with some football players—I never watch sports, so I don't even know their names—and they mistake me for a cactus. It's pretty silly but the producer called up Paul and made a nice offer."

"Who cares if you have to put on a monkey suit and swing from a tree branch? It's the Super Bowl, for crying out loud. Congrats, that's fantastic. I'll be in Palm Beach for a *Nylon* cover shoot."

"Nice. Who's the girl?"

"No idea. Whichever 'it' whore is making people moist these days. Being that I'm the same age as Betty White, I can't keep up anymore."

"Yeah, almost-twenty-eight is ancient, Ty," joked Callie. She hopped out of the water and whisked a towel across her body. "Are you in the mood to go to Barneys? I'm having a retail craving."

"I can't believe that's even a question. Do peas come in a pod? Let me take a quick dip first."

"Take your time. I'm going to shower off and call my mom." She sashayed through the kitchen and popped her daily Wellbutrin. Her new psychiatrist, Dr. Freisch, was a snooze compared to

Dr. Holtsclaw, but she'd gladly take someone sincere over a fame-chasing nincompoop any day.

Ring!

Callie answered the phone. "I was just about to call you, Mom."

"We must be on the same wavelength," said Virginia. Callie would never have predicted that Candice's overdose would begin the mending of her relationship with her mother. They still weren't close—not the way Callie had always pictured mother–daughter relationships being—but they spoke on a more frequent basis and in softer, less abrasive tones. It was a beginning. "Say, Cal, I have a question for you. Next month will mark the one-year anniversary of Candice's sobriety and her parents are planning a little celebration. Very intimate, just family and a few close friends. I know how busy you are these days, but this is a big milestone for her and—"

"Count me in," Callie said.

Virginia gasped. "You'll come? To *Michigan*?"

"Of course. I do return from time to time, you know, Mom."

"I know, I know. But it's not exactly your favorite place and what with you taping your show and you mentioned you wanted to jet off to Paris for a break. . . ."

"Filming doesn't resume for several months and Paris will always be there. I want to support Candice. This hasn't been easy for her."

"It certainly hasn't. Well, kiddo, that's fantastic. She's not aware of any of this, so it will be a wonderful surprise. And I haven't seen you since last year, so I suppose you could say I have a double agenda."

"Then it all works out perfectly," said Callie. "I wouldn't miss it for the world."

47

"Holy Christ on a cross! What the hell are you doing here?" Candice lunged from the sectional in her parents' living room straight into Callie's arms. Her gusto nearly toppled Callie over.

"I thought I'd pop up in your neck of the woods and help you celebrate your milestone. Congratulations," Callie said. She was struck by Candice's glow; the whites of her eyes were brighter, her hair held a varnishlike luster, and the hollows under her eyes and in her cheeks had filled out. Sobriety clearly agreed with her.

A year had passed since Candice's move back to Michigan, "with my tail between my legs," as she phrased it. She was determined not only to hop back on the straight and narrow, but stay there for good. Family and friends were not disappointed; squeaky-clean had become her middle name, and with her addictions under control, she resumed her psychology studies at Michigan State. Ten pounds heavier and infinitely healthier, Boyd was back.

"You look fantastic, Candy."

Candice beamed and twirled her raven strands. "*Gracias.* Of course, if you had a strict diet of zero drink, drugs, or dick, you'd look pretty healthy, too. The only thing I'm on these days is my mother's treadmill. At the rate I'm going, I may as well join the nunnery."

"You're doing great. I'm very proud of you and I want to show my support, so here I am, guns blazing, ready to throw down in the Motor City."

"I love it! I hope you don't mind Shirley Temples; my parents don't keep a stitch of liquor around. It's better for me that way—no temptation. Out of sight, out of mind. And to tell you the truth, after a year, I have no desire to touch anything mind-altering. I'm really getting off on this whole sobriety thing."

"Good for you," said Callie.

"Speaking of getting off, who's the latest panty creamer in your life?" Candice's eyes flashed wickedly.

"Honestly, Candy, no one. Zilch. I may have to join you in the nunnery."

"Oh, c'mon, last we spoke was months ago; you mean to tell me since then, with a hit TV show and this body, you don't have any men on your leash? I don't believe it, mama. Not a word of it."

"I swear. Tyler's my main man."

"Humph," Candice scoffed, "*she* doesn't count." Candice and Tyler had never been chummy, not before she spun a 180 and not after, either.

"Have gay, will travel. Besides, I've been so busy working, I don't have any time to devote to a relationship."

Candice's eyes bulged. "Who said anything about a relation-ship? What about just a lay every now and then?"

"One-nighters aren't my style. Been there, done that, not for me anymore. I'll leave those to you," Callie said.

"I told you, I'm not allowing a random penis to obstruct my vi-sion right now. School and twelve-step meetings—that's about it for me. Pretty dull, huh? Look at all the crap that went down when I was obsessed with Lars. That prick, I swear, was part of my down-fall. I don't need any male complications."

"Not at this stage. Keep on doing what you're doing, because it's definitely working."

"That, along with my vibrator," Candice quipped. "Working like a charm."

"Do I hear a Miss Callie?" Lara, Candice's mother, rushed out of the kitchen with a towel in her hands. "My goodness! How are you, honey? It's been quite some time." She inspected Callie up and down before giving her a squeeze. "Smokes, you look terrific. If only I had been born with your metabolism. You know, you look heavier on television. Why is that?"

"The camera adds ten pounds, Mom," Callie said. She often re-ferred to Lara Boyd as "Mom"—though not in Virginia's presence—and felt she understood her better than her own mother. Lara was warmer, gentler, more nurturing. True, Virginia was learning to be less abrasive (more so than Callie ever remembered) but it hadn't happened overnight and without much sweat. Lara, on the other hand—with Lara the rapport flowed freer.

"Does it? So in other words, I'd look like an elephant on-screen?" Lara chuckled and patted her stout torso. "I'm top-heavy, that's my problem. Candy and I both. The big difference, though, is she has a waist and I most definitely do not." She clutched the girls' forearms. "Come with me, my little chickadees. Dinner is just about ready and we're eating on the patio. Just a small group of us, about a dozen, nothing fancy. Since I've got all three of my kids with me—four, counting Cal—I don't need much else. I love this time of year. We have the loveliest autumn here, just beautiful, and I want to soak it up before it turns cold. I have to confess, Callie, your mother told me you were flying in but I didn't want to spoil the surprise for Candy. Where is your mother, anyway? I spoke to her last week and she said she and Tony would definitely make it."

"They'll be here soon. Tony took her to a doctor's appointment and they're running a little late. I drove here straight from the airport," said Callie.

"Say no more. Those offices are always running behind. It's ludicrous. Callie, you eat pork, don't you? I thought so. I've whipped up some chops and ribs and all the staples of a Midwest feast."

"Midworst, she means," whispered Candice, and Callie giggled. They joined the rest of Candice's family at the table. Her two brothers, nineteen-year-old Luke and twenty-year-old Shane, eyed Callie like a buttery cob of corn.

"*Wow,*" Shane said, taking Callie's hand in his. "I haven't seen you in a couple of years, Callie, not since you got all famous. You look g-g-great. We watch your show *all* the time."

"All the time," echoed Luke. "*Cheerleader Chronicles* is my favorite. Every Wednesday night, *bam,* there I am, chillin' in front of the TV. You've got the hottest chicks on that show."

"You're the hottest by far, though," Shane said.

"Like, *by far,*" added Luke.

Callie blushed and rubbed the back of her neck. "Thanks, guys, thank you. That's sweet."

Luke poured a glass of lemonade for Callie. "Here, want me to scoop you some of Mom's peanut coleslaw? I assure you, it rocks."

Shane threw his fork on the plate. "Dumbass, you know she's allergic to peanuts! God, you just got done saying you watch her show every week and you don't know that? She's allergic to peanuts *and* strawberries. She can die from 'em."

"No, no, guys, that's just my character," said Callie. "I'm not really allergic to those things in real life. Only on TV."

"Boys," Lara said, "why don't you let Callie relax? I'm sure she'd like to unwind without getting grilled."

"Really!" Candice huffed. "She didn't come to see *me* to get interviewed by *you*."

Callie jumped in. "It's okay. Really, I don't mind." And she didn't. She found their naiveté and flattery cute. Besides, the soft breeze caressed her face and the crickets had begun singing for the evening; she felt safe amongst the humble surroundings and familiar faces. If it made the brothers happy, fire away.

"Cool," Luke and Shane said in unison. They both shot a slew of questions faster than she could keep up with.

"What was Sal Saunders like to work with?"

"Was Gabrielle Manx as hot in person as she was in the movie?"

"Are you making a sequel to *NCA!*?"

"How do they come up with so much blood?"

"What's up with those cheerleader uniforms? In the movie your skirt is tiny—like, *tie-nee*—but on TV, man, you're practically in prairie clothes."

"Can you hook me up with the blonde? You know, the one with all the piercings?"

Candice's father, Joe, got in on the act. "Callie, I'm curious how much time they give you to learn your lines. I tune in from time to time and it's amazing how much dialogue you have to learn. Your memory must be excellent. That's a talent, for sure."

Candice flew to her feet. "Okay! Are we done yet? This is *my* shindig, *my* sobriety we're celebrating! It's about me, get it? *Me.* All of these stupid questions. Who cares? It's just a goddamned TV show." She stomped into the house. The silence at the table drowned out the crickets.

Lara broke the lull. "I'm sorry for that, Callie. She knows I don't tolerate that kind of language. I don't know what's gotten into her." She brushed her bangs away from her red face and avoided eye contact.

Callie folded her napkin on the table. "No worries. Why don't you guys eat up? I'm going to go inside for a minute." She searched for Candice and found her in the powder room sniffling in a tissue.

"Ohhh," Candice sobbed when she saw her friend in the doorway. "I'm an ass, Cal, I really am. I'm sorry. I just—it's really been tough for me. Here I am in Bum Fuck, Egypt, with nothing exciting happening. Back in L.A. everyone noticed me. I was Miss Social. I was a centerfold and in magazines and at all these glamorous events and parties. I was the belle of the ball! I always got the attention, way more than you. . . ."

I don't quite remember it that way, but whatever. "Candice, you've always been the competitive one in our relationship, not me. And it's not like I'm bragging, either; your family is interested in my job, that's all. They've known me since we were teenagers. You gotta admit, it's not every day a girl on a TV show sits down for a barbecue in Troy, Michigan. They're not used to that sort of thing."

"I know, but that used to be *my* world!" said Candice. "And it's gone. I'm fatter, man-less, and no one recognizes me anymore. I'm trying to make the most of my new life but I miss my old one, too. Like, a lot."

"I can understand that." Callie sympathized with her—she certainly wouldn't want to move back to Troy—but Candice's behavior was juvenile and her selfishness had, unfortunately, remained intact. Callie was angry she had bothered coming.

Honnnnnk! Candice blew her nose. "I'm not being fair. This isn't your issue, I know—it's mine. Look, why don't we—? Hold on, someone's at the front door. Your mom and Tony are here." She was greeted with a gigantic hug from Tony—a hug that, Callie thought, went on for several seconds too long to be kosher. But Candice didn't seem to mind.

"How ya doin', Candy? Lookin' good, lookin' good. As always," Tony bellowed. His eyes fondled Candice's chest, which was accentuated by her ribbed cotton tank. Tony DiPrizzio had always been, and forever would be, Candice's number one admirer. Throw her in L.A. or Luxembourg, Troy or Torino, at a buck twenty or ten pounds heavier—in his opinion, she was a goddess anywhere and at any weight. Callie rolled her eyes.

"How are you, kiddo?" Virginia planted a kiss on her daughter's forehead. "Where's my hug?"

Callie embraced her mother but was thrown off by her appearance; Virginia's dark eyes were puffy and pink, as if she hadn't slept in days. Her coloring was off, too—peaked, a far cry from her usual peaches-and-cream. But the biggest giveaway that something was amiss had to be her lipstick—or rather, the lack thereof. Her lips were bare, and she never so much as picked up the mail without her rosy pucker in place.

"Mom, what's wrong?"

Virginia waved an index finger in front of her face. "Nothing to worry about." To Callie's scowl: "Not now, Cal. Not the right time."

"Can we talk privately for a minute?" Callie whispered. "I'm pretty bent."

"Sure. I'll let Candice entertain her biggest fan." Virginia led her outside where her black Cadillac was parked and listened as Callie recounted the dinner debacle. "What a shame. Lara must have felt awful. I never pegged Candice as the jealous type, go figure. News to me."

"Let's just say it's been brewing since I booked the film. As if I had any say in who was cast. And I certainly didn't fly all the way here to be dumped on," fumed Callie. "It was totally embarrassing. And she calls me her best friend, if you can believe that."

"Imagine if you weren't."

"I'm over it. I can't change people and I shouldn't have to. But honestly, Mom, I'm more concerned with *you*. How are you? You look so . . . so tired and not yourself."

"I am," Virginia said quietly. "I am tired. I haven't been sleeping so well lately. Do I really look that bad?"

"Umm, no," Callie said delicately, "but I know you. I can tell something's off."

"I'll save it for another time. Trust me. We should go in and be polite. At least for a little bit."

"I don't feel like being polite and I'm in no mood for BS. Please, Mom, level with me; I woke up at four A.M. to sit on a smelly plane all day and this visit is off to a crappy start."

"Well, I have a confession to make: it's about to get worse."

"What do you mean?"

"You're always so impatient, Callie." Virginia swallowed. "I didn't want to tell you in this way, but, fine. I've been wheezing and coughing, having chest pains for a long time, now—too long to be normal—and I got checked out by Dr. Gerber a few weeks ago. You've met Dr. Gerber—I've known him for years. Well, I went back for more tests and today I received the results. The news isn't very good."

"Pneumonia, bronchitis, what?"

"Heavens, I wish. No, it's much more serious than that, but he says it's not hopeless. Not with my attitude. With my can-do spirit, we figure it's—"

"*Mother*—what is it?"

"Cancer. I have lung cancer, Cal."

49

Paul Angers paced across the shag rug in his office, back and forth, to and fro, his worn leather loafers creaking with every stride. "I don't want you to think I don't feel terrible about your mother's illness, Callie," he said into the phone. "My grandmother and favorite aunt had cancer, so I sympathize with you and your family. I truly do." *Creak.* "But the fact of the matter is you're due on set next month. And those aren't my orders, either—if it were up to me I'd tell you, by all means, stay with your mother in Michigan, stay as long as you need to—but a contract's a contract." *Creak.* "And while your dedication to her is very admirable, the suits aren't going to go for it."

Callie took a deep breath before speaking. "Paul, there's got to be something you can do. Why can't they shoot the other scenes that don't require me at that time?"

"They are. You're never required to be there if you're not needed—you know that. But they've planned everything out, Callie, and your scenes are scheduled to shoot the last week of October."

"Give me a break! Nothing in entertainment is exactly 'planned' or done by the book. Hollywood flies by the seat of its pants all the time, so why not now?"

"It's such short notice. . . ."

"Kind of like when I get a call, 'Hey, Callie, your schedule's changed. We don't need you on set next week after all—we need you at six A.M. tomorrow.' *That* kind of notice?"

"Yeah," Paul said sheepishly, "yeah, that kind of notice. I'll make some calls. Let me see what I can do."

"Thank you, Paul, I appreciate it, and I know you'll get this done." She hung up and plopped down on the bed in her mother's guest room. *Please. As if they can't be a little accommodating. I'm the star of the show, for crying out loud! And it's not like I'm calling in because of a hangover or a PMS attack. Jesus Christ. Why is this business so one-sided?*

C-A-N-C-E-R. The six-letter word grasped Callie's heart like a pair of tongs and squeezed it until she was nauseated. Her mother was never a smoker—and not her sisters or parents, friends or husbands. In fact, she couldn't tolerate anyone who smoked. Whenever Callie had indulged (behind closed doors) in her now-defunct habit, Virginia would snap, "I smell cigarettes! And don't tell me I'm wrong, either, missy; you've been puffing at some point in the last twenty-four hours, sure as a gun's iron." And she was always right on the money, too. Her sense of smell rivaled that of a K-9. If someone so much as lit up from across the street, she'd take off in the opposite direction like a bat out of hell. So, Callie agonized, how could this be? It was Stage II—she couldn't believe she was saying

"Stage II," as if she was referring to the neighborhood cinema around the corner—and the doctors were confident they could rope in the disease before it spread further. ("Surgery in three days followed up with chemo a month later," Virginia said. "Funny how you've been after me to update my hairstyle—you've always hated my poufy hair—and now I won't have any . . .") Callie had planned on a week-long visit but with the unexpected news, she extended her stay.

"Callie, kiddo, I love that you want to help me out, but you have a life back in L.A. and I don't want to screw anything up for you. You have an important job and—"

Callie interrupted. "It's not that important, Mom. Trust me, it's just entertainment. The sun's still going to rise and shine with or without a new episode of a stupid cheerleader show."

"Ssh, don't say that!" Virginia's well-sculpted brows furrowed. "You've worked hard to get to this point in your career, and at such a young age, too. Look at you, everything is at your feet—at the tip of those Fred Flintstone toes of yours. I know I never took this whole acting thing seriously in the beginning—don't forget I can admit when I'm wrong—but you've really done something special and I don't want you to blow that up. These opportunities are few and far between. Two years ago, if someone had told me, 'Mrs. DiPrizio, your daughter is going to make hundreds of thousands of dollars running around in a phony cheerleader skirt, killing people with a couple of pom-poms—well, let's say I would have told them to keep walking straight to the snake pit. But I gotta hand it to you, kiddo—you really have beaten the odds. The taste level could stand to be raised, that's for sure, but what do I know." Virginia couldn't understand sex as a commodity and Callie had given up trying to explain it long ago.

She picked up the new Hermès scarf she'd brought with her and caressed the silky threads. The gift had been intended for Candice but after her childish outburst Callie wasn't feeling particularly generous. It would be perfect, however, for her mother to wear— especially after her chemo treatments. She sighed and placed the scarf back in its box. Hopefully Paul would get back to her soon.

50

Grandma Esme cradled Callie's head in her lap and massaged her granddaughter's scalp with long, fluid strokes. The elderly woman never failed in soothing her, no matter how frazzled Callie was. Her grandma, she was sure, could restore world peace, given the opportunity. No question about it.

"Honey, your mother has a great team of caretakers, don't think twice about that," said Esme. "They're removing the tumor tomorrow and you'll get a chance to look after her for a couple of weeks before you head home."

"But, Grandma, it's the principle. A dumb soundstage in Burbank isn't going anywhere. The crew and cameras will always be there. My mother won't be. I want to be with her. I *want* to take care of her. I'm her only child. It's not like I have another parent on standby." Callie cursed herself for her tactlessness but Esme didn't seem to notice.

"I know, dear, I know. Mercy, life certainly does throw some curve balls, doesn't it? Maybe Paul will have good news for you."

"Maybe." *Rrrrring!* Callie grabbed her phone. Speaking of Paul. She stepped outside to take his call.

"Yeah, um, hi, there," Paul stammered. "Cal, I tried to pull some strings for you but I don't think it's going to work out. The Wilders really need you, as originally planned."

"Are you kidding? They can't work with me a little here, while my mom gets zapped with chemo? I mean, *really*?"

"I understand your frustration, but they'd really like you here on set. Money is time and time is money."

"In other words, they're demanding it, is that it?"

"More or less. Violating a written contract could really tip the applecart. Will and Wendell said to give you their condolences, however. And they wanted me to mention they just cast a new dynamite actor for you to spar with, an up-and-coming hotshot from Tennessee."

Those inconsiderate, morally corrupt Hollywood cretins. "Great," she mumbled.

"If there's chemistry, they may write him in as a series regular, but as it stands now, he's a recurring guest star. You're going to absolutely love Layla's evolution this season, the script is *fantastic* and you're getting a lot of juicy scenery to chew up. Callie, are you still there?"

"Yeah, I'm here." *Heaven forbid family should be put in front of money—oh, the horror!* "I guess it's settled, then. See you in a few weeks."

"Callie, I realize that—"

She hung up; the bullshit hurt her ears.

Rrrrring! Argh, that shrill clanging! She made a mental note to switch ringtones. *Rrrrr—*

Callie answered without looking at the caller ID. "Jesus Christ, Paul—what?" Silence. "*Hello?*"

The person on the other line didn't immediately speak but when he did, it was most definitely not Paul Angers.

"I figured I'd get your answering machine but I'm glad I was wrong. And all feisty, too, just how I remember."

The voice was unmistakable. The lilt, that distinct way of speaking—an irresistible combo of sweet and sinful. Callie's heart thrashed. She bit her lower lip but couldn't stop the smile spreading across her lips. Bedroom Eyes. *I'll be damned.*

51

"Well, well, if it isn't Mr. Marquardt," Callie said. That sexy devil. Why couldn't she tell him to go to hell as she had done back at Nobu? How dare he wait a full *year* to resurface? The nerve! But she couldn't say that. She couldn't find any cruel or witty words to say to him. Despite all of his shortcomings as a boyfriend, Callie had remained mad for him and he was the best thing she had heard in a while. "Sorry, I thought you were my manager calling back. How have you been?"

"Not bad, not bad at all. I've been busy producing a bunch of new artists—a jazz musician, a blues band. Established acts, too, of course. It's been great branching out in a different direction. I'm having a blast really grinding my heels in. And somewhere along the way I also found time to get engaged. I'm sure you've heard about all that, though."

Callie had indeed read about Bedroom Eyes's whirlwind court-ship with twenty-eight-year-old wannabe celebrity, Stephanie Schueller. The three-month romance culminated with a diamond on Stephanie's ring finger. Specifically, a Fancy Intense Yellow rock, pear shaped, 4.5 carats cradled in 18k two-tone gold. Not that Cal-lie admitted to keeping track, of course. Judging from the bits and pieces she gathered, the Ohio native wouldn't know the difference between a diamond and a lump of yellow-painted coal. ("She's not necessarily stupid," Callie had remarked to Tyler, "just more or less a piece of trash. Stephanie opens her mouth and a trailer park falls out.") "No, I haven't heard anything about it," she said.

"Really, now? Hmmm, I figured everyone had heard. Those silly rags, especially the British ones, keep us splashed on their covers. Anyhow, we broke up. Specifically, *I* broke up with *her*."

"I'm sorry to hear that, Evan. Gosh, that's too bad. What hap-pened?"

"It's for the best," he sighed. "She was just too much mainte-nance. It was a berserk, go, go, go kind of thing—we were always on the move, there was always some sort of drama going on. What goes up that fast is bound to come crashing down, I suppose. I like a girl to be more low-key. But enough about her. Let's talk about you. Everywhere I turn I see your gorgeous mug and I want to know for myself how you've been. And I was tired of waiting on your fine ass to call me so here I am calling you. So, Miss Lambert— how are you?"

Callie broke down and told him about her mother's health crisis.

"Good Lord. Sweetheart, I'm so sorry."

"Thank you. The irony is that this is the one time I actually want to be in Michigan and I can't be. Can you believe it? Go figure."

"That's the way the chips fall. God, I've missed the sound of your voice, Callie."

Damn you, Bedroom Eyes, for catching me in a vulnerable state! Stay strong, girl. Do not let him work you.

"Let's talk about us," he said.

"What do you mean by 'us'? Last time I checked, there hasn't been an 'us' in quite some time." Callie kept her tone devoid of emotion.

"That's just the thing; maybe there should be an 'us' again. I miss you, baby. I really, honest-to-God miss you. Have for quite some time. Christ, I really fucked things up for us and never gave you a proper apology."

"Correct on both accounts," she said coolly.

"Let me make it up to you. Why don't we get together when you get back? Or better yet, I'm taking off to London next week for a few appearances. Only a couple of days' worth, a concert and some meetings, then I'm free to do as I please. Why don't we take some time off and pal around Europe? Have you ever been to Greece?"

You know damn well I've never been to Greece. "Nope."

"We can take a tour. Go to Mykonos, where your grandmother's roots are. How is Grandma Esme, by the way?"

"Grandma is fine, thanks. She's always keeping busy playing cards or baking or watching her soaps. Healthy as a horse."

"That's good to hear. I adore that woman, do tell her hello for me. So, picture the two of us in Mykonos. I'll rent a villa right on the Aegean Sea. We'll do nothing but soak up the sun and lie around naked and we—"

"Evan," Callie said sharply, "I just got done telling you my mom has cancer. And, anyway, there is no 'we.' No 'us.' So just forget it, it's not going to happen."

"You cannot tell me you don't think about me or you don't care for me, Callie. I don't believe it for a second." His low, melodic drawl made Callie's body crawl with goose bumps. "I know you miss me.

Let's try this again and I promise, I won't disappoint you this time around."

Don't do it, don't do it . . . or should I? He may have changed. . . .

"Give me one week and see if I can't change your mind. Come on, you little tease, I dare you."

God, that sounds soooo sexy. . . . Argh . . . "Evan, I don't think—"

"One week, that's all I ask. Seven days alone with me in Greece and then make your decision. Let me redeem myself."

Fuck, that sounds fabulous. . . . Redeem yourself all day long, Bedroom Eyes, till the sun sets. With my legs spread, redeem away. . . . No, don't let him. . . . Or should I? "I can't do that, Evan. I'm sorry, but the answer is no."

"But I'm not used to hearing 'no,' doll."

"And I'm not used to being taken for a fool, Evan. Get it?"

"Gotcha," he sighed. "Well, can't say I didn't try, can you?"

"It was great hearing from you but I really have to go."

"Likewise. Later, sweets. Take care." *Click.*

Callie groaned. It was easier walking a tightrope made of dental floss than maintaining self-control with Evan. She didn't know whether to congratulate or kick herself. Mostly, she felt like doing the latter, but there was no reason for him to know that. As deep as her feelings ran for him, her pride easily doubled that.

52

Her limbs tingled as if needles poked her arms and legs, dozens at a time. She sat on her icy hands to warm them but it did nothing to remedy her prickling fingertips. Her breathing, quick yet labored, made the oxygen rush to her brain. A cement block pressed against her chest, she was sure of it. Why else would it be so difficult to breathe? The more she focused on a breathing technique, the more light-headed she became. The fluorescent lights of the hospital definitely didn't help. Concentrate on an object, Callie thought; that's always helped in the past. *Focus on that blue scarf the woman sitting across from you is wearing. Let your mind go blank and center in on that cool, monochromatic turquoise. Soak it in and abandon all the worries swirling through your brain. That's it, girl, good job. See how easy that is? What a pretty shade of blue. . . .*

"Mr. DiPrizio?" The doctor interrupted Callie's meditation.

Tony jumped to his feet. She had never seen her stepfather's three-hundred-pound frame move so quickly. "Your wife's lobectomy went just fine. Smooth sailing. She's still out and is resting comfortably."

"Thank you, Doc, thank you. I was sweatin' bullets for a minute there," Tony said. He pulled a handkerchief from his Wranglers and wiped his brow.

"Thank you, Jesus," Aunt Margaret said. She sat next to Callie and dabbed her Maybelline-enshrined eyes with a Kleenex.

Ahhhhh. Callie exhaled and her breathing returned to normalcy, thanks to the doctor's news—or maybe it was because of that milligram of Xanax she'd chewed when the panic attack came out of left field. It had been months—a year, easily—since she remembered experiencing an episode. This one was particularly bad. No matter; things were under control. She swigged her bottle of Fuji.

"You see, honey?" Grandma Esme whispered, and patted Callie's knee. "Everything's going to be fine, dear. Just fine. Your mother has an angel up there looking after her, you can bet your little bottom on that."

"Dad is watching over her for sure." Callie flashed a broad smile and made her dimples pop. Was she ever flooded with relief! "I'm going to call Tyler, Grandma, and let him know. He wanted me to keep him posted." She fluttered out of the waiting room and dialed his number.

"I'm glad it went well, skank," Tyler chirped. "That's one obstacle out of your mom's way. I was wondering when you were going to call. Lord, my panties were starting to bunch up."

"You and me both. The operation took longer than we anticipated."

"I'll say it did. About five hours instead of three."

"So, what's new with you and Hell-aye?"

"Nothing new, just holding down the fort and playing with my pussy," said Tyler. "No one to play with it for me since all the men in Los Angeles are either insane or in the closet. Same old, same old. Had a shoot today with *Elle* and one of the male models tried to convince me he was straight with a girlfriend. What, do my eyes and ears look like they don't work anymore? Just a big ol' screaming bottom. Every one of those models—I mean *everyone,* even the girls—had an eight-pack, at least. Made me sick. Humpty Dumpty is going on a diet ASAP."

"Please, Ty, you're a rail."

"Yeah, a rail with a spare tire and it ain't too cute. Oh, I almost forgot, I have a question for you: Do you sing?"

"A little, I guess. I sang in a class play once."

"That's not saying much," Tyler said. "I'm not musically inclined but when I bust a note in the shower you'd think Celine Dion was visiting. I mean can you sing reasonably well? Reason I ask is I have a client who manages an all-girl group and she's looking to replace one of the bitches who dropped out."

"An all-girl group? Tyler, are you kidding me? I'm an actress, not a teenybopper. Why would I want to join a band?"

"Heavens to Betsy, settle down. I just want to know if you can carry a tune, not carry my children. Victoria, the manager, mentioned she likes your look, that's all. No reason to bite my head off."

"Sorry, I'm just a little tense. Singing isn't anything I've ever thought about pursuing, Ty."

"I realize a Grammy isn't most likely in your future, but you never know—it could be fun. Singing isn't much different from acting—entertaining is entertaining. Money is money. It's all the same."

"I'll keep it in mind, thanks."

"You big whore. So, when are you coming home?"

"Two weeks. I tried to get my hours rescheduled so I can be with my mom when she starts chemo but the powers that be aren't exactly working with me on that."

"You're surprised? They've got you locked in and they're not about to let their meal ticket call the shots. Is what it is, skank. All right, I need to clean up; I'm going out with someone after work. A date, I guess you could say."

"*Date?* Didn't you just tell me you didn't have anyone because they're all crazy or in the closet?"

"I sure did. He's a writer, for one—most writers are hermits and crazy as loons—and two, he's still legally married. So, technically, he's both of those things. I'm not expecting much, trust me, but I am bored. What am I supposed to do, twiddle my twat by my lonesome every night?"

"That's more than I'm doing these days," Callie said glumly.

"Puh-leeze. You always end up with someone sooner or later, unlike yours truly. I find a man as often as a lunar eclipse occurs. Give your mother a kiss for me and hurry your rank ass back to Cali, where you belong."

53

"Cut!"

Callie slackened her shoulders and cracked her knuckles. The first day of filming the new season was off to an über-slow start. It was Brant Van Zant's tenth "cut" in an hour and only the first scene of the day. His style was much more relaxed than previous directors Callie had worked with and the polar opposite of Tom Johannesburg's franticness. The cast and crew had walked on pins and needles around Tom but Brant had the effect of making everyone feel they were treading on ultra-plush carpet.

A lighting complication prompted a thirty-minute delay and Callie helped herself to a cup of coffee at the craft service table. A sandy-haired, twentyish man of average height stood next to her and dumped packets of Sweet'n Low in his brew.

"You're going to overdose on saccharin." Callie grinned.

The man returned her smile. His teeth, while white, were crooked; the imperfection added a roguish quality that offset his pretty boy looks. "In the South, we like our spoon to stick straight up. Mitch Gracie, pleased to meet you. I'm the new kid, guess you could say."

"Callie Lambert. Pleasure. So, you're my new nemesis?"

"That's right. I'm the resident asshole on the block."

"Hmm. I see."

"I'm here to make Layla's life a livin' hell—and maybe teach the cast a thing or two in the ways of acting."

Callie scowled. *Real funny, you big hick. Grow some manners.*

Mitch continued. "I'm not used to scenes takin' so long. My background is theater, where everything's in chronological order."

"What kind of theater?" she asked.

"Drama, mostly. I was Brick in *Cat on a Hot Tin Roof* for two years."

"Broadway?"

"Off-Broadway. Been livin' in L.A. close to six months now. Can't say I'm too impressed with what I've seen so far."

"Why is that?"

"Not my style. The folks here really feast on their own bullshit."

"Not all of us do," Callie said.

Mitch guffawed. "From what I've observed, ninety-nine point nine nine percent do. I don't get off on makin' people feel like hell just so I can pretend I'm swingin' a ten-inch bat. What you see is what you get. Straight shooter. None of this phony Hollywood bullshit. What about you? You probably like your ego stroked, I bet. You're used to everyone fawning all over you, tellin' you how pretty you are." His dimples gave Callie's a run for their money. She was just as struck by his brashness as she was by his impressive biceps.

"That's a little presumptuous, wouldn't you say?" she said.

"Not at all." He downed his coffee and tossed the Styrofoam in the trash. "You've been in L.A. awhile, now, haven't you? Obviously you've been successful so I'm sure you're used to lots of brownnosers. But just to let you know, I don't play that way. I don't plan on kissin' your ass and I don't expect you to kiss mine."

"Good," sniffed Callie. "Because the only thing I was thinking is what a prick you are. It must be a Southern thing."

"No, darlin', it's a Mitch Gracie thing. I just don't give a damn." He sauntered off.

Callie's lip curled. *You cocky motherfucker.* A cocky motherfucker with a mighty tight ass. She wondered how many scenes she had the displeasure of filming with the Hick Prick and was thankful he was only a guest star. She whipped around and collided with a tall blonde.

"Whoops, my bad," the girl said.

Callie did a double take; the hazel orbs and high cheekbones resembled those of a certain infamous and deceased blonde Callie had known well. The face was squarer and her features lacked refinement, but nevertheless, the likeness was uncanny. "Wow," Callie muttered. "You look just like—"

"Gabby Manx, right? I know. I get that all the time. Ever since I dyed my hair." Her voice dripped of the Midwest.

"Are you an actress?" Callie asked.

The girl tucked her bleached extensions behind her protruding ears. "Kinda. I was a model and now I'm crossing over. The typical model-turned-actress thing. Let's just say I'm working hard at establishing myself."

A model, really? With those ears and that jaw? "Good for you."

"Yeah. I'm blessed, I'm very blessed. But I got nothing on you yet. I remember reading all about you when the whole Manx murder went down. And every time I log on to *Diva Dish with David,* there's always some tidbit about you. I feel like I know you already. I *love* your show."

"Thanks."

"Your delivery is in*cred*ible. You're the best part of *Cheerleader Chronicles.*"

Callie's cheeks reddened. "Aww, thank you so much."

"But I pictured you prettier in person."

Callie's smile froze. "Come again?"

"Some people are just more photogenic than others—and then some people have the best of both worlds—they're photogenic *and* stunning in person. It's not a bad thing, it's just . . ." She cocked a hand on her hip and jutted out a bronzed leg. "I guess it's just the model in me. I notice the small things, the details. I expected something a little different after seeing so many pictures of you, that's all. I don't know how else to explain it."

Callie's eyes narrowed. "You don't say."

The blonde laughed again and adjusted the waistband of her short shorts. Her legs were ridiculously long and out of proportion— like a giraffe, Callie thought. She desperately wanted to slap the smile off the girl's Juvederm-stuffed lips.

"So, blondie, are you hanging out on set because you have an actual part or do you just like being the token bimbo?"

"Neither. I'm visiting my boyfriend, Brant."

Callie didn't know whether her sarcasm had sailed clear over the girl's head or if she was adept at playing it cool. "Brant Van Zant?"

"Yep, we've been dating for a couple weeks now."

Jesus Christ. How original. Dating the director. "Lovely. Maybe he'll give you a part."

"Oh, you can plan on it. He promised me a role. Obviously he's not much to look at, but neither was Tom Johannesburg and if it worked for Gabby . . ."

If it worked for Gabby. Bitch, please. This wasn't the first time Callie had met a Gabby imitator. Manx mania was still thriving, from the silliest gimmicks ("The Great Gabby Look-Alike Pageant") to the crassest (The Gabby Halloween costume, complete with a ridiculously large padded bra and stick-on bullet wound) to somewhere in between (a line of Gabby-inspired blond wigs). "Gabby had *talent,* though," Callie said. "Most copycats don't."

"Oh, trust me, I have talent, too. Many talents, actually. Just ask Brant. Ha ha."

"What part of the Midwest do you hail from?"

"Aww, man, do I really have an accent? I've been working hard on getting rid of it but I'll have to work harder. Toledo." The blonde grabbed a Twizzler from the craft service table and bit the tip off. "My talents have taken me all the way from the toilet bowls of Toledo to the beds of Bel Air. Ha ha. No complaints from anyone, either, I may add. I guaran-fuckin'-tee that one. Ha ha."

What's so funny? Callie wondered. She prayed the giraffe would choke on her licorice. Who did this tacky slut think she was, anyway? "What's your name?"

"Stephanie."

Stephanie Schueller. Of course! That explained it. *No wonder I smell garbage.*

"Wouldn't it be *amazing* to work together?" Stephanie continued. "Maybe you can put a word in for me. Not that I haven't sealed the deal with Brant. But it can't hurt, you know?"

Callie pointed her finger like a pistol. "Great idea. You can count on it."

"Fan-fucking-tastic. Thanks! I'll see ya around." Stephanie skipped off, all six feet of her, Twizzler dangling from her mouth.

54

Callie curled her legs up on the living room couch and read her script with a snarl.

> *EXT. Forest—NIGHT*
>
> Layla and Wade face each other, both prepared for a smack-down. She does a high kick but he blocks her with his arm and flips her on her back. She drops to the ground with a thud. Wade stands over her, chest heaving. He catches his breath while staring into her eyes and then, without a word, kneels beside her and kisses her. Layla protests but he doesn't care. He hungrily devours her lips until she fully surrenders. He unbuttons her blouse and it's clear by her arched back that she desires him as much as he desires her. They paw each other, feverishly.

Ugh! Really?! She pictured Wade, aka Mitch Gracie, smelling like hay and tasting like soot, or worse, manure. Did he really think that aw-shucks, I'm-a-take-no-shit-kind-of-good-ol'-boy attitude was charming? She'd have to set him straight on that, just in case it wasn't clear during their first meeting. Another self-important head case with a bloated ego.

Tyler stormed in the house wearing a white tracksuit and an ear-to-ear grin. "I just had the most fantabulous workout. Look at this." He exposed his waist and pinched the skin. "The fat is melting away and this bitch is bulking up. Yes, it's true, ladies and gentleman, Tyler Bragg is actually—dare I say it—gaining *muscle*."

"Your abs looks amazing. That trainer is really working you."

"She sure is." He plunked down next to her. "Really knows her shit, too. Between my new body and my new man—this skank is one happy camper." Tyler's first, second, and third date went so well with Timothy, the writer, they decided to become exclusive. "It works out perfectly. Timothy plays hermit writing his screenplays all day while I'm busy slapping on gloss and lashes. Seeing each other after work is the perfect amount of time together. Normally I'd get sick of seeing someone nearly every night but with him it's different. I just can't believe how well we mesh together."

"What's going on with the wife?"

"Who? Oh, her." Tyler waved his hand in nonchalance. "Their divorce will be final in six months. They've been separated for years but never bothered legally calling it quits. I can't help thinking a certain tall, good-looking makeup artist must have influenced that. You know, it's bonkers, I don't even feel like going out and partying anymore; it's like I've transformed into my grandmother overnight. All that's missing is my Metamucil. But hey, I'm not complaining. Even our names fit well together—Tyler and Timothy. Cute, isn't it?"

"Very," Callie said absently.

"Why the long face? Did your vadge finally dry up?"

"It's been dry awhile now, I don't know where you've been." She tossed her script aside. "My new love interest is this cocky hillbilly who makes my skin crawl. We've only filmed one short scene together so far, we barely spoke a word on set. But tomorrow we have a sex scene and I'm not exactly looking forward to it."

"With your salary, I'd have no problem doing that. Matter of fact, if he's hot, I'd do it for free. Let me rephrase that—I *would* have done it for free, back when I was on the market. Just suck it up and pretend the hick is Matthew McConaughey."

"He's hotter than McConaughey. A little on the short side, but hot. As soon as he introduced himself, though, I wanted to run for the hills. He grates on my nerves. Have you ever met someone you can't stomach, right from the get-go?"

"Yeah, Candice," Tyler said with a wrinkle of his nose. "That crazy needs a serious dose of Ritalin. Have you spoken with her since her last flip-out?"

"No. And I don't plan on it, either. I swear, all those drugs must have deep-fried her brain. She's totally unreasonable and I just can't win."

"I'll second that one. If you told her, 'Hey, girl, Prince Albert is sending a private plane for us at noon, be ready,' she'd have a hissy it wasn't arriving at eleven thirty. She's impossible. Don't think the spots on that leopard are going to change just because she cut out her extracurricular activities."

"Yeah, I've come to that realization. Anyhow, I'm dreading this sex scene, Ty."

Tyler turned his head so quickly, his hat dipped over his brow. "Ummm, come again? You bump uglies with Gabrielle for the camera—all the money in the world couldn't pay me to do that—but you can't fake a little hetero action for cable TV?"

"With Gabby it was different."

"I'll say it was different—it was *lesbian*. Who am I speaking with here, Martina Navratilova?"

Callie shrugged. "It felt natural."

"Nothing natural about lesbianism. It's against God's will."

Callie chuckled. If Tyler had only known about her Christmas rendezvous with Gabrielle. He'd likely birth a cow. "It's easier when you're comfortable in someone's presence, that's what I'm trying to say."

"Think of basking in the presence of that check, skank—that should make it real easy for you. Cha-ching! Fake it till you make it. Do your job, cash the check. Another day, another dollar." Tyler's reasoning was practical, as always. Kicking ass and kissing hotties—not a shabby way of earning a living, she thought with a smile. So maybe she'd have to plug her nose to get through making out with the Hick Prick—big deal. It couldn't be *that* bad, and it could be a lot worse. She made a mental note to make sure there was a bottle of Listerine on set.

Tony wiped his eyes. His tears mixed with the grime under his nails produced an inky film on his hands. "We did the best we could," he said. "Your mother really put up a fight." Callie had never seen her stepfather weep before—ever—and his voice shook with emotion. "She was a helluva woman. The toughest woman, bar none, I've ever known."

Callie stood in front of him. Silent. She couldn't find the tears to cry or the words to express any feelings—she couldn't *feel* any feelings. Her lips were rubbery and when she moved them no sound escaped; her vocals had abandoned her, like a deaf-mute. Frozen. Her motor skills were nonexistent and so she remained still, like an upright mummy. . . . *Why am I not upset? I feel nothing. In fact, I don't even care. Why wouldn't I care? My mother is dead and I don't care?*

"*Les yeux sans visage . . .*"

She couldn't tell who was singing or where it was coming from. Tony was the only person in the room and it certainly wasn't him.

"Aren't you going to say anything?" Tony said. The vein in his temple pulsated and his brow swam with perspiration. "You must have a lot of questions, so go ahead, ask away. Damn it, say somethin'—what's wrong with you?"

"Les yeux sans visage . . ."

There was that voice again; she hadn't imagined it the first time. Callie parted her lips. Tony tilted his head forward, waiting, willing the words to come out of her. But, still, nothing . . .

"Eyes without a face . . ."

The music snapped Callie's eyes open. She checked out her clock radio—8:00 A.M.—and shot out of bed. Shit! How on earth had she managed to oversleep? She was sure she had set the alarm for six. Four messages from production waited on her cell. She dialed Kathy, the first AD, as she floored her BMW.

"Callie! Good, you're alive." Kathy sounded chipper.

"Alive and well, thanks."

"That's a relief. We were wondering when you'd surface; everyone was worried. So where the fuck are you?"

"I'm driving over the Canyon, Kathy, and I promise, I'll be there soon. I'm so sorry, I—"

"You were due on set almost two hours ago." The relief in Kathy's smoker warble gave way to irascibility.

"Trust me, I know," Callie said. "I'll be there in twenty minutes, tops. I promise."

"Mmm-hmm. Good luck in rush hour. Go directly to makeup when you get here and—you didn't hear it from me—avoid the Wilders. They're floating around on set. Just a heads-up."

Damn it. Of all the times the Wilder brothers could be on set they picked that hour, on that day—not the day she was an hour *ahead* of her call time, oh, no. "Gotcha. Thanks, Kathy." She flipped on the radio and cursed at who blared from the speakers: Billy Idol. Damn it. Her dream wafted back to her conscience. Chill out, she told herself; for being on her third chemo treatment, Mom wasn't feeling too awful, all considering. Or so Callie was told. "I'm a tough cookie, Cal, you know that," Virginia reassured her. Not that her mother would own up to feeling shabby . . .

Callie slapped the dial on the dashboard. What a lousy way to start the day.

56

"Oh, lookie here." Anna, the key hairstylist on set, plucked a hair off of Callie's head. "Guess what I found?"

Callie looked down at Anna's hand and gasped. Nestled between her plump, ebony fingers was a gray hair. "You've got to be kidding me! I'm not even twenty-six yet!"

"Sweetie, ain't nuthin' you can do about it. I started going gray when I was sixteen. And look at my head now." Anna shook her curls. "Thirty years later, I'm nothing *but* gray. Grab a bottle of color and call it a day. We all gotta deal with it at some point. Like doing your taxes."

Anna tossed the strand but Callie could see it poking out of the trash like a red flag, if ever there was one. *I'm officially old. Over the hill. Past my prime.* She scowled at the offensive, wiry perpetrator in disbelief. Her father had gone gray at the quarter-century mark. Apparently, neither he nor his daughter inherited Grandma Esme's amazing genetics.

"You know who's got some mighty fine hair," continued Anna, "is that new one, Mitch. Thick, wavy, just gorgeous. And here he is, too." Mitch Gracie walked in as Anna clipped an extension to Callie's head. "Mornin', handsome. How you doing today?"

"Doin' fine, Anna, just fine, thank you." He smiled and the skin creased around his suede brown eyes. He took a seat next to Callie.

"Sasha had to run to her car but she'll be back in a minute to fix you up," Anna said. "Not that you need much help in the styling department. We were just saying what perfect hair you have."

Mitch ran a hand through his tresses. "My mama never wanted me to cut it when I was younger. My sister and me, we looked like a couple of overgrown cactuses runnin' around. Howdy, Miss Callie."

"Humph." Callie barely managed an audible greeting. Between oversleeping, her nipples aching from her period, and her newly gray situation, she was in no mood for small talk.

"I'm lovin' the hair today, Anna," Mitch said. "Nice work."

"Why, thank you. You cats have that hot and heavy scene today and I want it to be extra full and sex-ay." As if Callie needed reminding. Anna took the bobby pin out of her mouth and secured a section of Callie's hair. "I gotta spray the bejesus out of this hair. It can't be falling from all the steam generating from you two."

"No need sweating it, Anna," scoffed Callie. "We just may need a little help producing heat, even."

"No doubt," Mitch snickered. "Callie's so used to filming lesbian scenes, she may need a little help in this department."

Anna blissfully pinned away. "I guess that remains to be seen.

Seems to me filming a love scene with a man would be much easier than with a nekkid woman. But I don't know, I've never been an actor."

"Neither has Callie," said Mitch with a wink. "She just whips her top off and flings her hair around a little. Not too much acting required, is there, Lambert?"

Callie stared straight ahead, stone-faced. "Kind of like with your off-off-*off*-Broadway gems. All those Tony winners under your belt, Sir Laurence Olivier."

"Acting comes easy to me. It's second nature. I get inside the character's head and"—Mitch snapped his fingers—"*boom*. Magic happens. Instantaneously."

Wow, big word. "How fortunate for you," Callie said.

"It is, isn't it? Same as how playin' a half-naked bimbo comes so easy to you."

Anna jerked her head from one actor to another, back and forth like she was watching a game of Ping-Pong. "You two need to take this outside? What's with all the attitude?"

"You'll have to ask her, Anna. Callie, here, doesn't care much for me. Wish I could tell you why."

"Maybe because you're a conceited know-it-all who needs to learn when to keep your mouth shut. You know, Mitch, not every thought that springs into your head needs to be spoken," Callie spat. She squeezed her eyes shut while Anna waved a can of hair spray around her head.

"Lawdy," Anna whispered. "I wish I could find time to be so silly. You two are too much. Okay, Miss Thang, you're good to go."

"Thanks, Anna. I'll catch you in a few hours." She hopped out of the chair and ran smack-dab into Will Wilder.

57

"Callie! Just the girl I was looking for. Got a minute?" Will said.

"Of course." Callie followed him into his office. "What's up?"

Will shut the door and took a seat. "What's with the late start?"

"I know, I know," Callie sputtered. "I'm sorry, Will. I totally understand you being angry and I promise I won't—"

He held up his hand. "Ssh, slow down, take a deep breath. Look, you're flustered right now and I know you're going through a tough time with your mother and all. How is that going, if I may ask?"

"Mom is doing well. She's had a few treatments since they removed the tumor and her doctors are very pleased. It's a work in progress, of course . . ."

"Of course."

"But she's doing better than expected. We spoke yesterday and she was very upbeat."

"That's great. I'm just checking to make sure you're doing okay," Will said. "It's my job. We want you to bring your A game."

"I know. I'm hanging in there."

"Good. Look, we all love you—in my book, you're golden. I have no desire to make a mountain out of a molehill. But let's not make a habit of showing up two hours late. Deal?"

"Deal."

"Excellent. So, Wendell and I have been doing a lot of thinking; we're tossing around a few ways of spicing up the storyline. *Cheerleader Chronicles* needs a little something, a little oomph. The network wants more fireworks. I don't mean more T and A, per se—after all, it isn't HBO—but it could use an arch. Another dynamic. What do you think?"

"I think that sounds interesting," Callie said carefully. "Like, what—casting a new love interest for me?"

"No, no, no. We're pleased as punch Mitch is on board. Six episodes, maybe more. We'll see how ratings go. Spike conducted a poll the other day asking what the fans would like to see more of and the answer given was: a villain." Will placed the tips of his fingers together on his desk, prayerlike.

"But we have villains, Will. Every week we have villains."

"I mean someone steady. Someone you love to hate. Catch my drift?"

"As in a supporting character? That's great. A Hamsburg-type would be perfect. Maybe you can get Sal to reprise his role."

Will shook his head. "He wanted too much moola before we got picked up for a full season—now forget it. No, more like another Kiki to your Layla. That's what worked so well with the movie—your dynamic with Gabrielle. Obviously, we can't duplicate the chemistry but we can take note. What the show needs is another female, a Lex Luthor in a skirt. Chicks equal ratings and seventy-five percent of our audience is male."

"Wouldn't it be more exciting to have a different guest star every week rather than the same old actress?"

"That's the problem—we need the excitement of a familiar rivalry. I'm talking raw theatrics, someone you can really gnash teeth with. The old-fashioned good-versus-evil routine to make viewers tune in."

"But don't the viewers tune in to see *me*?"

"Of course they do. But think of how many more will tune in to see you *and* your rival. Tension makes for good television."

"But that will take away from my character, won't it?"

"On the contrary; I think it will only add to your character's development. It could raise a whole new set of issues no one ever knew existed with Layla."

"Um, I don't know. . . ." Callie tried to wrap her head around sharing the spotlight with a new lead actress. "It's difficult picturing anyone other than Gabby playing Kiki."

"Agreed. It's impossible. Besides, you took out Kiki in the film, so bringing the character back isn't even a possibility. We were thinking, however, of writing in the role of Kiki's long-lost sister—now *that* could be hot. No one in direct competition with you, of course."

"Maybe that would make for an interesting twist, Will. . . ." Why had she doubted her importance? She mentally smacked herself for feeling and sounding so insecure.

"This is your show and we want you happy. And when we make money, we're all happy. So we're thinking, how great would it be for the long-lost sister to be a Gabby two point oh?"

"I don't follow."

"There's a pretty blond actress we've tested who's a dead ringer for Gabby. Sorry, bad pun. She's very green and rough around the edges but there's something interesting about her. She's got the right attitude—bitchy and badass—and she's physically imposing. She could provide the right contrast with your character."

Callie's stomach sank. "You wouldn't be talking about a girl named Stephanie, would you?"

"Why, yes, I am. You know her?"

"We met last week. She was wandering around the set."

"That's right—she was visiting Brant. I'm not kidding myself, I know damn well she's the poor man's version of Gabby. If Gabby was Monroe, then Stephanie's Jayne Mansfield—no, forget that, not even Mansfield. Mamie Van Doren, let's say. But she could work. She's not a name, which means we're getting her dirt cheap."

Of course. Everything in entertainment boiled down to money. "Sounds like you're pretty set on her. When does she start?"

"Not for a few more weeks. She hasn't even been written into the script yet."

Callie bit her cuticles.

Will chuckled. "Don't worry, Callie. It's *your* name that appears right after the title, not anyone else's, and certainly not hers. And don't forget—higher ratings means bonus time."

She sat up straighter. "Bonus?"

"That's right, my dear. Bonus with a capital *B*."

Callie was suddenly excited. "I like the sound of that, Will."

Will leaned back in his chair and smiled. "I knew you would. As I said, money makes everyone happy."

New actresses popped up all the time. So what? It was the nature of the business. She chalked up her lack of assurance to hormones and stress. A needy, temperamental actress equaled obnoxious and she despised self-indulgent prima donnas—the

Candices of the world. Naturally, everything would be fine—why wouldn't it be? There was only one Callie Lambert. *Bitches, hear me roar.*

Hours later, she was reunited with the Hick Prick.

Whack!

Mitch Gracie's face reverberated from the force of Callie's hand. He cranked his fist back but before he could return the hit she planted another one. She took a step back and swung a high kick but he blocked her with his fist. Callie fell. His eyes blazed and held Callie's contemptuous stare. And then, like a hawk sweeping to nab his prey, he dropped to his knees and kissed her.

Callie caught her breath. *Mmmm, he smells like pinecones and leather.* She kissed him back, at first mildly and then with abandon, swiping her tongue along his and sucking on his lips. Those pillowy, savage lips of his . . . He unbuttoned her top and she moved his hand lower down her body, between her legs. This wasn't so bad. . . .

"And cut." Brant removed his headphones. "Back on your feet. We'll take it from the top of Scene Five again, guys. Nice work. You two look good together. Have you been practicing behind our backs?"

"Very funny, Brant," Callie said. With reluctance, she tore herself from Mitch. She felt flushed—dazed, even. She hadn't expected to feel aroused. *Tingly.* Was it her self-imposed sexile that made her wild, or the man himself?

"Just a suggestion," Mitch whispered. "When I lean in to kiss you—"

"Yes?" she said eagerly.

"It may be more interesting if you put up more of a fight. Make me work for it a little more. Hey, Brant?" Mitch turned to the director. "How's the timing on our kiss?"

Brant chomped his gum and mulled it over. "You could slow it down just a little. Take your time with it. Remember, this is a culmination of all their pent-up hostility."

"Gotcha. Kind of like when I finally hooked up with my girlfriend. I worked so hard gettin' down her pants, I should have earned a certificate in Blue Balls 101," Mitch cracked.

Callie pictured a gingham-happy Pippi Longstocking on Mitch's arm, since he disliked the Hollywood kind so much. But that was beside the point—it wasn't about the girlfriend's looks or his relationship status. In fact, it wasn't about Mitch at all; for the first time in nearly two years, she felt fire for someone other than Evan Marquardt. (Mr. Quick Dick, the New York revenge lay, didn't count.) Suddenly, with crystal clarity, she saw a future without the pesky Brit shackled to her vagina. Yes! It *was* possible. Her body pounded with elation and recharged mojo. She wanted to tear through the soundstage and shout the news with a televangelist's fervor: *I'm hot for someone other than Bedroom Eyes!* Revelations were happening and miracles were alive and well in the City of Angels. Hallelujah!

58

Revealed: 20 *Celeb Plastic Surgery Shockers!*

Callie stood in line at CVS and scowled at the cover of *Got It!*
The cover photo wasn't the most flattering—her mouth hung open,
as though caught mid-sentence, and her skin was oilier than a pan
of Wesson. She recognized the bandage dress from the premiere of
NCA! but little else of the photo jogged her memory. What an awful angle, she thought; her shoulders looked uncommonly broad,
like a linebacker's. She glanced around to make sure no one was
watching her—in a hat and True Religions, she blended in with all
the other L.A. bums—and swiped the magazine from the rack.
There, on page 35, was a half page devoted to her nose. The article
featured a still from *The Cheerleader Chronicles* and an old snap-
shot, easily five years old and obtained through God-knows-who.

Callie Lambert hasn't always been so picture perfect. *Got It!* discovered a pic of the then 21-year-old starlet and her shorter hair wasn't the only thing different! "Judging from this older photo, it appears Miss Lambert has undergone a rhinoplasty at some point before her TV career," Miami-based plastic surgeon Dr. Liam Bowersox tells us. "The before photo demonstrates a thicker bridge with a noticeable bump. In the after shot, Miss Lambert shows off a more camera-friendly look: a thinner, smoother bridge, turned up slightly at the tip. The effect complements her face and gives her a more streamlined profile. In addition, her lips appear to have been plumped by an injectable filler—but that could also be a makeup trick. Whoever did her work—kudos to him or her for showing restraint and not going overboard." We concur, Doc. Job well done, Layla!

Callie contemplated informing the editor that not only were her lips 100 percent hers, but they were 100 percent fabulous, too—thank you very much—before reconsidering. No sense giving the press more ammo and labeling herself a bitch. Besides, if her pucker looked luscious enough to be confused for fake, why complain? She was learning to choose her battles. Fame was a double-edged sword; the attention stroked her vanity but made her self-conscious, too. She could stomach and even delight in the occasional write-up but couldn't bear being chased by the media. Luckily the initial insanity following the release of *NCA!* had all but evaporated—the paparazzi had an unending supply of fresh meat to stalk. Callie was thankful for all of the Hollywood bimbettes getting pregnant or a DUI—or both. The more girls courting the press, the less pressure put on her. She thought back to more simple times, when a Labatt's and making fun of drunk callers on QVC made her happy; leading a nondocumented existence wasn't so bad after all. But the tradeoff—the free designer clothing, comped dinners and five-star hotels, front-row tickets to concerts and fashion shows—wasn't too shabby, either, she reminded herself with a smile. In fact, life was pretty damned good.

She paid for her box of Nice 'n Easy and joined Tyler for a massage at the Spa Montage. Afterward they grabbed a bite at their favorite Beverly Hills people-watching spot, the patio of McCormick & Schmick's.

"I'm so relaxed, you could stretch me like a pretzel," said Tyler. "That massage was fabulous. We need to make this a monthly priority. Weekly, even. I can never have enough 'me' time."

"Mmmm. I needed that, too. I've been working fourteen-hour days lately."

"Has the trailer lady started?" Tyler said.

"Stephanie? Yeah, her first day was yesterday. And yeah, she's just as obnoxious as I thought she'd be. I'd rather deal with a yeast infection. The typical look-at-me, I-never-got-enough-attention-when-I-was-a-little-girl syndrome. Typical actress."

Tyler rolled his eyes. "Say no more. I know that type to a T. Those bitches infiltrate the biz like a rampant case of the clap."

"But here's the thing—I'm looking at a hundred-thousand-dollar bonus if the show climbs an additional ten percent in ratings, Ty. So I can't complain."

"Lord, tell her to come work with me—I could use a raise. Here"—he lifted his glass—"cheers, skankazoid. To health and wealth."

"Yes. To health and—"

"Tammy, look!" cried a man at an adjacent table. His worn Cardinals T-shirt barely concealed his tummy. "There's the gal from that cheerleader show." He and his wife craned their necks to inspect Callie. She slid farther down in her seat.

"Ugh, tourists," Tyler grumbled.

The woman made her move. "Excuse me, miss; I don't mean to bother you while you're eatin', but I gotta tell you my husband and I watch your show all the time! Your forehead don't look nearly as big as it does on TV."

Callie forced a smile. "Thank you."

"So what's it like?"

"It's a great show to be a part of," Callie said. "I'm really fortunate to have a steady gig and be a part of something so fun." Typical question, pat answer. *Yawn.*

The woman's eyes were bugged with so much adrenaline, she looked as though she'd pounce on Callie at any moment. "No, I mean what's it like being famous? Having people recognize you and takin' your picture? It must be so excitin' and make you feel special."

"Not really." The blank look on Tammy's face prompted Callie to continue, sans bullshit. "It's not like any of those people love me. And at the end of the day, that's all that matters."

"Huh? What's all that matters?" Tammy asked.

"Love. Without it, life isn't complete. And I don't know why— maybe because I can't wear it or smell it or spend it—but it's easy to take for granted. Trite but true. Love is what remains. The rest of that stuff—money and magazine covers and designer this and that— it's sweet, don't get me wrong. But it's not *real*. Know what I mean? It's not tangible. I can't take it with me."

"Not unless you're Egyptian," Tyler chirped.

Tammy's weathered face was soaked in confusion and she turned back to her equally clueless husband.

"I've never heard you so unguarded before," Tyler whispered. "You threw that poor thing for a loop."

"Well, it's true. It may not sound glamorous or be what she wants to hear, but come on—what else can I ask for?"

"A man," Tyler said. "A big, hot, strapping man to sweep you off your feet. That's next on your agenda."

"Nah," she demurred. "Trust me, I'm not looking. I've got enough on my plate."

"Ha! That's what you said before meeting what's-his-name. When you're not looking, that's when you find someone. Which explained why I couldn't find anyone for the longest time—bitch was trying way too hard."

"Everything in due time. Right now, I'm exhausted just being me." She attacked her Caesar and ignored the Missouri natives' ogling.

59

One, two, one, two . . . Callie placed a gladiator sandal along the edge of the infinity pool, one in front of the other, as though balancing on a beam. Arms straight out, clutch in hand. Brant Van Zant's house buzzed with Hollywood movers and shakers. She had met a good handful of the guests at one point or another through work but Callie wasn't in the mood for superficial gabble. Tyler was supposed to have joined her but had to cancel at the last minute for a client.

("Tyler, I implore you, come to Palm Springs," Barbara Hickey said. "A friend backed out of presenting an award at an architecture gala tonight and I'm filling in for her. This old face is screaming for your magic."

"Sorry, Barbara, can't do it," Tyler told her. "I'm going to a party tonight.")

"Surely you can change your plans," scoffed Barbara. "I'll arrange for a car to pick you up at your house and drive you here."

"I already told Callie I'd go with her."

"And, young man, I'll triple your rate."

"What time is good for you, Barbara?")

A woman's nasally voice rose above all other partygoers—ugh, Stephanie Schueller. Like a hyena on steroids. She rushed over to Callie and dragged her by the forearm.

"Come here, Callie, there's someone I want you to meet. That French guy who owns that magazine you were in. He's gonna invest a buttload of money in the franchise. You gotta meet him. And from what I hear"—Stephanie lowered her voice—"his dick matches his bank account."

Callie found it extremely difficult to be fond of Stephanie but impossible not to be grateful to her, too; thanks to the addition of the new character, Blaze, Callie's bank account was thriving more than ever. *The Cheerleader Chronicles* soared 30 percent and Paul Angers was able to get her contract rewritten, guaranteeing her $125,000 per episode. She didn't know if longevity was in store for Blaze (the Wilders claimed they weren't sure, either, but wanted to keep Stephanie on board for the remainder of the season) but hoped the blonde's storyline involved a gun or knife or nuclear explosion in the near future.

"Guess what that publicist, Sherri Finstad, managed to do?" Stephanie said. "Go on, take a guess."

"I have no idea."

"It involves something we both have in common."

Callie couldn't think of a single quality the two shared. "No clue."

"She scored me my first real interview! The cover of *Tell Us*. And I even mention you in it."

"I can hardly wait to read it." She reluctantly let Stephanie guide her over to Brant. He mingled with a small group of people drinking and smoking at a wrought-iron table. The smell of tobacco clouded the crisp night air.

"Mr. Roo-sew," Stephanie trumpeted, "meet Callie Lambert."

Yves Rousseau was sandwiched between two statuesque Latinas but rose when Callie approached. He raised her hand to his lips. "*Bonsoir, mademoiselle.* At last I have the pleasure of making your acquaintance." He raised her hand to his lips and his wide-set eyes flickered.

She hadn't yet been introduced to Mr. *Coquette* himself—they had missed each other by mere minutes at the celebration for her pictorial the previous year—and was struck by the Frenchman's style. Yves was a walking billboard for Parisian luxury; his silk tie was perfectly knotted and his full head of salt-and-pepper hair and swarthy skin emphasized the starkness of his white Givenchy suit. Any air of aloofness disappeared when he smiled; his dimples gave Callie's a run for their money. Of course, there were those scandalous rumors—he threw marathon sex parties every weekend and liked to keep his two girlfriends, Inez and Anita, tied to his bed, naked, for days at a time, allegedly—but Callie found him nonthreatening. Sexual, to be sure, but harmless.

"Likewise, Mr. Rousseau—"

"Yves," he interjected. "Please, *mademoiselle,* call me Yves. Everyone does."

"Yves," Callie said, "may I have one of your cigarettes?"

"But of course." He whipped a smoke from his gold case and lit it for her.

Callie took a deep drag. Ahhhhh. She was light-headed; it had been awhile since she last savored a nicotine rush. "*Merci beaucoup.*"

"*Mon plaisir, ma chère,*" Yves said. He brushed a fallen ash off the lapel of his white linen suit. "Your diction is very good. You studied French, no?"

"Just in high school for a few years. If that counts."

"Of course that counts, absolutely. You have lovely coloring. What's your background? Mediterranean, I suspect."

She nodded. "Yes, Greek. I—"

"Isn't she great, Yves? Her skin tone is in-fucking-credible," said Stephanie. "The makeup team always has to drench me in body makeup just so I have a little color and look remotely human but, nope, not Callie. She's got a tan for days."

Yves ignored the interruption. "You were saying, *mademoiselle?*"

"On my father's side, yes."

"So is one of my girls." He pointed to one of the Latinas. "Anita is part Greek."

"Only the good part," Anita purred.

"Don't let the good part fool you; this woman is *all* bad. Fantastically bad." His dark eyes out-burned his cigarette. "Callie, you *must* pose for me again. You were such a smash, the best-selling issue of last year and the top seller in all of Europe! I've put in several calls to your agent and you've ignored me."

"I'm sorry, Yves. I'm just not into nudes anymore."

"You should be—everyone else is. *I* certainly am. Name your price."

"It's not a question of money."

"Impossible. *Everything* boils down to money. Sex and money, that's what makes the world tick."

Callie looked away. "I don't know, Yves, I'm not really into—"

"*Je t'en prie*—I beg of you—name your price. *Coquette* needs Callie again."

But Callie doesn't need Coquette. "I'll think it over."

"You Americans make everything so difficult," he moaned. "*Très difficile,* when it need not be."

Stephanie chimed in. "Mr. Roo-sew, Callie is dying to hear all about your investment idea."

Brant shushed her but Yves didn't seem to mind. "Yes, yes, it's true. I've been giving much thought about financing a follow-up to *Nympho Cheerleaders.*"

"A sequel? I haven't heard anything about this," said Callie.

"Yves has a meeting with the Wilders next week," Brant said. "Under my direction—*NCA! Part Deux.* Great news, isn't it? You'll be a huge part of it, naturally. You and *Nympho* go hand in hand, like hotcakes and syrup."

Callie wasn't crazy about the sound of that; she was tired of being associated with anything overtly sexual, especially something carrying the word "nympho." All eyes were on her, impatient for her response. "Umm, wow," she said. "That's fantastic."

Stephanie bobbed up and down on her seat cushion. "Isn't that awesome? Yves says we can do *Coquette* together, too, as a tie-in. Another pictorial, only better."

"And bigger," Yves said. "A double layout, I'm thinking. Maybe even a double issue—you on one cover, Callie, and Stephanie on another. Big, big—I want to go *big.*"

"Wonderful," Callie murmured absently. She puffed the remainder of her cigarette.

"I have many tricks up my sleeve, oh, yes. Many different ways to entice *mademoiselle.* You say no to one offer, I come up with another idea. You say no to that, I come up with ten different ideas. One way or another, I get my way. You see, I do not believe in losing—and besides, I've never been remotely good at it, anyway." Yves laughed and the others joined in.

"Excuse me, I need to use the ladies' room." Callie walked to the front of the house, where the valet was set up, and waited while they fetched her car.

"Hey," said a male voice.

She looked over her shoulder. The last person she'd expect to see—a forlorn-looking Mitch Gracie—stood a few feet away from her, hands shoved deep in his torn jeans. "Hey," she said. "What are you doing here?"

"I do manage to score a few invites around here, believe it or not. You look miserable, Callie."

"Funny, I was thinking the same thing about you."

"I am miserable. That's why I'm leavin'. My girlfriend dragged me here, in case you were curious. As you know, these shindigs aren't my forte. But she's visiting from Alabama and wanted to go to a chichi Hollywood party."

"Where is she?"

"I have no idea." Mitch shook his head. "None whatsoever. And I don't really give a rat's ass, either. I haven't seen her in an hour. Last I did see of her, though, she was getting a little too friendly with some Z-list actor she recognized from TV. Her phone is off, too, so she must be really enjoying herself."

Callie looked down at the driveway. "I don't know what to say, Mitch. I'm sorry."

"Nah, don't worry about it. I was planning on breakin' up with her after the weekend was over, anyway. I realized we weren't exactly compatible. Better now than later. So what are you so upset over? What, did you break a Louboutin?"

Callie's mouth dropped. "Oh my God. Did you actually say—?"

"Yes, believe it or not, I do know what expensive shoes are, Callie. I'm not *that* much of a redneck. Wait a minute, let me rephrase myself—I believe the correct term is 'Hick Prick,' am I right? A few birdies told me that was your special name for me."

She blushed. "Mitch, I—"

"Relax. As I told you when I first met you, I don't give a damn. Or a rat's ass. Or anything you wanna call it. So, answer my question—why do you look so pissed off?"

"To tell you the truth, I'm not one for these Hollywood gimmicks, either. They're always the same—a bunch of phonies stroking each other's assholes."

He tipped his head back and laughed. "I like that—strokin' each other's assholes. Phrased perfectly. You don't seem like one of those types to me."

"I'm not. That's the problem. And every time I go to one of these parties I'm reminded of that," she sputtered.

"You know, when we first met I assumed—wrongfully, I admit— you were high maintenance. I came off a little strong—"

"A *little*?"

"A lot. Yeah, I'll give ya that. But I stand corrected."

He's not so bad, Callie thought. With his quick wit and raw sense of humor, he could be quite entertaining to work with, actually. His unpretentiousness was authentic and refreshing and, dare she admit it, a little sexy. And those lips . . . those lush lips of his demanded to be kissed for days at a time.

The valet pulled up in a Jeep. "That's me. Well, princess, your head's on straighter than most. Just don't forget to keep that chin up. If nothin' else, just to piss 'em off."

"So when is your next call time?" she asked.

"I'm done, darlin'. I'm wrapped."

"Oh, I didn't know that. They're not bringing you back?"

"Not unless the Wilders wanna renegotiate with my agent. Which they could, I guess, but so far, they haven't. My last day on set was last week."

"Really? Why didn't you say something?"

"Why would I? Don't tell me you miss me already." He hopped in the front seat and propped his elbow out the window. "Since when does hell freeze over?"

"Humph." Callie stuck her nose up. Mitch laughed again, a devil-may-care chuckle that brought a smile to Callie's lips.

"Look at those dimples," he said. "A badass is never supposed to have dimples, you know. Not good for your reputation. See ya around." He pulled out of the driveway. Callie watched his teeth flash in the rearview mirror as he trailed down the winding road.

60

"*No?* What do you mean, no?" Paul Angers held his fork of lasagna in midair and gawked.

"I mean no. *N-O,*" Callie said. Their waiter brought another basket of bread over and she dove in. "I'm not interested in posing for *Coquette* again. Been there, done that."

"But Rousseau's offering three hundred thousand dollars, Callie—that's sixty higher than his last offer."

"I know, Paul."

"If you're holding out for more, forget it. He said that's as high as he's going. Take it or leave it."

"Then I'll leave it. It's not about money. Besides, Paul, I thought we were on the same page? We agreed I need to steer away from this kind of work before I get pigeonholed."

"And, trust me, I fully believe you need and deserve diversity in your work, Cal. That's never been a question for me and I've never doubted you. But think it over—three hundred grand is a whole lot of dough."

She sighed. "Tell me about it. Sometimes I wonder if I've lost my marbles."

"You can say no until the cows come home, but when they dangle that cash in front of you, all bets are off."

"It brings out the whore in me, is that what you're trying to say?"

"Brings out the whore in all of us—me, you, and Jane Schmoe. There are no exceptions where a large lump of cash is concerned."

"But I'm not hard up for cash, Paul. What if I don't want to do it for *any* amount?"

"Here's the sticky part," Paul said carefully. "Rousseau is insisting you do another layout for the magazine if you want to do the sequel."

"Let him insist all he wants," she said. "Maybe I don't even want to do the sequel, did he ever think of that? Besides, Rousseau doesn't call the shots."

Paul cleared his throat. "Actually, yes, he does. The Wilders agree that in order to be part of the film you have to do the magazine, too. A package deal, so to speak. They're going to stipulate it in your contract."

"Come again?"

"Rousseau is financing it, Callie—ten million of his own. He figures, tie in the two projects together. First and foremost, he's a businessman and he wants to guarantee his investment is a smart one."

"So it's a Catch-22?"

"In so many words."

"Jesus Christ!" Callie threw her bread on the plate.

"Look, no one's holding an Uzi to anyone's heads, so let's not get too upset. You always have options, Callie—you're never trapped." Paul gave a halfhearted, half-hopeful smile.

Rat bastards. She swigged her Chardonnay. "What else do you have for me? Anything new going on? How about that romantic comedy I was up for?"

"The one opposite Clooney?"

"Yeah, that one."

"Clooney dropped out and since he's not attached to it anymore they've decided to recast the whole thing from scratch. Unfortunately, it doesn't look too promising."

"And the indie project? The one about the single mother?"

"I passed on it because they rewrote it as a stripper. Full nudity required." Paul pulled a magazine out of his briefcase. "And then we have this little gem. I'm assuming you haven't seen it yet."

Callie scanned the cover title. *Stephanie Schueller: What Evan Taught Me, Why I'm the Next Big TV Star, and Why Cheerleaders Are So F***ing Hot.*

"Just when I think you're done bearing bad news, Paul, you turn around and hit me with more. How much garbage does she spew?"

Paul flipped through the pages. "Oh, plenty. Here's a lovely part: 'Callie is pretty cool—like, she's not a bad chick—but she's not all that talented, to be honest. She's quite fake, actually. Everything about her is fake, including her tan. The makeup crew uses, like, ten bottles of tanner just to give her decent color. And let's be honest, the only reason she got big is because of Gabrielle Manx. She basically just rode the coattails of Gabby and screwed a famous singer to get to where she is today. And I'm not hating her for it. I mean, I had a relationship with Evan, too, bigger than the one she had—I've still got the rock to prove it. But I don't buy that whole "I'm so private" act of hers. She's told so many people I know that sex with Evan was, quote, eyeball-rolling. So why not just come clean? Why play coy with reporters and act like it didn't happen? Just admit it: yeah, I fucked him, yeah, it was good, yeah, he made me more interesting. Anyway, I can't respect that. I've worked my ass off for everything I've got and I haven't taken any handouts *and* I keep it real.'"

Callie's jaw clenched. "That hideous, low-rent bitch. I'm going to vomit."

"Can't say I blame you. She definitely has some whoppers. Sherri Finstad hooked that whole thing up."

Callie thought back to the dinner at the Waverly Inn. "'Eyeball-rolling,' huh? Sounds like Sherri needs to learn to keep her trap shut."

"I'm calling Sherri and telling her to take it down a few notches. Schueller's handlers, too. You know Will and Wendell—any publicity is good publicity."

Callie struggled to keep her voice at a low pitch. "You can tell the Wilders to go fuck themselves, Paul. And tell Yves to do the same. I'm not going to be bullied into doing something I don't want to do. If they want to stand by a pathetic fame fucker like Stephanie, I want nothing to do with any of them."

"I have a better idea—why don't we wait until you're good and sober to make these decisions? Sleep on it a little while."

"God, these people, I swear! Take your pick from douchier to douchiest."

Paul rubbed his chin. "That sounds like a movie—*Douchier and Douchiest*. Where have I heard that? Someone must have run that title past me recently. Hmm. Anyhow, no rush, but why don't you think over everything with a clear head." Paul called the waiter over. "Can we get some water, please? And do me a favor—throw this away for me."

The waiter ditched the magazine while Callie tossed back another glass of wine. "Paul," she slurred, "I'm washed up. Why are you still with me? I'm done. *Finished.*"

"What the hell are you talking about?" he said.

"I've got a one-way ticket to Nowheresville. Go save yourself and abandon ship."

Paul took her glass away from her. "Take it easy, now. You're being ridiculous."

"I mean it," she moaned. "My bosses hate me, I can't book another gig to save my life, and my taste in men is disgusting. How did I become so repugnant? What happened to me?"

"I'll tell you what happened to you, young lady," he said sternly. "It's called success. You'll net a million and a quarter this year alone, easy. *That's* what happened to you, and last I checked, it isn't something most actors cry over. The actors I represent would kill— probably kill me, even—to have what you have. Look around us. Not too long ago you were one of these guys. Or did you forget?"

Callie gave the restaurant a once-over. A waiter at a nearby booth spilled a plate of spaghetti, barely avoiding his customer's lap.

"Count your blessings, Cal, and remember where you came from. It can all go away so fast. Here, have some water and sober up. No one wants to hire a hungover actress with bloodshot eyes."

She slugged the water and Paul drove her home.

"Chop it off. Chop it *all* off, Tessa," said Callie. "A good nine, ten inches."

Tessa held a chunk of hair up. "Are you sure? That's a lot of length. Maybe we should start off with baby steps and add a few layers."

Callie shook her head. "I need a big change. Something refined and Grace Kelly–ish, only a brunette version. Let's go for the whole shebang at once. I'm donating my hair to cancer victims, so it's a win–win all the way around."

"Terrific." Tessa tied a smock around Callie. "What about the studio? They won't care?"

"The season wrapped and I don't have any immediate projects on the horizon. Besides, it's not in my contract that I can't cut my hair. Weight, yes—I can't gain more than ten pounds, not like *that* would ever happen—but it says nothing about hair."

"Last time you were here you mentioned your mother was getting a wig. How did that turn out?"

"I'll find out next week when I pay her a visit. Knowing my mom, the wig will be bigger than her own natural hair—she's always loved it poufy."

"Too much volume can be a bad thing. I try to convince women that bigger isn't necessarily better."

"I've been telling Mom that for years."

"How is she doing?"

"She's tired—some days are better than others. She says sometimes she wants to stay in bed all day and other times she has tons of energy. Up and down like a roller coaster."

"I can only imagine. Are you going to see Candice while you're there?"

Callie's eyes hardened. "No. I told you about our last encounter, didn't I?"

Tessa seized a pair of scissors from her arsenal of supplies. "The barbecue? Yes, you told me. Gosh, I haven't seen Candice in a long time. Last time she sat in my chair was a good two years ago." *Snip.* A wad of Callie's hair landed on the floor.

"I'm stripping all negativity from my life, Tessa, be it man, woman, or anything in between. Out with the old, in with the new." Callie watched another hunk of her precious locks plunge to its death. *I hope I didn't make a mistake. Damn it. Too late now.*

"Then this new do is the cherry on top," said Tessa. "You have the bone structure to pull it off, too. It will look *fab-u-lous.*"

Tessa was right; Callie adored her new look; it was sleek and sassy, but best of all, a complete departure from her usual style. No sooner had Tessa put down the hair dryer than Callie was out the door—her acting class with Deirdre Coleman was in fifteen minutes and, per usual, she was running late. She zoomed down Wilshire. Damn it—how could she possibly get from Beverly Hills to Lookout Mountain in such little time? She veered onto Crescent Heights and directly into a pothole. The crater was as wide as it was deep. *Splat!* A rear tire busted.

"Shit!" Callie screeched. She pulled over and switched on her flashers. Damn it all. She may as well kiss nine hundred bucks—Deirdre's hourly rate—good-bye. Essentially a pair of killer heels or a weekend at the Ritz or a third of her end of the rent. Pissing money on anything stupid, regardless of how much she sat on, was a major pet peeve of Callie's; her Midwest sensibility wouldn't allow it.

Beep!

A Jeep's horn made her jump. The vehicle pulled to the side of the road, behind her car. "Callie?" Mitch Gracie poked his head out the window. "Havin' trouble?"

"Whatever gave you that idea? I just thought I'd admire the potholes up close," she grumbled. "What are you doing here?"

He had already popped her trunk to get the spare. "I live here. In that peach house over there." He pointed to a Spanish home north up Crescent.

"No kidding? Small world. Mitch, don't worry about it, I'm calling a towing company—"

"Towing? Don't be silly. I'll have this thing changed in a minute. I'm from Alabama, princess—we're not afraid of gettin' our hands dirty."

"I *really* appreciate it. Thank you. I can't believe the timing—I'm running late to acting class and what happens? I get a flat. There's no way I'm going to make it in time now and she charges an arm and a leg. Grrr." She called Deirdre and paced along the curb.

C'mon, c'mon, pick up. She got the answering machine and dialed the number again. Finally, Deirdre answered.

"Take your time," Deirdre said. "I could use an extra half hour with this kid I'm working with, anyway. He needs a *lot* of help. Like pulling teeth, this one."

Excellent. Callie breathed a sigh of relief.

Mitch worked on her tire, as apt as a professional mechanic. "You know, I almost didn't recognize you with that new hair. It looks good on you—brings out those eyes."

"You like it?" She flicked the ends of her bob. "I literally just got it chopped. I needed a change. It's like I'm twenty pounds lighter."

"It makes you stand out from all these chicks in L.A. with junky-lookin' extensions. Like they bought 'em at the dollar store."

"I never want to blend in with the pack—especially if the said pack looks like a load of illiterate tramps."

He peeked at her from over his shoulder. "That could never happen. You couldn't blend in if you tried. So how's the show going? Have you strangled Schueller yet or did you just leave her black and blue?"

"Ha. Was it that obvious I didn't like her?"

"Obvious? Anyone with working eyeballs could see it. It couldn't be more obvious if you had 'Schueller sucks' scrawled on your ass," cracked Mitch.

"I think she's an acquired taste."

"You don't have to be diplomatic with me, you know, Callie. I'm not exactly gonna go squeal to the big guys. Or the press, for that matter. Come on—tell me how you really feel."

"A bottle of Boone's Farm has more elegance than that STD," Callie sniffed.

"Now, *that's* more like it! I like it when you tell it like it is—goes with my no-bullshit philosophy. I met her but never worked with her, thank God. I'd take nails on a chalkboard over listenin' to her yap any day."

"She's the Wilders' new golden girl," Callie sighed. "I swear, they probably installed a toilet seat in her dressing room made of solid platinum."

"It's not about you—remember that. I filmed a part in a movie last month and I'll never forget what an older actor told me. This eighty-year-old, John Wayne–lookin' man. I love listenin' to old folks; they always have such sage advice. He's been in the business for sixty years and he said to me, 'Mitch, the thing I learned early on in this business is that you can't take anything personal. There's always some asshole on your heels itchin' to get ahead—and they're gonna be more talented and better-lookin' and probably younger than you. That's the way it's always been and that's the way it always will be. Get used to it straight off.' Try not to let it get under your skin too much."

"Good point."

Mitch reached for a towel in the trunk and wiped his hands. "There ya go. Don't drive too much on this spare—you'll need to get a new one put on as soon as you can. But at least now you can get around."

"Thank you so much, Mitch. Bizarre you drove past me, huh?"

"Strange coincidence for sure. Glad I could be of assistance. Drive safe." He walked to his Jeep but spun back around. "I'd like to take you out sometime."

"Why, Mr. Gracie," Callie said with mock surprise, "are you actually asking me out on a *date*?"

"I am, yes. I most definitely am. Before you slip away again, can I get your number?"

It took a split second for her to mull over the question. "Let me find something to write with." She found a scrap of paper and pen under the driver's seat. "This is my cell. Call me anytime."

"I will. You can plan on that. I'm flying to Buffalo tomorrow to shoot a new flick—a few weeks, maybe a month—but when I come back, what do you say we get together?"

She smiled. "I say I'll be looking forward to it."

"Good to hear it. You know, it's funny—when we first met it felt like we couldn't be any more opposite, but my gut tells me we have more in common than I originally thought. You're all right, Callie— you're different."

"Different?"

"Yeah—that's a compliment. Different as in cool and smart and real. I like different. Puts you miles ahead of the Schuellers of the world." He showed off his crooked grin.

"Thanks, Mitch."

"Take care of yourself, darlin'. See ya soon."

62

The panic in Grandma Esme's voice crackled through the phone. "Honey, I just heard the news. I can't believe it."

Callie stopped mixing a batch of cookie dough and dropped the wooden spoon in the bowl. "The news?" she said, and gripped her iPhone tighter.

"Yes, dear. What a shame."

Callie racked her brain—what was Grandma talking about? Her urgency was alarming. Esme was usually so placid and low-key. It could only mean one thing. She stared out her kitchen window, paralyzed. "Grandma, what are you getting at?"

"I'm just surprised it ended like this, honey. I didn't expect it, especially since things were going so well."

"I don't understand. Is it Mom? What happened, Grandma?"

"No, no, I'm not referring to your mother, dear. She's been fine, thank goodness—we had a nice conversation yesterday afternoon."

Phew. "What's wrong, then?"

"I was just doing the dishes and heard the news on TV. I forget the name of it, but one of those entertainment shows played a clip about you."

"Grandma, I've told you, you have to take those programs with a grain of salt. Let me guess—I'm in the hospital, either because of malnutrition from my crash diet or withdrawals from Botox."

"No, honey, nothing like that—besides, I've learned not to pay any attention to such far-fetched rubbish. I'm referring to you being dropped from your show."

"Hold on—I've been *dropped*? As in fired?"

"He didn't use that word, I don't think. He said, 'It's official—Callie Lambert won't be returning to *The Cheerleader Chronicles*.' A heavyset woman—Cheryl or Sharon something—said that you and Wilder Productions have made a joint decision not to renew your contract."

"Joint decision"? Ha! "Sherri, was that her name?"

"That's it. Honey, is this true? Why didn't you tell me?"

"Grandma, I swear, this is the first I've heard of it."

"Really, now? They mentioned some other actress—said she was the only cast member who'd be returning. A really cheap, tall blonde. Does that ring a bell?"

"It certainly does," Callie muttered.

"My, the only reason that show was any good was because of *you*," Esme huffed. "Can't they see that? How can they do this? Surely they can't all be fools!"

Callie had been prepared for grave news by the sound of Esme's voice and was thankful it wasn't serious. It troubled her far more that her grandmother was so upset. "It's just the way the ball rolls,

Grandma. Please don't let it get to you. My friend, Mitch—I told you about him the other day—he talked about this same thing. 'You can't take it personal,' he said. And I can't."

"But they're disposing of you like garbage. *That's* what really gets my goat."

Her cell beeped—it was Paul Angers. "Grandma, my agent's calling."

"Take it, honey, and call me back when you can."

Callie switched over to the other line. "So, is it standard for actors to hear they've been fired on the news or am I a lone exception?"

"I just got done reaming the Wilders a new asshole," Paul said. "I found out like you."

"And?"

"And since you decided not to do another pictorial—which is fine, it was totally your call—their response was to write you out of the sequel and any subsequent sequels and also pass on renewing your contract." Her silence prompted Paul to continue. "I'm just as furious as you that they chose to release a statement before calling us."

"Actually, I'm not furious at all, Paul. You'd think I would be—I mean, I'm pissed they didn't have the decency to call me first. But not *that* pissed, all things considered." Why on earth weren't expletives rolling off her tongue? Was she ill? *Why am I so calm?*

"I wish I had better news for you. Honestly, I truly do. But nothing is a guarantee. And with Schueller gaining popularity . . . they thought that focusing on Blaze as the main storyline was the way to go. They like you and have enjoyed working with you—"

"But they don't like me enough to keep me around if they can't get their way," Callie finished. "Especially if Stephanie comes cheaper."

Paul sighed. "They're fully aware of their options. Look, you had a great run—a great run. And to call it anything less would be untrue. But it's really tough to please everyone *and* yourself at the same time. Now's as good a time as any to regroup and charge your batteries. Decide what game plan's best for you—what you really want in this business. This could be a blessing in disguise. In fact, I can't think of a better time to take a break. When you come back from Paris, we can figure everything out. This is the perfect time for you to . . ."

Callie drowned Paul out and her thoughts drifted an ocean and thousands of miles away. Tyler had accomplished a longtime goal of doing makeup at a fashion show in Paris. His boyfriend, Timothy, was joining him and Callie had decided it was the perfect opportunity for her to go, as well. Last-minute trips were right up her alley. Let Hollywood—and the dizzying effort it took maintaining a career—wait; she was overdue for a bona fide vacay. A few days with her family in Michigan followed up with three weeks in the City of Light, a perfect span of time for de-L.A.-ing. Expanding her horizons was as much a necessity as drinking H_2O; she *needed* to experience life beyond the bubble of Los Angeles and get back to basics—to sleep late and spend the afternoon reading a book at a sidewalk café. To admire a Monet or the *Mona Lisa* and feel the cobblestones scrape under her shoes' soles while something fresh— anything but the stench of gasoline—filled the breeze. And, oh, yes—there was also the business of getting to know that intriguing, tight-assed smart aleck, Mitch. Who knew where that would lead? Perhaps nowhere. Or perhaps, just maybe . . .

The smog clung to the air like a wispy negligee. Callie looked at her front yard; the sun skimmed the Hollywood sign and poured through her open window. She tipped her face in the rays and felt nothing short of blessed.